The
Blended
QUILT

The

Blended
Quilt

WANDA &
BRUNSTETTER
& JEAN BRUNSTETTER
New York Times BESTSELLING AUTHOR

SHILOH RUN  PRESS

An Imprint of Barbour Publishing, Inc.

Cover Design: Buffy Searl
Model Photography: Richard Brunstetter III
Scene Photography: Doyle Yoder

Published by Shiloh Run Press, an imprint of Barbour Publishing, Inc., 1810 Barbour Drive, Uhrichsville, Ohio 44683, www.shilohrunpress.com

Our mission is to inspire the world with the life-changing message of the Bible.

ecpa Member of the
Evangelical Christian
Publishers Association

Printed in the United States of America.

To the Log Cabin Quilt Shop.
Thanks for helping us create Sadie's beautiful Blended Quilt.

I have learned, in whatsoever state I am,
therewith to be content.
PHILIPPIANS 4:11

Chapter 1

*S*adie Kuhns sat on her parents' front porch, gazing at the coneflowers, petunias, daylilies, and garden phlox blooming in the flower bed closest to the house. As lovely as they were, they didn't compare to the hibiscus, plumeria, and bird-of-paradise she'd seen blooming on the Hawaiian Islands she and three of her friends had visited four and a half years ago. In some ways, it seemed like the trip had only been a few months ago. It was one of the most thrilling experiences of Sadie's life—something she would always remember and desire to tell her children and grandchildren about.

"I'll need to get married first," Sadie whispered. Out of the four young Amish women who'd gone on that cruise, Sadie was the only one still single.

Since I'm being courted by Wyman Kaufman, I have the potential of getting married, she thought. *Of course, he has to ask me first.*

Wyman was quite a handsome young man, in addition to being fun to be with. His only flaw was that he became easily bored and couldn't seem to stick to one job. It worried Sadie, because if her boyfriend was unable to commit to a profession, maybe he would get tired of her too. Also, if Wyman couldn't stay with a good job, it was unlikely that he could support a wife and children someday. It would mean their future together may not take off at all.

Sadie was glad that Wyman, who'd held several jobs over the last year, now worked at his father's feed store. She hoped he would stay put, because it was steady work. The business did well and provided an income for Wyman's father, Ernest, as well as for Wyman and his brother, Michael.

Sadie's best friend, Ellen Zook, who ran a local bed-and-breakfast with her husband, Rueben, had recently mentioned that Wyman might not be the best choice for Sadie, since he seemed so unsettled.

Sadie pursed her lips as she placed one hand against her chest. *Maybe what I need is something encouraging to do for myself that will distract me from the unsettled feelings and concerns I have about Wyman and the way our relationship has been going.*

A hummingbird swooped past her head, and Sadie ducked, her thoughts scattering. Seconds later, two more hummers zipped past and joined the first bird at one of the feeders hanging from the porch eaves.

Even with all the bird action in their yard and at the feeders, her life seemed predictable and boring. Maybe it was time to begin making a new quilt—something different than anything she'd made before. Sadie had learned to quilt when she was a girl and enjoyed quilting in her free time. Sometimes she created her own patterns for quilts, which she then sold or gave to friends and family members as gifts.

She tapped her chin. *I wonder if I could come up with something that's part Amish and part Hawaiian. That would certainly be different. I'll need to think on it awhile, but the idea certainly has some appeal. I wonder if anyone would buy a quilt like that.*

Sadie rested her chin in her hand and tapped the side of her face. *Since I will probably never go on another trip to Hawaii, maybe I should keep the quilt for myself as a remembrance of the wonderful time I had visiting the beautiful Hawaiian Islands.*

Sadie nearly jumped out of her chair when the screen door opened and slammed shut, dispersing her thoughts a second time.

"There you are, Sadie. I thought you planned to help me do some baking this morning." Mom moved over to stand in front of Sadie's chair and gave her a rosy-cheeked smile. "Or would you rather do something more to your liking on your day off?"

"I'm happy to help with the baking, but when we're done, I may get out my sketch pad and try to come up with a new quilt pattern. Unless you have something else you need me to do, that is," Sadie added.

"Once we're done in the kitchen, you're free to do whatever you want." Mom's metal-framed glasses slipped off the bridge of her nose, and she paused to push them back in place. "You're such a helpful *dochder*, and you work hard all week at your job in Shipshewana, so you deserve some time off to do as you please."

"*Danki,* Mom. I appreciate your understanding."

Sadie thought about her job at the hardware store, where she'd been working for nearly six years. As much as she enjoyed her position, there were other things, like quilting, that she would much rather do.

As she rose from the chair and followed her mother into the house, Sadie's mind swirled with the possibility of making some sort of blended quilt.

✳

By the time Sadie finished helping her mother bake several batches of cookies, as well as some sticky buns, her stomach had begun to growl. She glanced at the kitchen clock and realized it was almost time to fix lunch.

"It's not quite twelve yet, but is it okay if I fix myself something to eat now, so I can head over to the sewing room and start making preliminary plans for my new quilt?"

"Of course." Mom placed her warm hand on Sadie's arm. "You can eat whenever you're ready. In fact, I may make a sandwich now and sit down with you."

Sadie grinned. "That'd be nice." Since her sisters, Jana Beth and Kaylene, both a few years younger than Sadie, were working at the trailer factory where their father was also employed, it felt nice for Sadie to have this time with Mom. She and her sisters still lived at home, so she rarely got to spend any time alone with her mother.

It wasn't that Sadie minded having her sisters around. She just enjoyed being able to visit with Mom without anyone interrupting, as Kaylene, who'd recently turned eighteen, often did. Sadie sometimes wondered if her sister did it on purpose, to keep the focus on her. Kaylene had always been a chatty child, and monopolized their mother's time whenever she could. Even Jana Beth, who was two years older than their younger sister, had a hard time getting in a word whenever Kaylene was in the room.

Sadie's older brothers, Saul and Leland, who lived in the area, were both married. Leland and his wife, Margaret, had two children, and Saul and his spouse, Rebecca, had recently become parents of a little boy. Sadie didn't see her brothers every day, nor did Leland and Saul occupy much of their parents' time. They both kept busy with their jobs and seeing to the needs of their own families.

Sadie pushed her thoughts aside. While she and her mother put their ham and cheese sandwiches together, they talked about the mild temperatures they'd had for the past week.

"Normally June is one of our hottest months," Mom commented, placing her sandwich on a plate and setting it on the table.

"True, but the weather patterns change from year to year, and I, for one, am enjoying the cooler weather."

"Same here."

Sadie set her plate in front of her usual place and joined Mom at the table. They bowed their heads for silent prayer, and afterward both picked up their sandwiches and took a bite at the same time.

Sadie chuckled. "Like mother, like daughter, huh?"

"Jah." Mom bobbed her head. "Guess we both must be *hungerich.*"

"I sure am hungry. I worked up an appetite when the kitchen filled with those delicious aromas."

"Same here." Mom set her sandwich down and took a drink from her glass of cold buttermilk.

Sadie's lips curled, and she wrinkled her nose. "I don't know how you can drink that horrible-tasting stuff."

"I love it." Mom smacked her lips in an unladylike fashion. "I've been drinking *buddermillich* since I was a little girl and my *daadi* first introduced me to it."

"I don't mind it in biscuits or pancakes, but I could never drink buttermilk straight down the way you do."

"We all have different tastes—in food, in things we enjoy, and even the kind of friends we choose." Mom looked over at Sadie and smiled. "Speaking of friends—will you and Wyman be going out for supper this evening? I know you often do that on your day off."

"Jah, he made plans to pick me up at five thirty." She paused to take a drink of water then set her glass down. "I care deeply for Wyman, but I sometimes wonder if he's the right man for me."

"You mean because he's not as tall as you?"

Sadie shook her head. "The fact that he's a few inches shorter doesn't bother me so much—at least not anymore, like it did when we first started courting. After all, Dad's almost two inches shorter than you, and it's never seemed to be a problem."

"Not now, but your father was self-conscious about the difference in our heights when we first began courting."

"What made him change his mind?"

"I'm not sure—he never really said. He just stopped talking about it." Mom took another bite of her sandwich. "What exactly are you bothered about concerning your relationship with Wyman?"

"He's unsettled. Wyman's only working for his *daed* because he can't make up his mind what he really wants to do. He's gotten bored with every job he's had and will likely get tired of working at the feed store." Sadie drew a breath and released it with a huff. "If he never settles down to one job, he might get tired of me too and will start looking for another girlfriend."

"I don't think you have to worry about that. I've seen the way that young man looks at you."

"How's that?"

"With puppy dog eyes. And he hangs on every word you say."

Sadie snickered. "You're *iwwerdreiwe*, Mom."

"I'm not exaggerating. Wyman is in love with you. There's no doubt about it."

"Maybe so, but it doesn't put my mind at ease to know that the young man I care about is so unsettled. The truth is, Wyman may never ask me to marry him or find a job he's truly happy with."

Mom reached over and patted Sadie's arm. "Just give it to God and pray about things. That is what the good Lord wants us to do."

Sadie nodded instead of expressing her feelings. While she believed in God, she became impatient whenever she prayed for something and an answer didn't come right away. It was a test of her faith to wait for anything—especially something she'd been praying about for a while. Even if Wyman proposed marriage, unless he could prove to Sadie that he'd settled down, she would have to say no. Sadie would not be happy or feel secure in a marriage if her husband kept job hopping.

✳

Wyman wiped the sweat on his forehead with the back of his hand. At the beginning of the day, the feed store had been busy with customers, and he'd kept moving. He had helped load his fair share of feed, along with help from his brother, Michael, but for the last two hours, Wyman had stood around in the stuffy building, staring at the clock on the far wall of the main room.

I'm not interested in doing this kind of work. Sure would like to be doing something different. He brushed at some dust on his trousers. Right after lunch, he'd carted two sacks of dog and cat food out to a buggy and loaded them for a middle-aged Amish woman. Every hour since had dragged.

Wyman glanced over at his father, counting some of the inventory and writing it on a clipboard. Michael had gone to the office to get orders ready for some customers needing feed delivered. Wyman figured since they were the only ones in the store at the moment, there would be no concerns of customers listening in. "This job is boring," he muttered.

"What was that, Son?" Dad turned and looked at him.

"I'm bored here and want something different."

"If that's the case, you can set the broom aside, and I'll find something else for you to do."

Wyman shook his head. "No, I mean, this kind of work doesn't suit me."

Dad's dark eyebrows shot up. "What does?"

"I'm. . .uh. . .not really sure." Wyman avoided looking directly at his dad. "Think I oughta give you my two weeks' notice."

"You're kidding, right?"

"No, I'm not. I thought I could do it, but workin' here is not for me."

"You should give this more thought." His father's voice deepened.

"I've given it a lot of thought, and this isn't what I want to do."

"You've been doing a good job, and the customers like your contagious smile and the humorous stories you like to share."

Wyman dropped his gaze to the floor. "Sorry, but I think it's time for me to try something else."

Dad gave a heavy sigh. "Okay, Son, if that's how you feel, then I'll start putting my feelers out for someone to take your place."

Wyman looked up and watched as his father gave a shake of his slightly balding head. Carrying his clipboard, Dad shuffled toward the back of the store where the office was located.

At least I got the announcement over with. Dad may not understand my reasons for quitting, but he didn't try to talk me out of it, and I'm glad. I have to do what I believe is best for me, and if I continue working here, it'll drag me down.

Wyman felt an unexpected release of tension as he set the broom aside. *If I stayed here, it wouldn't be long before the fun-loving side of me would disappear and none of the customers would like me.*

He pulled his long fingers through his thick crop of hair as his thoughts went to Sadie and her pretty auburn hair. Since this was Friday, he'd be seeing her later this evening and would make good on his promise to take her someplace special. He'd made all the arrangements for a driver to pick them up.

Wyman couldn't wait to be with his girlfriend again, but after tonight he might not be able to take her to expensive restaurants for some time. Truth was, ever since he'd purchased a new buggy, with financial help from his brother, Wyman had been spending beyond his means. Some weeks, like this one, he either hadn't made a payment to Michael or could only pay half of what he'd promised. Wyman had done some fast-talking to get his brother to loan him money to help purchase the new rig. Since Michael was married, and he and his wife, Lovina, had two small children, he'd been hesitant to help Wyman out. But after promising to repay his debt as quickly as possible, Wyman had succeeded in talking his brother into chipping in to help him out. Michael had always been good with his money and kept a steady job at the feed store, so Wyman had seen no reason not to ask for his brother's financial assistance.

Sure hope Michael won't be upset when I tell him I don't have enough money to make a payment to him this week after all. Wyman picked up the broom again and gave the floor in front of him a few more passes. *Sadie deserves a nice meal at a special restaurant. Sure hope she won't be upset when I tell her that I'll be leaving this job in two weeks.*

The last time Wyman had quit a job she hadn't been happy about it. But Sadie had gotten over it, and everything seemed to be fine between them. Besides, he'd have a new job soon, so Sadie would have nothing to worry about.

Wyman let go of the broom handle with one hand and scratched behind one ear. *Maybe I shouldn't say anything to her yet. Might be better to wait till I've landed another job to mention that I quit working here.*

Chapter 2

*H*ow's it going?" Sadie's mother leaned over her shoulder, looking at what Sadie had drawn on her sketch pad.

Sadie pivoted in her chair and looked up at Mom. "Not very far, unfortunately. I can't decide on what patterns to include that give the feeling of both the Amish and Hawaiian cultures."

"This one is nice." Mom pointed to the Lone Star pattern Sadie had sketched in one area of her notebook.

"Jah, but it doesn't fit well with the Bread Fruit I've sketched over here." Sadie pointed with her pencil to the Hawaiian pattern.

"I see what you mean." Mom tapped Sadie's shoulder. "Keep working on it. I'm sure you'll come up with something you like."

"I hope so. Now that I've decided to create a blended quilt, I won't quit until I come up with the right combination."

"I'll leave you to it, then. I need to walk out and check for mail and also go to the phone shed to see if we have any messages."

"Okay. Enjoy your walk in the fresh air and sunshine." Sadie glanced toward the window. "Looks like another nice day."

"For sure." Mom moved toward the door but paused and turned to look at Sadie again. "You should try to get some fresh air and outdoor exercise today too. As the day progresses, it's bound to get stuffy in here."

"If it does, I'll take my work out on the porch."

"All right, then. I won't disturb you again unless there are any letters or phone messages for you." Mom gave a wave and headed out the door.

Some time went by as Sadie continued to draw several more designs and patterns. Glancing at the clock on the far wall, she was surprised to see that it was three o'clock already. She'd need to set this aside soon and get ready for her evening out with Wyman. He'd said he would be taking her someplace special for supper, but she had no idea where it might be.

It doesn't really matter, she told herself. *I'm just looking forward to spending time with him and hearing how things went at the feed store this week.*

The back door opened and closed, and Sadie turned to see her mother enter the room with a stack of mail.

"A letter came from your friend Mandy." Mom held it out to Sadie. "I figured you'd be eager to read it and find out what she and her family have been up to lately."

"Jah, most definitely." Sadie pushed her chair back and stood. "Think I'll take it out on the porch and read it there. If you'd like to join me, I'd be happy to read it out loud."

"Of course. I'm always interested in hearing what your friend from Kauai has to say."

Sadie followed her mother out the door, and they took seats in the wicker chairs. Then Sadie tore open the envelope and began to read:

> *"Dear Friend Sadie,*
>
> *"Aloha! I hope this letter finds you doing well. We are keeping busy as usual with the bed-and-breakfast, although things are always a bit slower during the summer months than the winter when people from the mainland are eager to leave the cold weather behind and exchange it for sunshine and warmer temperatures."*

✳

Sadie paused to shake off a fly that had landed on Mandy's letter.

"Maybe I should go inside and get the *mickebritsch*." Mom started to rise from her seat.

"Don't bother with the flyswatter. It probably won't land in a spot where you can get it anyway." Sadie wrinkled her nose. "Those pesky bugs are the worst part of summer."

Mom bobbed her head.

"Now back to Mandy's letter:

> *"One of the reasons I'm writing is to share our good news with you. Ken and I are expecting our second child, and we're very pleased. The baby is due the last week of December, or maybe he or she will be born on New Year's Day. Now wouldn't that be something?"*

Sadie stopped reading again—this time to see her mother's reaction.

Mom smiled. "I wonder if Ken and Mandy will make another trip to Middlebury to see Mandy's family after the *boppli* is born."

"Probably not right away, but I bet Mandy's mother will decide to go to Kauai to help out either shortly before or right after the baby comes."

Mom nodded. "Miriam will be most eager, and maybe Isaac will be able to take time from his job and go with her." She waved her hand at another troublesome fly. "I'm sure Mandy told her parents right away, and I wouldn't be one bit surprised if they haven't already booked their tickets for a cruise to Kauai so they can be there before the end of December."

"I wish I could go and help out, but I've already used my vacation time for this year. Besides, a trip like that is expensive, even if a person stays in one of the less expensive rooms on the cruise ship." Sadie sighed. "Truth be told, I'll probably never make another trip to the Hawaiian Islands."

"You never know." Mom's tone was encouraging. "You never dreamed you'd get to go the first time, but it happened."

"True." Sadie resumed reading Mandy's letter, commenting from time to time about her friend's enthusiasm concerning the expansion of her family, detailed information about the produce and lovely flowers growing in their garden, and some humorous things that happened at the B&B. By the time Sadie finished Mandy's letter, she and Mom were both laughing out loud.

"Well, as nice as it is to sit outside here on the porch, I need to get ready for my evening with Wyman." Sadie stood. "I want to get showered and changed into something more presentable than this before he gets here." She gestured to the dark green frock she'd put on that morning, which she'd managed to sully with flour and cookie batter when she and Mom did their baking.

"Go right ahead and get ready for your date. I'll be starting supper for us here as soon as your sisters and father get home from work." Mom left her seat too, and they both went inside.

Still clinging to Mandy's letter, Sadie hurried up the stairs to get ready to greet Wyman. Tomorrow when she got off work, she planned to stop and see Ellen. Perhaps she'd also received a letter from Mandy.

❋

In his eagerness to see Sadie, Wyman's knee bounced in time to the music playing on his driver's radio. Floyd Witherspoon, who frequently drove for Wyman's family, had a large, fifteen-passenger van he often took out when he did Amish runs. Tonight, however, since Wyman and Sadie would be his only passengers, Floyd had picked Wyman up in a midsize car. There was plenty of room in the backseat, and Sadie and Wyman would have it all to themselves. Wyman hoped Floyd would keep the music down as they made the trip to Winona Lake, where the Boathouse Restaurant was located. He didn't want to compete with whatever song was being played while trying to visit with Sadie.

I hope she doesn't bring up the topic of the feed store, Wyman thought as they neared the Kuhnses' place. *I don't want to accidentally let it slip that I've decided to quit and look for a new job. It could spoil our evening if Sadie doesn't understand my need to find a job that I really enjoy. She likes her position at the hardware store, so why shouldn't I look for something I like too?*

"You nervous about something?"

Floyd's question pulled Wyman's thoughts aside. "Uh, no. . . What makes you think I'm nervous?"

"The way your right leg keeps bouncing up and down."

"Oh, that." Wyman's face warmed as he placed one hand on his knee. "I was just keepin' time to the music."

"I see. Thought maybe you were gonna propose marriage to your girlfriend tonight and were having second thoughts." Floyd looked over at Wyman with a silly grin.

"I do want to marry Sadie someday, but I'm not ready to commit to it yet."

"How come? You've got a steady job now, working for your dad, right?"

Wyman's Adam's apple moved up and down as he swallowed hard. He didn't dare say a word to Floyd about putting in his two weeks' notice today. This driver was a gabber, and he'd no doubt spill the beans to Sadie and anyone else he would converse with soon.

"Did you not hear my question, or are you choosing to ignore it?"

Wyman looked at Floyd. "I don't have enough money saved up for marriage," he answered honestly. "I'll ask Sadie to marry me when I feel ready to support a wife."

Floyd shrugged his broad shoulders. "It's really none of my business. Just thought I'd ask."

Wyman didn't comment. To his relief, they were pulling onto the Kuhnses' driveway. This was not a topic he wished to discuss with his driver.

When Floyd pulled close to the house, Wyman got out of the car and hurried onto the front porch. He'd no more than lifted his hand to knock when the door swung open and Sadie's sister Jana Beth greeted him. "Sadie's still upstairs getting ready, but she'll be down soon. Would you like to come in?"

Wyman glanced at his driver's vehicle, the engine still running. No doubt he was anxious to be on their way, same as Wyman. He'd made reservations at the restaurant and didn't want to be late. Since it took about an hour to get there, they needed to go now.

Maybe I should have told Sadie where we were going instead of making it a surprise. Wyman stepped inside the open door but remained in the hall. He hoped he wouldn't get trapped in a conversation with either of Sadie's folks.

"Did you want to wait for Sadie here or go into the living room and take a seat?" Jana Beth asked.

"Umm. . .guess I'll wait right here."

"Okay. I hope the two of you enjoy your evening." She turned and disappeared into the other room.

She's probably going there to tell the rest of the family that Sadie's date is being unsociable. Wyman glanced toward the steps at the end of the hall. *Hurry up, Sadie—time's awasting.*

A few minutes went by; then Sadie descended the stairs, dressed in a rust-colored dress with matching apron and cape that complemented her pretty auburn hair.

Wyman drew a quick breath. "You ready to go, Sadie?"

She nodded, fingering the ties on her stiff, white head covering. "I'll just pop into the living room and say goodbye to my folks. Do you want to come with me?"

"No, that's okay. I need to tell my driver something, so I'll meet you by his car."

Sadie shrugged. "All right. I'll see you out there."

Wyman hurried out of the house and opened his driver's door. "Sadie will be here soon and then we can go," he told Floyd.

"Okie-dokie."

"Oh, and don't forget. . .Sadie doesn't know where we're going, and I want it to be a surprise."

"Have no fear. I won't say a word."

Wyman glanced toward the house and felt relief when his pretty girlfriend stepped out the door. He could hardly wait till they were sitting at a table inside the Boathouse Restaurant, looking out at beautiful Winona Lake.

✳

Kosciusko County, Indiana

I wonder where we're headed. Earlier, Sadie watched their driver take them out onto the highway from Middlebury. Some time had passed since then, and her curiosity had increased. *I honestly thought we'd be going to a local establishment, but here we are still traveling down State Route 15.*

Sadie sat next to Wyman in the backseat as he held her hand. She peered out the passenger window, looking at the sights while they chatted. Sadie felt excited about spending this evening with Wyman. When he'd first picked her up, Wyman said he had arranged a little surprise for her, and she grew more curious with each passing mile.

After more time passed, they exited and approached Winona Lake. She'd been here before with her family, but it had been a few years ago. They'd come to have a little fun away from home and done some shopping and gotten takeout from an establishment to have a picnic lunch at the lake. Sadie thought it was a pretty place, and she liked the peacefulness here. She remembered how during their meal she'd observed several people out riding bikes and others in boats tootling around on the water. It had turned out to be a warm, beautiful day, and she'd had a great time with her family.

I'm having a nice time right now with Wyman. Sadie looked over at him and smiled. He winked and grinned back at her.

The car slowed and turned into the entrance of the Boathouse. She sat up straight and waited until the vehicle pulled up front.

"Is this where we will be eating?" she asked.

"Jah. I hope you're okay with it. I know we've talked about coming here in the past." Wyman gave her hand a tender squeeze before letting go of it.

"I'm totally fine with the idea of eating here." Sadie reached for the door handle.

They both climbed out of the car, and Wyman talked to Floyd before he drove from the lot.

Sadie was tickled over being at this lakefront restaurant, and she followed him in through the entrance. The place had a warmth about it as she looked around at the oak woodwork. The entry floor was covered with a grayish tile that met up near a doorway to her left. Sadie noticed it was an entrance to a gift shop.

Oh, fun. Maybe we'll have time before the meal to go in and have a look around.

Wyman stepped up to the host and inquired about their reservations. His blue eyes sparkled as he smiled at Sadie.

"It'll be a few minutes, but we'll call your name when the table is ready," the man said.

Wyman put his hand against the small of Sadie's back. "We have some time, so why don't we step into the gift shop and have a look around?"

"That sounds *gut* to me." Sadie grinned and headed in.

Wyman stayed near as they made their way through the store.

"These are a fine-looking pair." Sadie held up two glass ducks and inspected the intricate detail of the quality etching. Then she set them back down.

Wyman picked up the pair. "I'll get these for you, so you'll remember our time here at Winona Lake."

"You don't have to buy them. They are a little pricey, so I can look for something else."

"Nope. I'm getting these."

"Thank you." She appreciated Wyman's generosity and attentiveness this evening.

When he'd finished paying at the cash register, Sadie heard his name being called. "Wyman, we need to go—our table is ready."

They returned to the podium where the host waited. "You two can follow me." He took them to a spot by the window.

After being seated, Sadie set aside her handbag and the box with the ducks in it and focused on Wyman. He looked so handsome in his light yellow button-down dress shirt and black vest. She couldn't help staring at him. "This is a nice place you picked out for us, and the view is wonderful." Sadie even admired the tall ceiling overhead, with big dark beams placed every few feet apart.

The sun shone in from the row of windows, filling the long seating area with abundant light. Sadie noticed a pair of mallard ducks swimming by on the lake. "Look, Wyman, aren't they a handsome pair?"

"Jah. They remind me of the glass ones I bought for you."

"I can't get over how nice this place is," she commented.

"I was hoping you'd like it. I thought this would be a good spot to eat our meal."

"It is. I appreciate the view of the lake."

"Me too."

Soon a waitress came over to see to their drinks. She took their orders and gave them each a menu before retreating. Wyman opened his and began to scan the choices. Sadie did the same, but seeing the prices, she thought it might be best to order a salad or bowl of soup. Her thinking ceased when Wyman spoke again.

"Sadie, let me just say that tonight I want you to order anything you want."

"Are you sure? Most things on the menu are kind of pricey."

"It's okay. I've got it covered." He reached over and tenderly patted her hand.

Sadie nearly melted at his sweet attention. It wasn't long after he'd said this to her when the waitress returned with their sodas. Wyman seemed ready to order, but Sadie still wasn't sure.

"Would you like me to go first?" He closed up his menu.

She nodded.

"I'll have the filet mignon with a baked potato and mixed vegetables.

Also, I'd like a side salad with ranch dressing on it."

The waitress wrote down his selections. "How would you like your steak cooked?"

"Medium rare, please."

She turned to Sadie. "What would you like for your meal this evening, miss?"

She pondered a bit before giving her answer. "I'll have the same thing he's having, but I'd like my steak cooked medium well."

"Okay, I'll get your meal choices turned in." The woman hurried off.

Out the window, Sadie watched a boat going by, wishing that she and Wyman could take a ride on the lake. She thought it would be fun to own a boat and be able to sail around Winona Lake whenever she wanted.

"How was work today, Wyman?" Sadie asked, pushing her unrealistic musings aside. No way could she afford to own a boat like the ones she saw on this lake.

"Just the usual—mostly loading up feed for customers, but I'd rather not talk about work right now." He leaned back in his chair and gazed out the window.

"Anything new happen this week that's not related to your job?"

"Actually, I've been installing new LED lights inside and outside of my buggy." He gave her a wide smile.

"I'll be eager to see how it looks. What evening should I come over?"

"How 'bout I come over to your place and show you?"

"Are you sure? I haven't been to your house in a while. It would be nice to see your folks and visit with them."

Wyman seemed to be mulling over her question. "I'd rather spend time at your place if you don't mind."

"Okay." Sadie sipped on her root beer. *He's acting a little odd, and I wonder where he got the money to bring me here tonight, not to mention buy new buggy lights. Maybe he got a raise or has been able to put some money aside.* She set her glass back on the table. *I'd like to find out what's going on.*

Chapter 3

Sadie had finished waiting on a customer when she saw Barbara Eash enter the hardware store. She noticed that her friend didn't have the children with her today.

I wonder what it's like to be settled down and sharing a home with the man you love. Sadie swallowed hard. *I really want a life with Wyman. He's so sweet and giving—especially the way he treated me last night. I felt like I was being spoiled.*

Barbara smiled as she stepped up to the counter. "*Guder mariye,* Sadie. How are you this beautiful Saturday morning?"

"Good morning." Sadie returned the smile. "I'm doing well. How about you?"

"I can't complain. My *mamm* volunteered to watch the *kinner* for me so I could get some shopping done today. One of the items I need is for Gideon, which I'm sure I'll find here."

"It's nice of your mother to help out when needed. I'm sure your husband's busy working today."

"Jah, he's always busy. And my mamm—well, she loves spending time with her grandchildren."

"It's been awhile since I've seen you. I was wondering if you'd heard from Mandy lately."

Barbara shook her head. "I have to admit, though, I don't keep in touch with her the way I should. She's busy raising her family and running a B&B with Ken, and I'm busy with my children, so there's not much time for writing letters anymore."

Sadie hesitated to mention the news she'd received from Mandy the other day but decided to go ahead and share it. "I got a letter from her, and she said that she's expecting another boppli."

"That's *wunderbaar*. I bet they're *eiferich*." Barbara's tone sounded genuine, and her blue eyes looked sincere. Not a shred of jealousy in her expression because Mandy had told Sadie the news and not her.

"Jah, she and Ken are very excited." Sadie figured Mandy had probably written Barbara a letter too, and she hadn't received it yet.

Barbara leaned on the counter. "Not to change the subject or anything, but I was wondering how things are going with you and Wyman these days. Are you still seeing him regularly?"

Sadie gave an enthusiastic nod. "He took me out for supper last night to the Boathouse Restaurant at Winona Lake."

Barbara's dark eyebrows lifted high on her forehead. "That must have been nice. Your boyfriend's obviously making good money working for his daed."

I hope he will keep making good money, and that we can hopefully start a future together soon. "I'm sure Wyman's father is paying him a decent wage, and I'm thankful that he's settled in there and seems to enjoy working at the feed store. It gives me hope that we might finally have a future together."

"Has he asked you to marry him?"

"Not yet, but I'm sure it's only a matter of time."

"That'll be good. When he does, let me know, because I've been praying things will work out between you two. And just think, Sadie, you could soon be an old married *fraa* like me, Ellen, and Mandy." Barbara grinned and winked. "Well, maybe not old, but you know what I mean."

"Jah." *I would love to be Wyman's wife,* Sadie thought. *But only when he's ready and has proved that he can settle down and stick with one job.*

✳

Middlebury

After work, Sadie planned to go to Ellen Zook's place for a short visit. It had been nice seeing Barbara today, and now she looked forward to seeing another good friend. She was happy for them but couldn't help feeling a bit envious that they both had loving husbands.

Just bide your time, Sadie told herself. *Someday Wyman will ask you to marry him.*

A welcoming breeze caressed Sadie's face as her feet pedaled her bike along. It had turned out to be a warm afternoon. *I'm glad Ellen can work from home and be able to take care of her family too.*

When Sadie pulled her bicycle in front of Ellen and Rueben's bed-and-breakfast, the first thing she noticed was the lovely pots of colorful petunias decorating the front porch. While the B&B wasn't on her normal route home from work, it wasn't far out of the way either.

She parked the bike, making sure it was secure, before hurrying up the stairs and rapping on the front door. Moments later Ellen answered, holding baby Irene, who had been named after Rueben's maternal grandmother.

As Ellen opened the door wider, the sun pouring in made the hair peeking out from the front of her *kapp* look like spun gold. "It's good to see you. Please, come in."

"Are you sure? I mean, if you're busy right now, I can drop by some other time."

Ellen stroked her ten-month-old daughter's rosy cheek. "We have no guests coming until this evening, so I've been enjoying some quality time with my little one this afternoon. You are most welcome to join us."

"I'd like that." Sadie eagerly followed her friend to the cozy living room, and they took seats on the sofa. She gazed about the well-appointed room that smelled of fresh roses. Sadie noticed the long-stemmed pink flowers that had been put in a pretty glass vase and placed on a side table.

She looked back at her friend, cradling the baby. The pacifier in Irene's mouth moved rhythmically. Sadie couldn't help watching the cute baby.

"How have you been?" Sadie and Ellen spoke at the same time.

Sadie chuckled. "Why don't you go first?"

"Okay." A few strands of Ellen's blond hair had come loose from the bun at the back of her head, and she reached up to tuck them into place before caressing her daughter's chubby arm. "I'm feeling fine physically, but the responsibility of running the B&B while taking care of Irene can be pretty tiring. So in addition to the woman we hired to clean and service the rooms, we've recently brought in another person who does most of the cooking."

"That makes sense—especially with this being tourist season. I remember how, when I helped you out here a few times after Mandy and Ken moved to Hawaii, things sometimes became a bit hectic." Sadie reached over and took hold of the baby's hand. "Would you mind if I held her?" *I hope one day I have such an adorable boppli.*

"Of course not." Ellen handed her daughter to Sadie. "She's not one bit afraid of strangers, so you can hold her anytime."

Sadie chuckled. "I'm not really a stranger. I come by here often enough that Irene should recognize my face."

"I know." Ellen leaned closer to Sadie. "It's your turn now. What have you been up to lately?"

"I've been working on a new quilt design, but before I tell you about that, I was wondering if you've heard from Mandy lately."

Ellen nodded. "I got a letter from her yesterday."

"I received one too."

"Did she mention that she's expecting another boppli?"

"Jah. Mandy seems quite excited about it."

Ellen smiled while reaching over to touch the tip of her little girl's nose. "And with good reason. Every child born is special in God's sight, and I look forward to the day Irene has a baby brother or sister."

"I understand. I look forward to becoming a mother someday too." Sadie gave the child a tender caress.

"Has Wyman asked you to marry him yet?"

Not this question again. I have nothing new to tell her. Sadie shook her head. "But I'm sure he will when he's ready."

"Ready financially, or when he's settled down enough to take on the responsibility of being a husband and someday a father?"

"Both." Sadie pulled a tissue from the box on the end table by the couch and wiped some drool off Irene's chin. "Is she teething?"

"Jah. I have to watch her 'cause she'll put anything she can get her hands on into her mouth." Ellen leaned against the sofa cushions. "Is Wyman still working for his daed?"

Sadie bobbed her head. "He took me to the Boathouse Restaurant in Winona Lake last night for supper, and we ordered one of the most expensive meals. So I assume he's making good money at the feed store, and if that's the case, then maybe it won't be long before he feels ready for marriage."

"I wouldn't be surprised. Now please tell me about this new quilt pattern you're working on."

As Sadie held Ellen's baby firmly on her lap, she went into detail about her plan to make a blended quilt.

✳

"Say, Wyman, before you leave the store, can I talk to you for a few minutes?" Michael motioned for Wyman to join him behind the checkout counter. The feed store was empty of customers, and the CLOSED sign had been put in the front window.

I can only imagine what Michael wants to ask me. He reminds me a lot of Dad, always needing to know every detail about my business.

Wyman gave the clock a quick glance. *How long is this going to take? I hope not too long.* "Sure, what's up?" He sauntered over to stand by his brother.

"There are two things I would like to ask you about, and since Dad's already gone home, I figured now's a good time."

Wyman's brows furrowed. "Is it something you don't want our daed to know about?"

"Let's just say I'd prefer that he not hear our discussion."

"Okay, what's on your mind?"

Michael pressed his lips together in a slight grimace. "Is it true that you put in your two weeks' notice with Dad?"

Wyman nodded.

"How come? I thought everything was going along fine with you working here."

"Well, it's not. I—I mean, nothing bad has happened. I'm just not happy doing this kind of work. I need to find something more to my liking."

"What would that be?"

Wyman shrugged. "I'm not sure, but I'll know when I find it."

Michael flapped his hand. "That's *lecherich*."

"It's not ridiculous. No one should have to work at a job they don't like."

"Our dad pays well, and if you quit without finding another job, how are you going to give me regular payments for the money I loaned you?" Michael pointed at Wyman. "Speaking of which—do you have the cash you promised to give me by the end of this week?"

It was only a matter of time. Why couldn't he have let it slip by this once? Wyman's chin dipped slightly, and he felt warmth creep over his ears and spread across his face. "Sorry, but I don't have it right now."

"When will you have it?"

"Soon—I promise it'll be soon." No way could Wyman admit to his brother that he'd spent the money he was supposed to give him on an expensive meal with Sadie last night. That would not go over well.

"You sure about that?"

Wyman didn't like the accusing tone of his brother's voice or the look of uncertainty in his eyes. He felt backed into a corner. "I said I'd pay, and I will, just as soon as I get my final paycheck from Dad."

Michael folded his arms as he stared at Wyman. "I think you ought to reconsider and continue working here."

Sometimes my brother even sounds like our father, but today he's being a little bossy. Wyman shook his head. "No way! I've already told Dad that I'm quitting, and what's done is done."

"Okay, it's obvious that I can't talk you out of it, but I expect the payment when you get your last paycheck—no excuses. I'm counting on the money so I can pay a few bills that are coming due. I also promised my fraa some spending money so she can go out shopping for some things she's been needing."

"I understand, and you can get that worried look off your face. I'll make good on my word."

Wyman squirmed under his brother's scrutiny. If he didn't come through with the money he'd promised, Michael would probably tell Dad about it, and then he'd have two family members upset with him.

Guess I'd better start looking through the want ads in the newspaper and see what jobs are available, he told himself. *If there's nothing to my liking, I may have to take another job I don't care about and work there till something better opens up. At least then I'll have some money coming in so I can meet my obligations and be able to take Sadie out for a nice meal once in a while. We both had such a good time last night. It'd be a shame if we couldn't do anything fun due to lack of funds in my bank account.*

Wyman thought about his decision not to tell Sadie that he'd quit his job until he'd landed a better one. He still felt it was the best choice right now. There was no point in saying anything that might cause her to become upset with him.

Another thought popped into Wyman's head. *What if Dad's already told Mom about my decision to quit working here? Once she hears the news I'd better wear earplugs for a few days, 'cause Mom's gonna be upset and will no doubt start hounding me about it.*

Chapter 4

Three weeks had passed, and on Friday, Sadie's day off, she decided to drop by the feed store to see Wyman. She'd been in the area shopping and had hoped to catch him during his lunch break. Wyman had been on Sadie's mind since this morning. She'd picked out a bright blue dress that he liked and even dabbed on a splash of cologne. Sadie hoped Wyman would be happy to see her and wouldn't be too busy when she arrived.

When Sadie entered the store, she found Michael behind the counter, but there was no sign of Wyman. She figured he might be in the back room or had gone out to make a delivery.

"Is Wyman here?" Sadie asked, stepping up to the counter.

The smile he'd first offered her faded. Sadie didn't know what to think as the silence dragged on. *I wonder why the sullen face.*

Michael pushed the invoice book in front of him aside and reached up to give his right earlobe a tug. "My brother doesn't work here anymore—but then you probably knew that, right?"

Oh no. . . Wyman, why did you do this? Sadie's fingers touched her parted lips as she shook her head. "Wh–when did he quit?"

"Three weeks ago he told our daed he wasn't happy working here and would be quitting in two weeks. So last Friday was his final day."

Sadie held her purse tightly against her chest. *Wait a minute; let me think. Three weeks ago I was excited about seeing Wyman and anticipating his surprise for me. That was the same day he took me to the Boathouse for supper, but Wyman never said one word about quitting his job at the feed store. He acted a bit strangely, but I dismissed it, thinking he was tired. Why didn't he tell me? Was he afraid I'd be upset about his decision?*

Sadie's fingers curled tightly around her purse straps. *I would have been upset, but not nearly as much as I am right now, learning that he quit three weeks ago and hasn't told me about it.*

"So my *bruder* never mentioned that he'd walked away from this perfectly good job?"

Michael's question halted Sadie's disconcerting thoughts. "No, he did not. Apparently when Wyman took me out for supper in Winona Lake, it was the same day he told your father he planned to quit, but he never said a word about it." She gave a frustrated huff. "Even when he came over to show me his new buggy lights last week, he never mentioned quitting his job here."

Michael gave his other earlobe a tug. "That brother of mine—I don't know what his problem is. He should have told you about his impulsive decision."

"One would think." Sadie leaned heavily against her side of the counter. "Guess I'm not as important to him as I thought."

"I don't think it's that. Wyman was probably worried about your reaction to the news."

"I'm not the enemy. We could have talked about it, at least."

"I agree, but—"

"Is he working someplace else?"

Michael shook his head. "Not that I'm aware of. Since my bruder still lives at home, I'm sure he would have told our daed if he'd found another job, and Dad would have mentioned it to me."

"How do your folks feel about him quitting?"

Michael's russet-colored eyebrows rose as he looked directly at Sadie. "Dad's not happy about Wyman's decision, but Mom hasn't said anything about it to me. I'm not sure she even knows. Wyman may have asked Dad not to say anything until he found another job. She was so happy when he started working there and might be *umgerennt* about this."

No more upset than me, Sadie thought. *I need to calm down before I speak to him, because I don't want to make matters worse.*

✳

"Have you found anything yet?"

Wyman jumped at the sound of his mother's voice, and he nearly dropped the newspaper he'd been looking at. *"Ach!* Mom, you shouldn't sneak up on me like that."

"I wasn't sneaking. I came out to get my horse out of her stall." She rested both hands firmly against her hips. "And what are you doing sitting out here in the barn on a bale of straw in the middle of the day? Shouldn't you be out looking for a job?"

Wyman lowered his gaze a few seconds and then looked up at her. "I guess Dad must've told ya, huh?"

"Jah, I've known for several days, but I was waiting and hoping you'd tell me that news yourself." She crossed her arms. "Why the big secret, Son? Didn't you think I had the right to know?"

He shook his head. "It's not that, Mom. I figured you'd be upset and I'd be in for a stern lecture."

"And well you should be, but I doubt it would do any good." She shifted her weight but kept her arms folded. "I love you, Wyman, but you're *unverlaessich.*"

"Because I want some other job rather than working for Dad? Is that what you think is unreliable?"

"Maybe a better word would be *irresponsible.*"

Wyman pointed to the Want Ads section of the paper. "Would I be looking here for a job if I was irresponsible?"

"You're looking because you're in need of a job, but you had a perfectly good one and tossed it aside like yesterday's garbage."

"I wasn't happy there, Mom."

"What about your *aldi*? How does she feel about you being jobless again?" His mother spoke in a stern tone, causing Wyman to feel like a little boy who'd done something to displease her.

"My girlfriend doesn't know. I haven't told her yet."

"How come?"

"I don't want to upset Sadie or cause her to think I'm not capable of providing for her if we get married."

She pointed at him again. "Which is precisely why you need a steady job—one you'll stick with and not run from when you get tired or bored of the work."

"If I had a job I really like I wouldn't get bored." Wyman folded the newspaper, tucked it under his arm, and stood. "Think I'll head over to Sadie's house and see her. She does need to know the truth, and there's no point in me hiding it any longer. News travels fast in this community, and if I don't say something soon, she's bound to hear it from someone else." He said goodbye to his mother and hurried from the barn. Wyman wouldn't take the time to get his horse out and hitch him to the buggy. He'd ride his bike over to see Sadie instead.

✳

Sadie pedaled her bike toward home so fast, it was a miracle her head covering didn't blow off. She felt tempted to turn back and head for Wyman's house to see if he was home but thought better of it. In her frame of mind, she might say the wrong thing and end up arguing with him. No, it was better to go home and think things through—give herself some time to rehearse what she would say when she did speak to Wyman about his deceit. He'd quit working for his dad and for some reason did not want her to know, so she needed to be careful how she approached the topic.

Pedaling into her yard, she stopped the bike by the front porch, where her mother was kneeling near one of the flower beds.

"You're back sooner than I expected." Mom turned to her and smiled.

"Did you get all your shopping done?"

Sadie lifted a plastic sack from the basket at the front of her bike. "Most of it, anyhow."

Mom's digging in the flower bed halted. "Okay, something has you upset. It's written all over your face. Did you stop by the feed store to see Wyman, like you'd planned to do?"

"Jah, but he wasn't there."

"Was it also his day off?"

"Oh, he was off all right. I spoke with Michael and found out that Wyman's no longer working there."

"What? Did I hear that right?" Mom's brows shot up. "And why is that? I thought he was content to work at his father's store."

"That's what I believed too, but I was wrong. Michael said Wyman wasn't happy working there so he decided to quit. He gave his notice three weeks ago."

"For goodness' sakes. What's happened to that man's way of thinking? Doesn't he realize the stress he's putting you through?" Mom removed her gardening gloves and shook the dirt off. "How's he ever going to be ready for marriage if he can't hold a job?"

"I know, Mom. . . . I know. I've wondered the same thing all the way here." She climbed off the bicycle. "Maybe he has no intention of settling down or asking me to marry him."

"Under the circumstances, that might be in your best interest, Daughter. My thoughts are leaning toward you staying away from him, but that's only my opinion. Do you what you feel is best."

Sadie couldn't deny the truth in her mother's words, but it cut her heart to think that she and the man she loved might never become husband and wife. If Wyman would just buckle down and stick with a job, Sadie could relax and stop worrying so much about her future. No way would she marry him if he kept changing jobs all the time, not to mention his deceit in not telling her about it. *I have to wonder if he's hiding anything else from me. How would I know if he is or isn't, when Wyman can be so good at deceiving me?* Sadie wiped the perspiration from her hands onto her apron.

"No comment on what I last said?" Mom stood up and moved over to stand next to Sadie.

"I can't make a decision on anything right now. I need to speak with Wyman first and hear what he has to say about this."

"Looks like that might be happening soon. Here comes your boyfriend now."

Sadie turned and looked in the direction her mother pointed. Her emotions ran amuck as she watched Wyman coming up the driveway on his bicycle. *I hope he has a good explanation to offer.*

✳

As soon as Wyman saw Sadie's wrinkled brows and pursed lips he knew it spelled trouble. *She knows. I'm not sure who told, but Sadie knows that I quit my job.*

He parked his bike next to hers and got off. Glancing briefly at Grace Kuhns and giving a nod, he turned his attention to Sadie. "Can I talk to you in private? There's something important I need to say."

She leveled him with an icy stare. "If it's about you quitting your job at the feed store, there's not much to be said."

"Jah, there is. I need to explain."

Grace stepped onto the front porch. "I'll leave you two alone to talk things through." She opened the screen door and disappeared into the house.

"Can we sit and talk awhile?" Wyman motioned to the picnic table on the front lawn.

Sadie nodded and silently followed him over to it.

Wyman took a seat on the closest bench, and Sadie sat on the other side of the table. She crossed her arms, and her rigid posture told him she was upset.

"How'd you find out I quit my job?" he asked.

"Michael told me. I stopped by the store to see you this morning, and your bruder said you'd put in your notice three weeks ago." Her chin quivered. "You knew that night you took me to dinner at the Boathouse, didn't you?"

I've gotta fix this, but where do I start? I have made a mess of things with the girl I love. "Jah, I knew." It was hard to look at her.

"Why didn't you say something?"

"I didn't want to spoil our nice evening."

"What about the day you came over here to show me the lights on your buggy? How come you didn't mention it then?"

Wyman squirmed under her scrutiny. "I was afraid you'd be upset. And I figured I'd find another job soon and then I would tell you."

"Have you found another one?"

"Not yet, but I will."

"What'll happen if you decide to quit that one too?" She emitted a deep, weighted sigh.

"I won't. The next job I take will be the right one, and I'll stick with it—I promise."

Sadie placed her hands on the table and folded them. "You know what I think, Wyman?"

"What's that?"

"I think you don't know what kind of job you really want. You may spend the rest of your life searching for something you'll never be satisfied with."

"Not true. When I find the right job, I'll stick with it for sure."

"I'll tell you what else I think." She leaned forward, resting her elbows on the table.

"What's that?"

"I think you don't care much for me, or you wouldn't have been so deceitful."

"Also not true." Wyman's face felt flushed. "I care deeply for you, Sadie, and I'm hoping—"

She held up her hand. "Until you figure out what's really important to you and you're ready to make some serious changes, I don't think we should see each other anymore."

He placed both hands against his hot, sweaty forehead, and his voice cracked with the emotion stirring in his soul. "Are you breaking up with me?"

She gave a slow nod. "Under the circumstances, I think that's the best decision for both of us."

"Well, I don't." Wyman stood. "If you'll just be patient with me—"

"I've been patient long enough." Tears sprang into Sadie's eyes as she left the picnic table. "I can't talk about this anymore. Goodbye, Wyman." She made a dash for the house and rushed inside before he could form a response.

Wyman stumbled toward his bike, got on, and pedaled out of the yard. *This can't be the end of my relationship with Sadie. She's the only girl for me, and I'll win her back somehow. . . . I have to.*

Chapter 5

*H*ow'd it go out there with Wyman?" Sadie's mother asked when she entered the house.

"Not good. We"—Sadie's voice faltered—"we broke up."

Mom gave Sadie a big hug. "I'm sorry, but maybe it's for the best. Perhaps he's not the man God wants for you."

"It was me who broke things off with Wyman." *Did I really make the right decision? Should I have waited longer to see if he would change his ways?*

Sadie sniffed and wiped her eyes. "Except for him skipping from job to job, Wyman has many good qualities."

"While I'm sure that is true, would you want to marry someone who can't make up his mind about the type of work he wants to do? What would happen if, down the road, Wyman quit one job but couldn't find another? Or what if he found a job that didn't pay well? Good-paying jobs are not always plentiful, you know."

Sadie blew her nose on the tissue Mom handed her. "I'm well aware, but I don't believe Wyman would take any job that didn't pay well enough."

Mom shook her head. "I don't understand. One minute you're saying you and Wyman broke up, and now you're defending him. You need to make up your mind."

"I have, but that doesn't make my decision any easier." She blinked as a few more tears escaped her eyes. "If he would only find a job and stick with it, maybe things could still work out for us."

"But Sadie..."

"I—I can't talk about this anymore, Mom. I'm going to the sewing room to work on my quilt pattern. Maybe a few hours of drawing and cutting out material will help me de-stress." Sadie hurried from the room. Although she did appreciate her mother's sympathy, Sadie didn't need to be lectured or to feel like she was being told what to do. *Mom doesn't understand how difficult it was for me to call things off with Wyman.* Sadie blew out a frustrated breath. *She doesn't realize how much I love him. But will my breaking up with Wyman wake him up, or is it time for me to move on to someone else?*

✷

Grace stood at the kitchen sink, staring out the window. She felt sure she'd upset Sadie with the things she'd said, but she'd only spoken the truth as she saw it. *I love and care about Sadie. It's difficult to see her struggle and be in pain over making what I think was a good decision.*

"If only my dochder could see it."

"See what, Mom? And which daughter are you referring to?"

Grace turned at the sound of Jana Beth's voice. "Oh, I didn't realize you were home."

"I just got here, actually. Came in to see if you needed any help with supper preparations." Jana Beth slipped on the apron she wore to do chores.

"Danki, that's thoughtful of you—especially since you've been working at the trailer factory all day and must be *mied.*"

"I am tired, but not so much that I can't offer to pitch in. I got off earlier than Kaylene and Dad today, so there's no reason I can't help you with supper preparations." She moved closer to Grace. "Which of your daughters were you referring to when I entered the kitchen and found you talking to yourself?"

"Sadie."

"Ah, I see. I saw her bike outside, so I assumed she must be home."

"She is."

"I'm surprised she's not in here helping you with supper."

Grace gestured with her head toward the hallway outside the kitchen door. "She's in the sewing room, working on a new quilt pattern."

Jana Beth rolled her pretty blue eyes. "How thoughtful. Doesn't she know what time it is?"

"Don't be so hard on your sister. She and Wyman broke up today, so she's feeling a bit stressed out." Grace took a potato peeler from the drawer and handed it to Jana Beth. "Would you mind peeling some potatoes while I check on the roast in the oven?"

"Of course. Let me wash my hands first, and I'll tackle the job." Jana Beth tilted her reddish-blond head to one side. "I'm sorry to hear about their breakup. Do you know what went wrong?"

"That's something you ought to ask your sister. If she wants to talk about it, I'm sure she will tell you."

"I won't say anything unless she brings it up."

"Even if she does, I'd be careful not to offer a strong opinion. She became upset when I voiced my concerns."

"Okay, Mom, I'll heed your advice. I sure don't want to upset her any more than she already is."

Grace opened the oven door to check on the roast and sent up a silent prayer. *Heavenly Father, please guide and direct each of my children's lives and help them to make wise choices.*

✳

When Michael entered the house, he found his wife in the living room, feeding their five-month-old son, Aaron, while their three-year-old daughter, Priscilla, played on the floor with two of her favorite dolls.

"How'd your day go at work?" she asked, smiling up at him.

He lifted his shoulders in a brief shrug. "It went okay, but we were busy most of the day. It would have been easier for Dad and me if Wyman had been there."

"I still can't understand what possessed him to quit a perfectly good job." Lovina placed Aaron against her shoulder and patted his back. It wasn't long before a noisy burp came forth. "I wonder what his aldi thinks about it."

Michael's mouth twisted as he shifted his stance. "Sadie didn't know until today."

Lovina blinked. "Really? Why not?"

"Because Wyman is inconsiderate and chose not to tell her. She came into the store looking for him, and you should have seen her stunned expression when I said he wasn't working at the feed store anymore." He paused a moment then continued. "It was awkward for me to be the one to give Sadie the news. I'm not sure what's going on with my brother lately. He's been making the dumbest decisions."

Lovina clicked her tongue. "Apparently."

Michael took a seat on the couch and beckoned their daughter to come to him.

The dark-haired little girl didn't have to be coaxed. She grabbed one of the dolls and ran over to Michael, hugging his knee.

He leaned over and picked Priscilla up, placing her in his lap. The little girl leaned into his chest as Michael stroked the top of her silky hair.

"I bet it didn't go over so well when you told Sadie the reason Wyman wasn't at the feed store." Lovina pursed her lips.

"You're right, and I wouldn't be surprised if Sadie didn't go straight over to our folks' place and give my changeable brother a piece of her mind."

"Do you think they'll break up over this?"

Michael shrugged again. "It's possible—maybe they already have. Sadie needs to feel that she can trust Wyman to keep his word and that he won't spend the rest of his life dissatisfied with every new job."

"There shouldn't be a bunch of new jobs. Wyman's twenty-four years old. One would think by now he'd be ready to settle down. You're only two years older than him, and look what a dependable husband and father you've turned out to be."

"Danki." Lovina's sincere smile nearly melted Michael's heart. He still couldn't believe that this lovely woman with jet-black hair and eyes the color of the clear blue sky on a summer day had chosen him above all the other potential suitors in their Amish community.

"Has your bruder found another job yet?" she questioned.

Michael shook his head, and when Priscilla began to squirm, he put her on the floor again. She scampered off, grabbed her other doll, and scurried from the room.

Lovina began rocking the baby. "Has Wyman made a payment this month on the money you loaned him?"

Oh no. I was afraid she would get around to asking me that. My brother is sure making life difficult for those who are closest to him. Michael rubbed his forehead where a dribble of sweat had formed. "Not yet, but he said he'd make a payment when he gets his last check from having worked for Dad at the feed store."

She pressed her lips together and patted the baby some more.

"I don't think it'll be too long a wait. And you know, Wyman may be a job hopper, but he's always been able to find work and get hired."

"Maybe not this time, though. He might be out of a job for a long while. Then what, Michael? How's he going to get you paid back if he's not making any *geld*?"

"Wyman will be making money soon. You'll see."

"I hope so, because there are bills to be paid each month, and I was counting on the money he would pay you this month to buy a few extra things we've been needing."

"I'll speak to him again soon." Michael stood. "I have a few chores to do outside before I take a shower. Then I'll help you fix supper."

Lovina shook her head. "There's no need for that. I can manage. You've had a long day at work and deserve some downtime this evening."

He moved across the room, leaned down, and kissed her cheek. "Don't know what I did to deserve you, but I'm glad you said yes when I asked you to become my fraa."

She smiled. "I'm glad I did too."

As Michael strode from the room, his thoughts turned to Wyman again. *I'm not sure what to do if that brother of mine doesn't find a job soon and give me some money. I sure don't want any of this mess to come between me and my fraa.*

✽

Sadie turned toward the door as the clattering of plates interrupted her work. It sounded like someone had begun setting the table for supper.

I'm glad I've been kept busy on my quilt pattern this afternoon. The distraction has been helpful. She had been staring at her drawing too long. It was time to go help Mom with supper. The most recent sketch she'd made was close to what she wanted, but it needed something else. Since she couldn't figure out what, there was no point in continuing to sit here fretting over it.

Sadie looked over at the pile of wadded papers near the trash and mumbled, "At least I've been trying to come up with something creative, despite feeling so drained and unhappy today." Of course, she'd done more agonizing over her situation with Wyman than she had over the sketch she had made during the past few hours she'd spent in the sewing room.

Guess I should've helped Mom with the meal preparations. Sadie frowned. *The food must be close to being ready. I'll go see what I can do to help.*

A tantalizing aroma coming from the kitchen filled Sadie's nostrils as she made her way down the hall.

"Everything smells good. How's it going in here?" Sadie asked when she entered the kitchen where Mom and Jana Beth stood working on a tossed green salad.

"We've got it under control," her sister responded. She looked over at Sadie and smiled.

Mom lifted the lid on the potatoes and poked them with a fork. "These are done and ready to be mashed. Supper is close to being served, so all we need is to get everyone in here to wash up and eat."

Sadie had to admit the aromas made her mouth water. She felt her body relax some in this cozy environment as she watched Mom drain the spuds and begin working on making her tantalizing mashed potatoes.

"How's your quilt design coming along?" Jana Beth asked. "Mom said you've been working on a new one."

"Okay, I guess." She folded her arms across her chest. "It's not quite what I want it to be, but hopefully soon."

The back door flew open, and Kaylene burst into the room. "Something's wrong with your *gaul*, Sadie. She's laying out in the pasture and our *hund*'s standing over her, barking like there's no tomorrow. I'm surprised you all haven't heard him."

Mom's brows furrowed. "I did hear the dog carrying on, but I figured he was chasing one of the *katze*."

Kaylene shook her head. "I saw no cats—just Rufus running in circles around Sadie's horse."

"This makes no sense. I'd better go see what's up." Sadie hurried out of the house, unlocked the pasture gate, and ran across the field. Kaylene was right—Daisy was down, and Rufus was carrying on like crazy.

"Come on, girl!" she hollered. "Daisy, get up!" Sadie's heart pounded as she approached and tried to shush the dog. Kneeling next to Daisy, she saw a terrible gash and blood on the mare's head. It appeared that Daisy, now lying ever so still, had run into the nearest fence post, because there was blood on it too.

Sadie called out to the horse again, but there was no response and no indication that Daisy was breathing. The poor animal had apparently died.

She reached out and stroked the mare's mane. "I'm so sorry. . . . I'm going to miss you, Daisy." Sadie's eyes overflowed with tears, and she began to sob. Her aunt Sadie Ruth, whom she'd been named after, had given her the money to buy this mare when she'd turned sixteen. Sadie's fondness for Daisy had begun the day she'd brought the gentle horse home.

Rufus came up close to her, no longer barking. He nudged his nose against Sadie's face and gave her a kiss with his slurpy tongue. It was little comfort as she remained there, processing this whole ordeal. Sadie felt steeped in the loss she'd suffered today and wished it could be turned around. Her day couldn't get any worse.

Chapter 6

Tears coursed down Sadie's cheeks as she stared at her horse's empty stall. *I wish she were here right now. I miss her so much.*

She could visualize Daisy standing there, nickering at her. The mare's harness rested on its hook, and the cleaning brush sat on a shelf nearby, still holding some remnants of her hair.

It had been two weeks since her horse died, and Sadie had not found a replacement for her. Truth was, she hadn't even looked. Horses didn't come cheap, and Sadie refused to borrow money from her dad or either of her brothers. Leland and Saul had enough to deal with financially, supporting their families.

Sadie couldn't believe she'd lost her boyfriend and horse in the same day. Her relationship with Wyman was over, and it still hurt like crazy. She had seen Wyman only once in the last two weeks, and that was at their biweekly church service. The fact that he hadn't come around or tried to make amends with her spoke volumes. He obviously didn't care that she'd broken up with him. It bothered Sadie to realize how unimportant she'd been in Wyman's life. If he'd truly cared for her, he would have admitted right away that he'd quit his job at the feed store instead of letting Sadie believe he still worked there.

She clenched her teeth so hard her jaw hurt. *If Wyman really loved me, he wouldn't have quit a perfectly good job.*

Sadie shuffled across the barn where the animals' feed was kept. Bales of hay stood tall, stacked neatly almost to the rafters. The smell of it tickled

Sadie's nose as she eyed a spot to take a seat. "I don't understand how one day things can be going along fine, and then it takes such a drastic turn."

Her throat felt swollen, and she swallowed a couple of times. *If Wyman wanted to keep courting me, he'd be over here on bended knee, begging for me to take him back.*

Sadie sank onto a single bale of straw sitting off to one side. *Would I weaken and resume my relationship with Wyman if he came over to see me with an apology?* She shook her head. *No, it would take more than him saying he was sorry for keeping me in the dark about his plans. Wyman would have to prove himself. He'd need to get another job and stick to it, without running off in search of something else for no good reason.*

Sadie closed her eyes. *I shouldn't be thinking about Wyman right now. His irresponsibility and lack of communication is the reason we broke up, and that's how it should stay. I need to keep my focus on something else and stop bemoaning this situation.*

She turned away from the empty stall and went to the area in the barn where her bike was stored. Looking out the barn door, she noticed her sisters and father coming her way. It was time for all of them to head for work, and no one could afford to be late.

✳

"Still no jobs available, huh?" Wyman's mother stood behind the chair where he sat at the table going over the want ads for a second time.

"Nope, not yet." Looking for another job had become discouraging, although Wyman wasn't about to admit defeat. The one thing that troubled him the most, besides not having any cash coming in, was that without a steady job there was no way he could get back in Sadie's good graces. He hadn't seen her since their breakup, except during church, but no words had been spoken between them. As far as Wyman could tell, Sadie hadn't even looked his way. As much as he disliked the idea, it was clear that for now at least, his and Sadie's relationship was over. Someday soon, however, he hoped to right that situation.

Mom placed her hands on his shoulders. "How long are you going to let this go on before you swallow your pride and ask your daed for your old job back?"

Wyman's hands curled into fists as he clutched the newspaper. "I don't want to work there, and even if I did, it's too late for that. Dad's already hired a new man to take my place." He turned in his seat and looked up at her. "You don't expect Dad to let Ira Yoder go on my account, do you? That wouldn't show much for his integrity, would it?"

She nodded. "Your point is well taken. But if business picks up, there might be room for three employees."

Wyman pushed his chair aside and stood. "Even if that should happen, I won't be asking for my job back." He strode toward the back door.

"Where are you going?"

"Outside to do some chores."

"But I thought you and your daed took care of all your responsibilities this morning before he left for the store."

"We did, but I'll find something else to do that will keep me busy—at least till noon." Wyman waved and rushed out the door. If he'd stayed in the kitchen any longer, Mom would have kept pestering him about not having a job and no doubt making all kinds of suggestions.

This is something I need to do on my own. He took the back porch steps two at a time. *My future lies in my hands, and no one else's.*

✳

Shipshewana

"Is it true that you and Wyman broke up?"

The question took Sadie by surprise as she restocked some shelves with small gardening tools. She turned and saw Gideon Eash behind her. It figured that he would know, since he was married to Barbara, whom Sadie had told when they'd visited after church last Sunday. She just hadn't expected that Gideon would show up at the hardware store and bring up this topic.

"Jah, it's true." Sadie took two small shovels from the box beside her and hung them in place on a metal peg.

"You ready to put your feet in the water again? I know a couple of fellows you might like, so I thought maybe. . ."

Sadie gave a vigorous shake of her head. "I appreciate your concern, but I am not ready to be courted by anyone right now." *Or maybe ever. If I can't have Wyman, I don't want anyone.* She hoped other well-meaning folks wouldn't try matching her up with someone now that she was no longer seeing Wyman. Beginning a new romance was the last thing on her mind. Focusing on work while she was here at the hardware store was good therapy, and at home she had her new quilt pattern to work on, which kept her occupied.

Is this the beginning of my friends trying to talk me into the idea of meeting someone new? I'm sure Ellen will be tempted to do the same thing when she gets the chance. Sadie attached some additional pegs to the board while she continued to muse. *Ellen told me before that Wyman didn't have his act together. Guess my friend was right about him all along, but I'm not interested in dating anyone else.*

"If you change your mind, let me or Barbara know, and we'll have you over for supper to get acquainted with one of my friends." Gideon grinned at her. "If you give yourself a chance, you might find that you actually like one of them."

Sadie shrugged and moved down the line to set out more tools. She hoped Barbara hadn't asked her husband to play matchmaker, but if she had, she'd find out when Gideon came home that he hadn't succeeded.

She shoved each of the hand tillers into place. *Doesn't my friend realize I may not want to start courting again?*

✳

As Wyman approached the hardware store, he was tempted to pull into the parking lot, tie his horse to one of the hitching rails, and go inside to seek

Sadie out. But he didn't want to embarrass Sadie in front of her employer, not to mention anyone else who might be shopping in the store. He had more common sense than that. Besides, what would he say to Sadie—that he still had no job and nothing to offer her except his undying love?

Wyman crooked his neck, attempting to look through the windows of the building as he allowed the horse and buggy to ease along. "I don't see her, but then she could be anywhere inside the store."

Turning his head back, Wyman gasped as he nearly drove into a pedestrian crossing the street. He stopped his horse and apologized to the elderly man before continuing on his way. *That was sure stupid of me.* Wyman gripped the reins and focused on guiding his horse through town.

When Wyman arrived at the bulk food store, he guided his horse into the parking lot and found an empty spot at the hitching rail. This place was usually busy with locals and tourists alike. Samples were offered at times for the patrons to try in a few places within the store. Sometimes it could get difficult to work one's way around due to the amount of people shopping.

Wyman had come here to pick up some baking supplies for his mother and hoped it wasn't too crowded. He wanted to get the shopping done and move on with his day, which included stopping at a few other stores in the hope that they might be hiring. At this point, Wyman would take almost anything, even if he didn't like the work. It would give him some money for expenses and to make payments to his brother. Also he wouldn't have to be at home all the time, listening to Mom harp on how foolish he'd been for leaving his father's store.

As Wyman entered the building, where everything from bulk items to individual grocery items was sold, he spotted a sign near the door: Help Wanted. If Interested See Store Manager.

Well, how about that. Maybe there's a position available to work in the warehouse and drive a forklift.

A sense of hope welled in his soul. He had no idea what the work entailed, but it didn't matter. With any luck he might get hired on the spot.

Hurrying past the shopping carts, Wyman stepped up to one of the cashiers. "Excuse me, but could you please point me in the direction of the manager?"

"I think he's in his office at the moment. It's at the back of the store." The young man behind the counter pointed in that direction.

"Thanks." With a sense of urgency, Wyman rushed down the first aisle, skirting around several shopping carts and the people pushing them. He hoped no one else had already been given the job.

When he reached a door where a sign read OFFICE, Wyman knocked. Several seconds went by; then a middle-age bearded Amish man opened the door. "May I help you with something?"

"Umm. . .jah, I'm here in response to the 'Help Wanted' sign by the front door. Is the position still open?"

"Has anyone explained what the job entails?"

Wyman shook his head.

"The position we have open is for a clerk at one of the front checkout counters. Have you done any clerking before?"

"Jah. I did that, among other things, at my last job."

"Okay, then. You can fill out a job application and lay the paperwork on my desk." The man gestured to a seat; then he handed Wyman a clipboard with a job application and a pen.

After filing out the paperwork, Wyman placed it on the manager's desk. "Any idea how soon I might know if I got the position?"

"Sometime in the next week or so. In addition to yours, there are several others who have also applied for this job. If you're chosen, you'll receive a phone call." The Amish man shook Wyman's hand and bid him good day.

Wyman said, "Thank you," and went back into the store to do the shopping for Mom. *Sure hope I'm the one who gets chosen for this job.*

✳

After she left work that afternoon, Sadie went to the fabric store. She'd decided to make part of her blended quilt in the Ocean Waves pattern. While many times she'd seen it done up in shades of blue, to represent water, Sadie thought the quilt would look nice in softer, more subdued colors. She picked out some dark and light beige material and took it up to the counter. Once the fabric had been cut, folded, and put in a plastic sack, it fit easily in her bicycle basket.

Now all I need to do is decide what to add to give it a partial Hawaiian theme, Sadie thought as she mounted her bike. She'd purchased a book of Hawaiian quilt patterns while visiting one of the islands, so she would see if one of those designs went well with Ocean Waves. If she couldn't come up with something, she'd give Mandy a call and ask her opinion. Since her once-Amish friend had been living on Kauai for a few years now, she'd probably know a lot about the lovely quilt patterns found there.

Sadie smiled as she pedaled toward home. She couldn't wait to start this project.

She lifted her hand in a wave as a horse and buggy going in the opposite direction went by.

Lately, Sadie had been picturing things in her mind that she'd seen on the island of Kauai and figured it might be the sort of inspiration she needed to make all of this come together.

For the moment, at least, Sadie felt a little better than she had since she and Wyman broke up. She lifted her face briefly toward the sky and breathed in. *Maybe my hobby of quilting is enough for me right now. Working on the blended quilt has given me a sense of purpose and joy.*

Chapter 7

Middlebury

*A*fter work the following day, Sadie went out to the phone shed to call Mandy. When her friend's sweet voice answered, Sadie heard Hawaiian music playing in the background. It was still hard to believe that one of her friends who had grown up in an Amish home was now a part of the English world and living with her husband and little boy on the island of Kauai.

"Aloha, Mandy, it's Sadie."

"It's nice to hear from you. Did you get the letter I sent, sharing our good news?"

"I did, and I wrote you back. Didn't you receive my note?"

"No, but then sometimes mail is slow coming from the mainland."

"In case it never arrives, I said I'm happy to hear you're expecting another baby, and I'll be eager to see you and your family when you're able to visit here in Indiana again."

"It won't be until the baby's old enough to travel, and of course, we'll choose a time when we aren't likely to be so busy at the B&B. If we came during the busiest tourist season, it would be a lot for Ken's mother to handle on her own."

"That's understandable."

"How are things going with you and Wyman these days? Has he asked you to marry him yet?"

"No, and it's not likely to happen." Sadie tapped her fingers along the edge of the counter where the phone sat. "We broke up."

"I'm so sorry. What happened?"

Sadie gave a quick explanation then changed the subject. "I've been keeping busy with a new quilting project, and I would like your opinion on it. That is, if you have the time to talk longer right now."

"Yes, I do. My son's down for his nap, and the two guests we have staying here right now are out touring the island for the day."

"Okay, good." Sadie scooted the folding chair a little closer and rested one elbow on the counter as she explained about her plan to create a blended quilt.

"What a wonderful idea. Your quilt will be a one of a kind, and I'm sure it'll be beautiful."

"That's what I'm hoping. I thought I'd use the Ocean Waves pattern for most of the quilt, but I need a Hawaiian pattern, or at one least that represents Hawaii, to blend with it." Sadie's words had been rushed, and she paused briefly to take a breath. "I was hoping you might have some ideas for me."

"Well, let's see. . . . You could use the Breadfruit pattern. Or there's also Hibiscus, Kukui Nut, Torch Ginger, or Pineapple to consider, as well as many more. I could send you a pamphlet I picked up at one of the quilt shops here. I'm pretty sure it will help."

Sadie tilted her head back slightly as she contemplated her friend's suggestions. "I'm leaning toward the Pineapple pattern, but why don't you go ahead and send me the pamphlet to look at, in case I change my mind?"

"Sure, no problem. I'll get it mailed out right away. If I send it Priority, maybe it'll get there early next week."

Sadie sat up straight with her hands clutched together and one foot bouncing up and down. Talking about this with Mandy gave her a renewed sense of excitement over her new quilt project.

✳

Wyman walked briskly toward the phone shed to check for messages. It was probably too soon to hear anything back from the manager at the bulk food store in Shipshewana, but there would no doubt be other recorded messages to relay to Mom and Dad.

When Wyman stepped into the small wooden building, he was hit in the face by a cobweb. "Ugh! Sure hope there's no spider attached." He took his straw hat off and swiped at the web, which drifted to the floor. Relieved when he looked down and saw no sign of any creepy crawlers, he pulled out the wooden stool and took a seat in front of the table where the phone and answering machine sat.

While Wyman didn't live in fear of spiders, they grossed him out—especially if one got too close to his face. The memory still lingered of the day when they were boys and Michael thought it would be fun to play a trick on Wyman. He'd been sleeping in the hayloft—his favorite place to take a nap—when something touched his nose. Of course Wyman woke up. When he opened his eyes and saw his brother standing over him with a stick, on which a big brown spider dangled, he had screamed so loud, their mother had dashed into the barn, shouting, "What happened? Has someone been hurt?"

Feeling a little foolish, and quite angry at his brother, Wyman knocked the stick from Michael's hand and shouted down from the hayloft: "No one's hurt, Mom, but someone's gonna be if he doesn't stop making himself such a *gebellert* to me."

Of course that statement had led to a strong lecture by Mom. In addition to telling Michael to stop pestering his brother, she'd reminded Wyman what the Bible says about not repaying evil for evil. Mom also stated that she would not tolerate her boys physically fighting with one another. While Wyman had never struck his brother, there were times when he'd felt like it.

I'll bet Michael feels like giving me a good smack for not paying him back the money I owe, Wyman thought. *Sure hope I find a job real soon.*

He clicked the flashing green button on the answering machine and listened to the first message. It was from Michael, asking if Wyman had found another job yet.

Wyman felt a tightness in his chest, and he pulled in a few deep breaths. "Wouldn't ya know it? I wonder if his fraa has been bugging him about the money I still owe and put him up to calling." Wyman tapped his foot on the bottom rung of the stool. *It'd be just like Lovina to insist that Michael keep after me till I finally pay up. Well, I can't pay what I don't have.*

Wyman hated to admit it, even to himself, but he'd probably been stupid for leaving the job at his father's feed store. *I shoulda stayed put, even though I didn't like the work. At least there I had a steady paycheck and a girlfriend besides.* He pulled his fingers through the back of his hair. *Dad's found someone else now, so it's too late to ask for my old job back.*

The other matter weighing on him was Sadie, and if she might find someone else who was interested in her. Wyman swallowed hard. *If I wrecked any chance of getting back with her, it'll be my undoing.*

Wyman listened to the next few messages—two for Dad and one for Mom—and jotted them down on the notepad. The last message caught him off guard. It was the manager of the bulk food store in Shipshewana, stating that the position for a store clerk had been filled, but he wondered if Wyman would be interested in stocking shelves. The pay was less than clerking, but if Wyman wanted the position, he could begin work tomorrow morning. While it certainly wasn't the kind of job he'd hoped for, it would be better than no work at all. Wyman couldn't help pondering about his first day on the job. "How hard can it be to work there?" He laughed. *Whenever I've shopped at the store, none of the workers appeared stressed out or seemed to dislike their jobs.*

Wyman couldn't wait to be employed at the bulk food store and see his friends come into the place. Several of them shopped there, and it would be easy to visit with friends or family members while working. It felt good to be smiling again and have a little hope bubbling over. *If I'm working, I'll be able to make payments to Michael again.*

He jotted down the number and called the manager right away. Since all he got was the man's voice mail, Wyman left a message stating that he would be willing to stock shelves and would report for work in the morning. He ended it by thanking the manager for offering him the job.

Wyman smiled, feeling a little more hopeful now. *When I'm done in here I'll head to the house and tell my folks the news.* Things were looking up, and if this job worked out, Wyman would not only be able to pay Michael back, but he might even have a chance to win Sadie back.

He picked up the phone to call Michael and leave a message but was surprised when Lovina answered. "Oh, um. . .I wasn't expecting anyone to answer the phone."

"Hello, Wyman. I just came out to check for messages."

Wyman couldn't miss his sister-in-law's curt tone of voice. He could almost picture her sitting in their phone shed with narrowed eyes and a pinched mouth. *I'm probably the last person Lovina wants to talk to.*

"I'd like to speak with Michael. Is he at home?"

"No, my husband is not home from work yet, but since you have me on the phone, there's something I want to say to you."

Oh, great. . .here it comes. Wyman sat silently waiting for Lovina's next words.

"It's about the money you borrowed from Michael. I'm wondering when you plan to pay it back."

"I should be able to make a payment in a week or so." He spoke through his teeth with forced restraint.

"Oh? Does that mean you've found another job?"

"Jah. I'll be working at the bulk food store in Shipshe. That's what I called about—to let Michael know that as soon as I get my first paycheck I'll give him some money." Wyman didn't mention what type of work he'd be doing. That part didn't matter. The important thing was, he would be able to start paying his brother back soon.

"I'm glad to hear you found employment, but there is something else I'd like to say."

"What's that?"

"I would appreciate it if, from now on, you don't ask my husband to borrow any more money. We have a family to care for and bills that need to be paid. It put a hardship on us when Michael took money out of our savings account to help pay for your new buggy."

"I realize that, but. . ."

"Please, let me finish." Lovina's harsh tone reminded Wyman of his teacher when he attended school as a boy. Whenever anyone in the class spoke out of turn, Maryjane's voice rose, her cheeks reddened, and she looked at the scholars with a pinched expression. If Wyman could view Lovina through the phone, he'd most likely see something similar.

"I'm listening," he mumbled.

"I am aware of the reason Sadie broke up with you, and I can't say as I blame her. During my courting days, if I had been seeing a man as irresponsible as you, I would have broken up with him too."

I can't believe she is bringing Sadie into this conversation. This call has nothing to do with her. Doesn't Lovina get that? I called to talk to my brother and sort things out with him, not her.

After taking a deep breath, he slowly released it. *My sister-in-law can sure be annoying.* Wyman's jaw clenched so hard his jaw ached. He often wondered what his brother ever saw in Lovina, other than a pretty face. She could be so critical sometimes and didn't think twice about saying what was on her mind.

"Are you finished?" he asked.

"Jah, that's all I have to say on the subject. I'll give Michael your message when he gets home. I'm sure he'll be relieved to hear that you found a job and will be making some money again."

"Thanks, and don't worry, Lovina—I won't be asking my brother for any more loans. If I don't have the funds for something I need, I'll either do without or figure out something on my own. I've gotta go now. Goodbye." Wyman hung up before she could respond. Although it wasn't the polite thing to do, at the moment, he didn't care if he had been rude.

He left the phone shed with the notepad to share the messages for Mom and Dad and sprinted all the way up the driveway and to the house. Wyman felt sure his parents would be pleased to know he'd gotten a job, but he hoped neither of them would say anything negative or condescending. The last thing Wyman needed was another lecture.

✷

As they all lowered their heads for silent prayer, Wyman closed his eyes. *I wonder what my folks will say about me landing a job and where I'll be working. I'm so relieved and can't wait to start tomorrow morning.*

The clearing of his father's throat brought Wyman out of his musings, and his eyes snapped open.

Dad dished a couple pieces of Mom's fried chicken onto his plate. "We had a busy day at the store. A lot of people came in to take advantage of the sales we had on several items today."

"Good to hear." She passed the chicken to Wyman and then dished herself a couple spoonfuls of homemade baked beans.

He helped himself from the bowl of macaroni salad and followed that with a couple servings of scalloped potatoes. "I checked the phone messages out in the shed. There's a list of the people who called you both on this slip of paper." Wyman passed it over to his mother.

"Danki for going out and doing this." Mom showed it to Dad. "I've been hoping to hear something from my sister. I'll give her a call after we're done with supper."

Dad looked at the paper. "At least the order I placed for the wheelbarrows is on its way."

Wyman waited a moment then spoke up. "I had a message too."

"Who called?" his parents asked in unison.

"The manager from the bulk food store in Shipshe."

"Hmm. . .what's up?" Mom tilted her head.

"I've been asked to start work there tomorrow morning."

Dad put two spoonfuls of baked beans on his plate. "What kind of work will you be doing?"

"Mostly stocking shelves." Wyman took a sip of his drink. "The clerk's position I'd applied for was taken already, but the boss said he had the other spot available if I was interested."

"I'm glad you found a job, Son, and that you'll be starting right away." Mom looked at him and smiled.

Dad nodded and continued to work on his meal.

It was a quiet for a while, and Wyman sensed his father's displeasure. He could only imagine what Dad had on his mind. Wyman lost his appetite as he kept glancing at his father. *I thought he'd be pleased. At least I won't be hanging around the house after today. My daed is a hard man to figure out.*

Chapter 8

*S*adie was working on her new quilt design when she heard the *clippity-clop* of horse's hooves. *Maybe Mom has company, although she didn't mention anyone coming by today. Of course, it could be one of my sisters-in-law. . . . I'd like to take some time and show them my project.*

When Sadie left her chair and went to look out the window, she was surprised to see Wyman's horse and open buggy coming up the driveway. Her mouth twisted. *I had no clue he'd be stopping by.*

She watched as he pulled up to the hitching rail, got out, and secured his horse.

I wonder what he wants. Should I open the door and greet him on the porch or wait until he knocks? Deciding on the latter, Sadie returned to her chair, but she didn't have to wait long before a knock sounded. She didn't move. *Maybe I'll let Mom answer it, since she's doing some cleaning in the living room, which is closer to the front door.*

When the knocking continued, Sadie left the sewing room and went to see why her mother had not opened the door. Looking into the living room, she quickly realized that Mom was nowhere in sight. She must have moved on to a different room with her cleaning supplies.

Sadie's jaw clenched. *I'm not even prepared to discuss getting back together right now, so I hope he's not here for that. Even if Wyman tells me he went back to work for his father, there are still unresolved issues we need to work through.*

A few more knocks, which had grown louder, prompted Sadie to step into the hallway and open the door. Wyman stood on the porch, face covered in a sheen of sweat. "Sadie, I'm glad you're here. I was beginning to think nobody was at home."

Sadie's attraction to Wyman hadn't changed, and the sound of his voice made her miss being with him. She couldn't help the allure of his sweet smile. Staying away from him kept her focused on making better choices.

"Mom and I are the only ones at home, and she's busy cleaning," Sadie glanced toward the door leading to the sewing room then looked back at him. "Since this is my day off, I've been working on a quilted wall hanging."

"Same here." His cheeks reddened. "I don't mean I'm workin' on a quilt. What I meant was that this is also my day off."

She tipped her head. "Oh? Have you found a job?"

"Jah. Can I come inside and tell you about it?" He stepped closer to her.

"Okay." Sadie inhaled the aroma of his cologne and contemplated. *He sure smells nice, but I will not weaken, no matter what he says.*

After Wyman entered the house, she closed the front door and moved away from him. "Let's go to the living room."

Wyman followed Sadie and seated himself on the sofa. Feeling the need to put some distance between them, she sat in the rocking chair. The room fell quiet, and Sadie felt a sense of unease between them. *I wonder what he has to say.*

He removed his straw hat and placed it on the cushion beside him. "I started working at the bulk food store in Shipshe two weeks ago."

"That's good. What are your duties there?"

"I got hired to stock shelves, but I've also been doing some cleanup when something's been dropped on the floor."

"I see. Do you like your new job?" Sadie looked at him but couldn't read his placid expression. Since Wyman hadn't enjoyed working at his dad's feed store, he probably wasn't too thrilled about working at the bulk food store either. In fact, Wyman had never liked any of the jobs he'd had in the past. If he had, he would have stuck with at least one of them.

He shifted on the couch and gave his shirt collar a tug. "It's okay."

"But do you enjoy the work?" she persisted.

Wyman shrugged his shoulders. "Not so much, but the job provides me with a steady paycheck."

Sadie stared at her hands, folded in her lap. *I bet it's just a matter of time and he'll be out looking for some other kind of employment. I doubt there's any kind of job that would satisfy him. He may spend the rest of his life going from job to job, always looking for something better.* She got the rocking chair moving. *Chasing rainbows—that's what my daed would call it.*

Wyman cleared his throat a couple of times. "Umm...so, since I've found a steady job, I wondered if you might be willing to give me another chance."

Your answers lack enthusiasm, and for that matter, my trust in you has not been restored. Sadie slowed the rocker and looked at him again. "You haven't been working very long, and I will need to think about it."

His shoulders hunched as he stared at the floor. "I kinda figured you might say that, but on the other hand, I'd hoped you might be more forgiving. Your response is similar to my daed's. He wasn't happy about me seeking other work either."

She stopped rocking and spoke in a clear voice. "In response to your first statement—this is not about forgiveness, Wyman. It's about you proving that you can be dependable and will not keep going from job to job. Two weeks at the bulk food store is hardly enough time for you to prove yourself in that regard. As to your last comment—you're right—I'm not pleased either, because you don't seem to understand what really matters."

Lifting his gaze, he opened his mouth as if to say something, but Sadie held up her hand. "Sorry, but I'm not done."

Wyman leaned against the back of the sofa with a groan.

"In addition to being undependable, you've been dishonest in not telling me you had quit working for your daed as soon as it happened. It was upsetting to find out secondhand."

"I understand, and I apologized for that. If you'll take me back, I promise never to keep anything from you."

Sadie wished she could believe Wyman and get back to the way things were between them before this all happened, but she still felt betrayed by his dishonesty and wasn't sure she could trust him anymore. He would need to prove himself first, and that would take awhile. "I need more time," she said. "I think it's best if we don't start courting again until we're both sure what direction our lives are going."

He leaned forward, one hand on his knee. "I already know the direction my life needs to go, and that's with you, Sadie. I love you, and—"

"But you don't know whether you can remain at a job and be content."

"Well, no, but for the sake of our relationship, I'm gonna try."

Sadie wanted to give in and tell him that they could resume their courtship, but common sense won out.

"Let's give it another month, and then we'll talk about it again. Okay?"

He gave a slow nod and rose to his feet. "Danki for hearing me out."

"You're welcome. I appreciate you coming by." Sadie followed Wyman to the door and watched as he ambled, head down, toward his horse and buggy. She hoped she had handled it well and made the right decision. If Wyman didn't prove himself in the month they'd agreed upon, she'd have to say goodbye to him for good.

✳

With a heavy heart, Wyman got into his rig and backed his horse from the rail. Sadie's answer was not what he'd wanted to hear, but at least she hadn't completely shut him out, so there was still hope. *I don't dare do anything to mess things up. One thing for sure—I can't quit my new job, no matter how much I may not like it.*

Wyman guided his horse in the direction of the feed store. *Guess I may as well stop by and make a payment to Michael. If I don't give him some money soon, Lovina will hound me about it again.* He grunted. *I'm sure glad she's my bruder's fraa and not mine. Don't think I could live with a woman as pushy and controlling as she is. Lovina's nothing like my sweet Sadie, that's for sure. Boy, I sure hope she agrees to let me court her again after thirty days are up. Don't know what I'm gonna do if she says no.*

✻

"It was nice of you to invite me to come here for supper," Sadie said when she entered Ellen's kitchen that evening.

Her friend smiled. "I'm glad you were free to come. We haven't had a good visit in a while. I'm anxious to hear how things are going for you these days."

"And I'm eager to know what's new in your world." Sadie grabbed a work apron and slipped it on. "What can I do to help? We can talk while we work."

"You can either help me peel the potatoes or set the table."

"I'll do the spuds first and then get out the dishes and silverware. Where do you want them set out—on the kitchen or dining-room table?"

"I think in here is fine. Since we have a few guests staying at the B&B this week and they're coming and going, I'd rather eat in the kitchen where it's more private." Ellen opened the oven door and peeked in at the roast. The delicious aroma wafted up to Sadie's nose.

"Rueben wanted me to cook some venison this evening. We had deer meat from when he went hunting last fall in our frozen food locker, so I figured tonight would work since we all like it." Ellen carried the sack of potatoes to the sink.

"I do like it, and I'll bet that venison will taste as good as it smells."

"It's a nice cut, so I hope it's plenty moist and tender. I also used a rub that came from Hawaii. Those island seasonings should give the roast some interesting additional flavoring." She handed Sadie a potato peeler and took one out for herself.

As Sadie stood in front of the sink removing the skins from the potatoes, she told Ellen about the design she'd chosen for her quilt. "It was Mandy's idea. While we were talking on the phone I asked for suggestions, and she mentioned several Hawaiian patterns. When she referred to the

Pineapple pattern, I knew right away that it was the one I wanted."

"Sounds like it'll go nice with the traditional Amish Ocean Waves pattern. One of our guest rooms has a quilt on the bed made up entirely of that pattern."

Sadie chuckled. "I know, since I made it for you."

A spot of red erupted on Ellen's cheeks. "Of course you did. I can't believe I'd forgotten that."

"It doesn't matter. You're so busy helping Rueben keep this place running and taking care of Irene, I don't know how you can keep track of anything."

Ellen nodded toward the desk across the room. "If I didn't write down all the things that need to be done, I'd probably forget many of them."

"Maybe not. You've always been quite organized."

"More so before the boppli came along, but I do my best to stay on top of things." Ellen rinsed the potato she held before cutting it into smaller pieces and placing it in the kettle of water by the sink. "Have you heard anything from Wyman lately?"

"Jah. In fact, he came by to see me earlier today."

"Have you two gotten back together?"

"Not yet, but there might be some hope." Sadie told her friend about Wyman's new job and the promise he'd made.

"Do you believe he'll stick to it—the job, I mean?"

Sadie shrugged and added a potato to the kettle. "The only thing I know for sure is that if he doesn't, I won't agree to let him court me again. I can't commit to a relationship with a man who doesn't take life seriously enough to stick to a job. I also require honesty between us above all things."

"I don't blame you." Ellen's brows furrowed. "I remember the way I felt when I learned that Rueben, who had called himself Rob during the time I spent on Kauai with Mandy, had grown up in an Amish home and had family living in Pennsylvania. I felt deeply hurt that he hadn't trusted me enough to tell me the truth about his identity."

"But you eventually forgave him, and now the two of you are happily married."

"True, but it wasn't until I saw a change in him that I allowed myself to make a commitment to marriage. I also went through a change during our struggle, because my first impulse was to try handling things in my own strength." Ellen's voice softened. "I began to go to God's Word for help and prayed often."

Sadie set the peeler aside and turned to face Ellen. "Will you pray for me, Ellen—that if Wyman and I are meant to be together, I will know beyond a shadow of doubt that I can trust him?"

"Of course I will." Ellen dried her hands on a towel and gave Sadie a hug. "I remember once, soon after Rueben and I were married, that I said to him, 'I hope someday my dear friend Sadie will find someone who will make her as happy as I am.' And I meant it. If things work out for you and Wyman, I'll be pleased. But if things go the other way, and you two break up for good, then I'll pray that God sends the man He wants for you—someone who will make you happy."

Tears welled in Sadie's eyes. "Danki for being such a good friend and knowing the right thing to say to make me feel better."

"You've always done the same for me."

The sound of a baby crying interrupted their conversation.

"Would you like me to check on Irene?" Sadie questioned.

"No, I'd better go. She probably needs to be fed and have her *windel* changed."

"Okay, I'll finish the potatoes while you're gone and get them cooking."

"Sounds good. Maybe by the time Rueben is back from the store, supper will be ready and we can eat."

After Ellen left the room, Sadie picked up the potato peeler and continued her task. *If things could work out so well for Ellen and Rueben, then why not me and Wyman? I need to pray about our relationship and trust God instead of fretting.*

Chapter 9

Two weeks later, on a sultry day in August, Sadie headed for the shoe and boot store in Shipshewana, using her mother's horse, Annabelle, as well as her carriage. She still hadn't replaced her old horse and figured it would be some time before she had enough money to afford a new one. Sadie's father had brought up the topic early that morning of a horse that might come available. It belonged to one of the ministers from their church district. She'd listened to him as they sat in the kitchen finishing breakfast.

It's obvious that Dad wants to help me find another horse, and it would free me up from using Mom's buggy. She's been such a good sport, allowing me to use hers, and I'm thankful for that. Sadie jiggled the reins and kept her eyes on the road ahead. *I'll be more than happy to do a favor whenever Mom needs my help.*

It wasn't hard to do some steady pondering when her mode of transportation moved along at five to eight miles per hour—not to mention the light traffic.

As she continued her travels down the road, guiding Annabelle at a steady pace, Sadie thought about Wyman and how he'd borrowed money from his brother in order to purchase a nice-looking buggy.

She grimaced. "I hope Wyman won't borrow any more money—at least not for a while. He needs to learn to save what he is making first. As it is, I'll be saving up for quite a while until I can afford what I need."

Even though Sadie's father had offered to help finance her purchase of a new mare, Sadie had refused his help, preferring to do it on her own. At least now, during the warm days of summer, and even into early fall, she could continue riding her bike a good many places. Perhaps before winter set in, Sadie would have enough money in her savings, without cutting herself short, to attend an auction and pay cash for a new horse.

"You shouldn't be too proud and stubborn to ask for help," Mom had told her this morning before she left the house. Sadie had argued, stating that if she lost her job, she'd be in the same predicament as Wyman—struggling to pay back the money he'd borrowed from his brother. Sadie was not about to put any of her family members in such a predicament, expecting to be repaid and being put on hold. She had more consideration than that.

The shoe and boot store came into sight, and Sadie pulled into their parking lot. She'd come here to buy new shoes for work—something comfortable since she was on her feet most of the day—and needed to concentrate on that.

There were two other horses tied to the hitching rail, as well as a van in the parking lot. Sadie figured it might be awhile before she got waited on, but that was okay. She could fend for herself unless they didn't have the size she needed out on the shelf.

When Sadie entered the store, she spotted Ezra Bontrager behind the counter, waiting on an English man. Ezra's wife, Lenore, who was Ellen's youngest sister, could be seen down one aisle, helping an Amish woman try on shoes for her little girl.

Sadie smiled, remembering how last year Ezra had taken a serious interest in Lenore, despite her being four years younger than him. She reflected on how Ezra's father-in-law had allowed the newlywed couple to take over running this store. Ezra used to have his cap set for Ellen but seemed quite happy with Lenore, so things had worked out well in the end for both sisters.

Sadie was reminded of what Ellen had said to her the night she'd gone to the B&B for supper—about how if things didn't work out between her and Wyman, God would send Sadie the right man. Maybe it was true, for

He'd certainly brought Ezra and Lenore together. Right now, however, Sadie couldn't see herself with anyone but Wyman. She was eager to know how he'd been doing since they had last talked, and she hoped he was still at his new job. *Think I'll stop by the bulk food store before I go home,* she told herself. *Then I can see for myself how things are going for Wyman.*

✳

Wyman ground his teeth together in an effort to keep his emotions under control as he cleaned up a mess where a customer had spilled a bag of popcorn on the floor. He had no idea what prompted them to bring it into the bulk food store and figured they may have gotten it at Yoder Popcorn down the road. The business sold several types of popcorn and often gave away free bags of popped corn to customers who came into the store.

He'd cleaned up other messes recently too—like a glass jar of honey someone had dropped on the floor. What a sticky ordeal, along with all the shards of glass that had gotten mixed into the thick substance. Wyman had managed to hold in his frustration over being the lowest-ranking employee to deal with the job. When he'd been hired to stock shelves, he hadn't realized he'd get stuck doing so much cleanup work too. After working only four weeks, he was already sick of the job.

If I didn't need a job so bad, I'd quit right now. It's ridiculous that I'm doing the bottommost job at this store. He'd worked on the second mess using the broom around the spill until he'd formed a pile. *Boy. . .I hope none of my friends see me cleaning this up. I wish I could be driving a forklift out in the warehouse instead.*

Wyman had finished sweeping up the last of the popcorn and dumped it in a bucket for disposal, when he looked down the aisle and saw Sadie heading toward him. He put on his best smile and greeted her warmly. *Maybe she's come to tell me that I can begin courting her again. Maybe I don't have to wait for two more weeks to hear her decision.*

"It's mighty nice to see you, Sadie. Are you done working at the hardware store for the day?"

She shook her head. "This is my day off, and I just came from the shoe and boot store. I decided to come by here before heading home to see how things have been going for you."

More than likely, she's come to check up on me—see if I'm still working here. Even though I'm not thrilled about this job, I won't let on. In fact, I am going to act positive about it. He only had two weeks to go before approaching her again about resuming their courtship and didn't want to say or do anything that might mess up his chances at getting her back. But Wyman kept his thoughts to himself. "I'm glad you came by, Sadie." His smile widened.

She grinned at him too. "It's nice to see you're still working here. How are you liking the job?"

"It's steady employment, and my boss and coworkers are nice."

"Good to hear."

They talked a short while, until Sadie said she needed to get going.

"Okay, I should get back to work too. I'll see you in a couple of weeks."

"I'll look forward to that."

They said their goodbyes, and as Sadie walked away, Wyman heaved a hefty sigh and swiped a hand across his moist forehead. *Sure hope I can keep my promise to her. If so, I'll be back in Sadie's good graces in no time. I've sure missed seeing her and spending fun times together.*

While she hadn't said she was ready to resume their relationship, Wyman took it as a good sign that she looked forward to seeing him. He felt certain there was still some hope of him being able to court her again. He'd sure come to realize that Sadie meant more to him than being happy at a job. So Wyman would continue to work here indefinitely if that's what it took, even if he didn't like it.

✳

When Sadie exited the store, she felt a sense of relief knowing Wyman still worked here. Maybe he meant what he'd said previously and did plan to change his ways. She certainly hoped that was the case.

As Sadie walked across the parking lot toward her mother's horse and buggy, she caught sight of an unkempt-looking young English woman approach an elderly woman, also English. In the blink of an eye, the younger woman snatched the purse out of the older woman's hand and started running.

I can't believe what's happening! Shock spiraled through Sadie as the scene unfolded. All the older woman, who stood with a panicked expression, seemed capable of doing was to shout, "Hey! Thief! Come back with my handbag!"

Sadie, who had always been a bit impulsive, not to mention a fast runner, dashed across the parking lot and grabbed the purse out of the perpetrator's hand. The young woman paused briefly enough to look at Sadie and blink a few times before running off. Sadie hadn't taken the time to speculate what the thief might do to her, but now the thought crossed her mind that she could have easily been knocked to the ground, because the other woman was a lot taller than her.

What a relief to have been able to retrieve the handbag from the purse snatcher! Sadie felt energized, watching the assailant run out of the parking lot and duck around a corner. *I'm glad I put myself out there and did what I did. At least the poor woman will have her property back.*

After Sadie gained her wits, she stepped up to the trembling older woman and handed her back the fancy-looking leather purse. "I believe this belongs to you."

"Thank you so much," she said breathlessly. "How can I ever repay you?"

"No payment is necessary. I'm glad I saw it happening and could catch the thief in time." The finely dressed lady looked around for a moment; she gripped her bag so tightly, the veins on her hands protruded. "Where is that thief? We should call the sheriff and report what happened."

"She's gone." Sadie pointed. "The young woman ran off in that direction, but she'll no doubt have disappeared by the time the sheriff arrives."

The woman turned to Sadie with a grim expression. "Are you saying we should let her get away with it?"

"No, but. . ."

The lady gave a gentle wave of her hand. "Don't worry about it. Thanks to you, I have my purse back, so that's really all that counts." She opened her handbag and reached inside, giving a careful assessment of the contents. "Everything seems to be here, and that's a relief. If she'd gotten away with my purse, I would have lost everything—my cash, credit cards, driver's license, and some other important information." She withdrew her wallet and plucked a crisp bill from it.

Sadie's eyes widened when the woman offered her one hundred dollars. "Please take this. It's a small way of saying thank you for coming to my aid."

"There's no need for that. I wouldn't feel right about taking your money."

"Oh, but I insist." The elderly woman thrust the bill into Sadie's hand and closed her fingers around it.

Sadie didn't want to appear ungrateful, but at the same time, her conscience would prick if she took the money. "I appreciate your offer, but instead of giving me a reward, why don't you use the money to help someone in need?" *I didn't expect to receive anything from my good deed. My intention was only to do right from a wrong.*

"I don't know anyone in need at this time."

Sadie was surprised this person of obvious means couldn't think of someone who needed help. She thought of her closest neighbor—Laura Mast. While the widow wasn't destitute, she lived with her son in the *daadi haus* and didn't have much money of her own. No doubt Laura would appreciate the hundred dollars to buy yarn for one of her knitting projects or perhaps some material for a new dress.

"If I take the cash, would you have any objections if I give it to a neighbor lady who doesn't have much money of her own?"

"I have no problem with that at all. Feel free to use the reward in any way you like." The woman glanced at her fancy gold watch. "I should be on my way. I have a dental appointment in half an hour and don't want to be late."

Sadie smiled and gave the lady's arm a gentle pat. "I hope God blesses the rest of your day."

"Same to you, young lady. I wish there were more people as kind and helpful in this world as you've been today."

Sadie said goodbye, and as she made her way to the horse and buggy, she reflected on the woman's final words. While she felt no pride in being told she'd been kind and helpful, it was a reminder that she should always put others' needs ahead of her own. Sadie looked forward to visiting her elderly neighbor and presenting her with the hundred-dollar bill.

She paused to offer a prayer on behalf of the girl who had taken the older woman's purse. *Dear Lord, please open that young woman's eyes and cause her to realize what she did was wrong. If she needs help in some way, then help her to seek it or put someone in her path to help guide the way.*

Chapter 10

Middlebury

C ome see what you think of my quilted wall hanging." Sadie beckoned her mother into the sewing room.

"Is it finished?"

Sadie nodded. "At least I think so, but I'd like your *mehne*."

"I'm not sure my opinion will count for much, but I'd be happy to see what you've done." Mom followed Sadie from the kitchen to the sewing room.

"Well, there it is." Sadie pointed across the room where her blended quilt had been draped on a quilt rack.

"Oh my. . .it's *schee*. Jah, so pretty—and what a creative job you have done." Mom placed her hand on Sadie's arm. "How did you come up with such an interesting pattern?"

Sadie walked over to the quilt. "When Mandy mentioned the Pineapple pattern, the idea came to me that it would go well with our Ocean Waves pattern." She gestured to the large pineapple in the center of the quilt. "I wanted this to be the focal point." Sadie touched the four corners of the wall hanging. "I felt it would work well to have smaller pineapples in each corner, with Ocean Waves throughout the rest of the quilt."

Mom leaned in for a closer look. "The combined fabrics certainly do blend well together, and I like the soft, muted beige, yellow, and green colors." She faced Sadie as a wide smile stretched across her face. "I believe you have a one-of-a-kind quilt that would sell well in any of our local quilt shops."

Sadie shook her head vigorously. "Oh no, Mom. . . I worked too hard on this quilt to even think of selling it. I want to keep it right here in this house, so I can be reminded of the wonderful time Ellen, Barbara, Mandy, and I had on our adventurous trip to the Hawaiian Islands." Sadie sighed. "I'll probably never be able to go there again."

Mom tapped Sadie's shoulder and spoke with a reassuring tone. "You know what I have to say about that, dear girl. Never is a long time, and no one can be sure what might occur in the future."

"I suppose, but it's just hard to imagine that I would be able to make another trip such as that."

"A trip to where?" Jana Beth asked when she and Kaylene entered the room.

"To the Hawaiian Islands." Mom spoke before Sadie could form a response. "I believe she longs to go back there again."

"Is that so?" Kaylene tipped her head.

Sadie couldn't deny it. Working on the blended quilt had sparked a desire to see Hawaii once more. These days her mind seemed to be taking more tours back through the places and times spent there on the islands. *If only I could go back and make new memories in Hawaii.*

Sadie's gaze lingered over her quilt. She would have to be satisfied with the pictures Mandy sometimes sent to her, Ellen, and Barbara. Even the pamphlets about quilts found on Kauai that Mandy had mailed to Sadie when she'd first started working on the wall hanging had caused a stirring in her heart. At the very least, she wished to know more about the islands she and her friends had visited when they were all single and carefree.

And now, I'm the only one who's not married and starting a family. Sadie lowered her head as she was reminded once again of her single status.

Her thoughts turned to Wyman. She felt concerned because she hadn't heard anything from him in almost four weeks, even though he'd said he would be back to talk to her again in two weeks. Maybe he'd given up on their relationship. He could even have moved on to some other job.

That could be why he'd made no contact with her, other than a brief hello after their last church service. Sadie had been tempted on more than one occasion to stop by the bulk food store and see if he still worked there but had decided to wait for him to come to her. The last thing she wanted was for Wyman to think she was checking up on him. For that reason she hadn't asked any of Wyman's friends or family members if they knew whether he was still employed at the bulk food store.

"What's that look of defeat I see on your face?" Mom's question pulled Sadie out of her moody reflections. "You just finished a beautiful wall hanging and should be quite pleased."

Sadie lifted her gaze in time to see Mom point to her new quilt. "Kaylene, Jana Beth, what do you think of your sister's new creation?"

Jana Beth's fingers touched her parted lips. "It's the prettiest *gwilt* I've ever seen. If it were a little bigger it would be nice as a bedspread."

"I agree. I love the colors, and the pineapple design goes really well with the Ocean Waves pattern." Kaylene blinked. "Know what else?"

"What's that?" Sadie asked.

"I think you ought to sell this wall hanging at one of our upcoming benefit auctions."

Sadie's mouth nearly fell open as she stifled a gasp. She could hardly believe Kaylene wanted her to sell the quilt—especially after having worked so hard on it these last several weeks.

"Your sister doesn't want to part with her blended gwilt," their mother interjected. "It reminds her of the trip she and her friends took to Hawaii."

"I don't blame her," Jana Beth put in. "If I'd made such a magnificent quilt, I wouldn't give it away or sell it either."

"Then what are you gonna do with the wall hanging?" Kaylene asked.

"I'm not sure about the future, but for now, I'm going to leave it draped on the quilt rack and put it in my room where I can see it first thing in the morning and before I go to bed." Sadie gave a decisive nod. "If I donate any of my quilted items for a charity event, it won't be this one."

"It's entirely your decision." Mom gave Sadie's shoulder a gentle tap. "Why don't you take the wall hanging to your room now? When you come downstairs, the four of us need to get started on supper before your daed gets home and says he's as hungerich as a *baer* and needs to be fed."

Sadie laughed along with her sisters. Most evenings when Dad came home from the trailer factory, he announced that he was hungry as a bear. She lifted her wall hanging from the quilt rack and started up the stairs. After they finished eating supper, she might walk over to their English neighbors' place and see if one of them might be willing to come over and take a picture of the new quilt. That way, if Sadie got a printed copy, she could send it to Mandy for her opinion.

A wide smiled stretched across Sadie's face as she stepped into her room and placed the lovely quilt on the end of her bed. She would bring the quilt rack up after supper, but for now, the covering could remain here. In some ways, Sadie wished she'd made a full-size bed quilt rather than a wall hanging, but that would have taken her longer to make.

Don't let yourself become full of hochmut, Sadie told herself as she took one final look at the quilt before leaving her room. It was never a good thing to let pride set in over anything a person said or did.

Maybe someday I'll make another quilt like this, only bigger. But for now that'll have to be put on hold.

She refocused. Lately, Sadie had felt the need to pray for her family and others whom she thought were in need. She'd prayed daily for Wyman in the hope that he would exhibit the desire for a good work ethic and a sense of commitment to her and his new job.

Sadie thought about the day she'd rescued the English woman's purse outside the bulk food store and how the lady had been appreciative and insisted on giving Sadie money. Doing the good deed and the praise she'd received could have gone to Sadie's head, even when she'd taken the money over to Laura Mast, who'd said she was thankful. Having been taught from an early age not to become boastful, Sadie strove to remain humble. She wouldn't let the compliments she'd received from her mother and sisters about the quilt fill her with an undesirable pride.

She closed her door and headed down the stairs to join the others.

＊

As Wyman headed for the Kuhnses' place that evening, his heart pounded in his chest, matching the *clip-clop* of his horse's hooves on the pavement. During the days that had passed since he'd seen Sadie, Wyman had opened his Bible and searched the scriptures. He found comfort in them while alone in the later part of the evenings. God's Word gave him food for thought too. He'd come to realize that his previous desires and actions had been selfish and immature. His focus needed to be on the Lord—making Him first in his life, and then the people around him whom he loved. Wyman even slept better after reading from his Bible and praying.

He'd waited four weeks to approach Sadie again and hoped she would be receptive to the idea of them resuming their courtship. Surely, after two months of working at the bulk food store, he had proved that he was serious about keeping the job. "I sure hope she'll believe in me," he said aloud. "Don't know what I'll do if Sadie breaks things off for good."

Wyman's horse, Benny, flicked his ears and whinnied, as if he understood. Or maybe it was because they had approached the Kuhnses' driveway and the gelding, having been there many times before, recognized the place. Added to that, Sadie's mother's horse, Annabelle, began to whinny from the corral and paced along the fence. Benny pulled hard to go toward the mare.

Wyman gripped the reins and kept his animal moving toward the hitching rail, where he got out and secured Benny. As he approached the house, Jana Beth stepped out onto the porch. "How are you doing, Wyman?" She smiled. "We haven't seen you for a while. Did Sadie know you were coming?"

He shook his head. "I wanted to surprise her and took a chance that she'd be home. Is she in the *haus*?"

"No, sorry. My sister went over to see one of our English neighbors about taking a picture of her new wall hanging."

"I see." Wyman tapped the toe of his boot. "Any idea when she'll be back?"

"I expect soon. She's been over there nearly an hour."

"Mind if I sit out here on the porch and wait for Sadie?"

"Be my guest." Jana Beth pointed at the wicker chairs. "I'd join you, but I need to help Kaylene finish putting the clean supper dishes away."

"No problem. I'll just wait here and relax."

She gave Wyman a nod before stepping inside.

Wyman lowered himself into a chair, leaned back against the cushion, and closed his eyes. Although it was a hot, muggy evening for the first week of September, the gentle breeze that had come up cooled the air some. He was almost to the point of dozing off when he heard footsteps coming up the porch stairs.

Wyman's eyes snapped open, and he leaped to his feet as Sadie approached. "Oh, good. You're back. I've been waiting for you."

"I wasn't expecting you'd come by this evening or I would have been here. Why didn't you call and leave a message for me?"

This was not the friendly reception he'd hoped to receive. Wyman wondered if Sadie's cool tone meant she wasn't pleased to see him. "Guess I should have given you some advanced notice, but I wanted my visit to be a surprise."

Sadie took a seat and gestured for him to do the same. "I thought you'd be coming by two weeks ago."

"I wanted to give it more time," he explained after they'd both taken seats. "Figured if I worked at the bulk food store a few more weeks that you'd be more likely to believe I meant what I said about sticking with a job this time."

Sadie folded her hands in her lap. "I see."

"You don't sound as if you're convinced. Do I need to work another month or longer before you'll consider letting me court you again?"

"It's not that. I just—"

"Have your feelings for me changed, or have you found someone you like better? Is that how far things have gone? Because if it is, then I wish you'd just say so before I make a big *narr* of myself, Sadie."

"You're not a fool." She shook her head. "I still care about you, Wyman."

He heaved a sigh. "That's a relief!"

Sadie leaned forward. "The problem is, we still haven't resolved the issue of you being untruthful with me."

"I wasn't untruthful. I just didn't say anything about quitting my job at Dad's store because I didn't want to ruin our evening at Winona Lake." He snapped both suspenders at the same time. "We've gone over all this before, Sadie."

"But you could have told me afterward."

"True. I just figured it would be better to wait and tell you after I got another job. That way you wouldn't be so disappointed in me."

She turned in her chair to face him directly. "Learning from your bruder that you'd quit your job at the feed store was a bigger disappointment than anything, Wyman."

He took hold of her hand. "I can't undo the past, but if you take me back, I promise it'll never happen again."

Sadie sat quietly, looking down at their joined hands. Several seconds went by before she looked at him with her lips slightly parted. "I forgive you, Wyman, and I'm willing to try again."

Heat radiated through Wyman's chest as he experienced a great sense of relief. "I promise I won't let you down this time."

Chapter 11

Kapaa, on the island of Kauai

When Mandy stepped outside the bed-and-breakfast to get the mail, she paused and drew in a deep breath to enjoy the delicate fragrance of the lovely tropical flowers growing in the yard. Mandy never grew tired of the beauty found on the island. She especially enjoyed all the plants, trees, and flowers the previous owners of the Palms Bed-and-Breakfast had planted and lovingly cared for. She missed seeing her dear friends Luana and Makaio but understood that they wanted to live close to their daughter and her family on the Big Island of Hawaii.

A pang of regret shot through her. By her own choice, Mandy had chosen to make her home here with her husband, Ken, and his mother, Vickie, while her parents and siblings lived in Middlebury, Indiana, and continued with their Plain way of life. It had been a difficult decision not to join the Amish church and remain on the mainland, but Mandy's love for Ken, as well as the island that had beckoned to her from the moment she'd arrived, won out in the end. Mom and Dad, as well as her four brothers, missed her presence, but they'd all come to grips with her decision to marry Ken and move to Kauai. Even so, there were times when Mandy felt homesick and longed to see her Amish family.

As she approached the mailbox, Mandy placed one hand against her stomach. She looked forward to visiting Indiana after the baby came and he or she was old enough to travel. Her parents would be surprised to see how much their grandson had grown, since they'd last seen him. Isaac Charles, whom they called Charlie, was a lively two-year-old now, and by the time he saw Mandy's family, he'd be three. Mandy took lots of photos of him and sent some to her family whenever she wrote a letter. She also called often and enjoyed talking to Mom, Dad, and sometimes her brothers.

"It's too bad a person has to give up something in order to get something," Mandy murmured as she opened the door on the mailbox and pulled it open. By living here, she had the enjoyment of running the B&B with Ken and his widowed mother and also being able to take advantage of warm weather year-round, not to mention the wonderful opportunity of going to the beach whenever they had time.

Mandy retrieved a stack of mail and carried it up to the house. After thumbing through the letters, she spotted one from Sadie. Eager to find out what her friend had to say, Mandy placed the rest of the mail on a small table near the front door. Then she took a seat on the porch glider and opened up Sadie's letter. Surprised to see a photo of a lovely quilt, she read her friend's message.

> *Dear Mandy,*
>
> *I hope this letter finds you and your family doing well. Everyone here is fine—including your parents, who came into the hardware store the other day.*
>
> *You're probably wondering about the enclosed photo—it's the quilted wall hanging I recently finished—the one I told you about that includes a traditional Amish pattern mixed with the Hawaiian pattern of a pineapple.*
>
> *It turned out quite well, and I've received positive comments from those who have seen it. If you're wondering how I got a picture of the quilt—I asked our closest English neighbor, Darlene, if she would come to our house and take the picture so I could send it to you.*
>
> *Ellen came by the other day, and when she saw the blended*

quilt, she brought up the notion that I should write a book and see about getting it self-published. Ellen suggested that the book would include Amish as well as Hawaiian quilt patterns that could be blended together, similar to the one I made, only with different designs.

I actually contacted a business in Ohio where they print books and other publications for people who want to self-publish. Of course there would be a lot involved in writing the book, not to mention the cost of having it printed, a cover design created, etc. So it's only wishful thinking at this point, and for now, at least, I'll keep enjoying my newest quilt creation.

Give my love to Ken, Charlie, and also Ken's mother. I look forward to seeing you when you're able to make another trip to the mainland.

Your friend,
Sadie

Mandy studied the photo. She was impressed with how well the quilted wall hanging had been blended. *No wonder Ellen suggested Sadie should write a book. She's a gifted quilter, and her ideas and the information she could offer about the similarities between Amish and Hawaiian quilts should be shared with others. Hopefully someday Sadie will find a way to make it happen.*

✳

Middlebury

Wyman looked forward to seeing Sadie this evening, but first, he had a stop to make. He needed to drop by his brother's place and make another payment on his debt.

As he urged his horse onward, Wyman thought about work today and how he'd been reprimanded for talking to one of his friends when he was supposed to be working. He had promised it wouldn't happen again and knew he'd better not mess up or he might lose his job. No way could he let that happen—not with things going so well between him and Sadie these days. He felt sure she'd begun to trust him again, and if he got fired or quit working at the bulk food store, she'd probably break up with him for good this time.

I will not allow that to occur, Wyman told himself. *I love Sadie too much to let her go, and as soon as I get Michael paid back, I plan to ask Sadie to marry me.*

When Wyman arrived at Michael's place, his brother's wife greeted him at the door. Seeing her made his stomach tighten. *I hope she'll maintain some pleasantness with me this time and not get on my case again.*

"Hello, Lovina." Wyman offered her his best smile. "I came to see Michael. Is he home from work yet?"

"Jah, but he's in the shower right now. If you want to wait for him to get out, you can have a seat in the living room." She stepped back from the open door and gestured in that direction.

"I'm in a hurry right now and would rather not wait, so I'll just give this to you, and you can let my bruder know I came by." Wyman pulled his wallet open, took out the money he'd brought to give Michael, and handed it to Lovina.

Instead of offering Wyman a smile, which was what he'd expected, his sister-in-law's chin jutted out as she crossed her arms and glared at him. "How much longer will it be before you can pay off the remainder of the loan?"

"I'm not sure, but since I'm working full-time, I'm hoping it won't be—"

"If you'd stayed working for your daed, you would have repaid the entire amount weeks ago. And if you hadn't been out of work so long after quitting your job at the feed store, you would have had the money to pay off the loan a lot sooner." Lovina's eyes narrowed into slits. "We have our own bills to pay, you know."

"I realize that, and I'm doing the best I can."

She looked at the bills in her hand. "I'd appreciate it if you could pay a little more next time. You need to get this debt cleared up before you end up quitting your latest job."

Wyman bristled as his tone deepened. "For your information, I have no intention of walking away from my position at the bulk food store."

Lovina unfolded her arms. "That remains to be seen. You're not dependable, Wyman, and you need to grow up."

Anger boiled in Wyman's chest, but he held his temper—as well as his tongue. If he said what he felt to Lovina, she'd tell Michael, who in turn would repeat it to Dad, and then Mom would hear about it. There was no point getting the rest of his family up in arms, so the best thing to do was leave before he said things he might later regret.

"Please tell Michael I was here and that I'll pay him the rest of what I owe as quickly as possible." Wyman turned and rushed out the door.

Boy, it's a relief to be out of there. Lovina can be unreasonable and so harsh at times. He quickly untied his horse. *I'm sure glad my girlfriend is nothing like my brother's wife.*

Wyman climbed into his buggy and released the brake. His whole body felt tense. *Maybe I should try to find a second job and work on my days off or evenings,* he thought as he headed down the road toward Sadie's. *But if I did that, there would be no time for courting.*

✳

Sadie sat in the living room, where she'd decided to wait for Wyman. She stared off toward her upstairs bedroom and wondered if there was any way she could share with others the pattern for the lovely wall hanging she kept in her room and tell about the similarities between Amish and Hawaiian quilts.

I sure can't publish a book. Her posture sagged. *Even if I took on a second job, I wouldn't make enough money to pay for a self-published book.*

She thought about the money in her bank account, which she had been adding to in order to buy a new horse. Even if she took that and didn't get a horse by the end of fall, it wouldn't be enough to pay for all the books she'd want printed.

"Concentrate on what's most important right now," Dad had told her the other night. "You need a horse for transportation. A book about quilt patterns and information concerning what you saw and did during your trip to Hawaii is not vital."

Sadie was sure Dad's words weren't meant to hurt her, but they had, nonetheless. She felt guilty for wanting to pursue the book idea Ellen had suggested, but her father didn't have to worry. If all went well, and she didn't need the money she'd been saving for something more important, Sadie hoped to buy a new horse by the end of October. That was, after all, the most important item on her to-do list.

The *clip-clop* of a horse's hooves drew Sadie's thoughts aside, and she moved over to the window to look out. She smiled, watching as Wyman directed his horse to the hitching rail and got out.

Not caring if she appeared too eager to see him, Sadie went out the front door and stood waiting for him on the porch. When he joined her a short while later, and she saw the way he avoided looking at her, she felt concern.

"What's wrong? You look umgerennt."

"I am upset."

"How come?"

"Just came from my brother's house, and I was forced to talk with his fraa instead of him."

"Did Lovina say something to frustrate you?"

"Jah, but that's nothing new. She's been harsh with me ever since I borrowed money from Michael to help me purchase a new buggy."

Which is precisely why I don't want to borrow money from anyone to buy a horse. Sadie didn't voice her thoughts. Instead, she took hold of Wyman's hand and led him to the other side of the porch where they took seats on the glider. "Want to know what I think?"

He gave a nod. "Always."

"You should get your brother paid back as quickly as possible so you won't have the loan hanging over your head any longer."

"I'm working on it and was even considering taking on a second job, but I decided against it."

"How come?"

"It would mean we'd hardly see each other anymore." Wyman leaned close to Sadie's ear and whispered, "I love you and want us to spend as much time together as possible. I'm hoping you want that too."

Sadie moved her head slowly up and down. "I love you too."

"Then let's not talk about me looking for a second job. Let's focus on enjoying each other's company as often as we can."

"I agree." Sadie felt a sense of weightlessness as they sat quietly moving the glider back and forth. She was almost certain that it wouldn't be much longer and she'd be getting a marriage proposal from Wyman.

They continued sitting on the porch, and Sadie noticed their English neighbor across the road, mowing his lawn. Carl waved at them from behind his gas-powered mower, while Sadie and Wyman visited and sipped the iced tea Mom had brought out a few minutes ago. But a short time later, Sadie noticed the machine sat running with Carl nowhere in sight. It seemed odd, and she continued to stare over at their yard.

"What are you looking at?" Wyman asked.

"I'm wondering where the neighbor is. Carl's been gone awhile and left his mower running."

He shrugged. "Maybe his wife is talking to him around back, or he could've gone into the house for something."

"Strange. . .Darlene's car is gone right now, and it's normally parked out front when Darlene is home." Sadie's brows wrinkled. "Maybe I should walk over there and check on him. Would you mind coming with me?"

"Sure thing."

They crossed the street and came up to the running mower. Sadie looked on the porch, hoping to see Carl, but he wasn't there. "Let's walk around the side of the house and see if he's there."

Wyman followed her in the dense heat, and as they rounded the back side of the house she saw her neighbor lying on the grass. Sadie dashed over to him and knelt down. "Carl, can you hear me?"

He appeared to be drenched in sweat and didn't respond to Sadie's question.

Wyman placed his hand on Carl's forehead. "His skin is clammy." He laid two fingers on the man's wrist. "His pulse is rapid." Wyman grabbed the cell phone from his pocket. "I'd better call for emergency help."

Sadie nodded. While she wasn't thrilled that her boyfriend carried the device, in this case, it was a good thing. She stayed by Carl's side and waited to hear what they should do, while sending up a prayer for her neighbor.

As Wyman spoke on his phone, Carl came to. He seemed confused about what had happened to him but made no attempt to get up, saying he felt dizzy and sick to his stomach.

It wasn't long before Sadie heard sirens coming their way. Wyman stayed on the phone with the call center until help arrived, while Sadie went to turn off the mower.

The paramedics arrived about the same time Carl's wife pulled in.

Sadie moved back, to allow the EMTs the room they needed. She spoke to Darlene briefly about what had happened.

Carl's wife dropped her purse on the ground and leaned in close to him. "I'm right here, dear. Don't worry about a thing—you're in good hands."

Once Carl had been stabilized, they brought over the gurney and put him on it. The lead paramedic looked down as he secured the stretcher. "Carl, we're going to take you to the hospital now. Your symptoms indicate that you're suffering from heat exhaustion, and we want to make sure you're okay."

"All right," he mumbled.

"I'll drive to the hospital as soon as I make sure the house is locked up."

Darlene picked up her purse.

Sadie placed a hand on the woman's trembling arm. "I'll be praying for you and Carl."

"Same here," Wyman added.

Darlene teared up. "I appreciate that. Thank you."

Sadie watched the middle-aged woman rush into the house, while her husband was taken from the side yard. She and Wyman walked out front as the EMTs put Carl into the ambulance. Soon, Darlene came out the front door and hurried to her car.

Wyman and Sadie crossed back to the other side of the street before the vehicles left the neighbors' property.

Sadie offered a silent prayer. *Lord, I'm glad You used Wyman and me to help Carl today. Please give this nice couple the comfort they need and be with the doctors who will treat Carl.*

Chapter 12

Sadie stepped into the phone shed to check for messages but left the door open. The early morning air was already so hot and humid she could hardly breathe, so closing the door was out of the question. As she took a seat in the stuffy building, it reminded her of several days ago when her neighbor across the road had suffered from heat exhaustion. Sadie had gone over to see Carl after he'd come home from the hospital. Darlene had thanked Sadie for her kindness and offered to take more pictures of Sadie's quilt if needed. Sadie wished everyone could see the importance of helping others.

Sadie clicked on the answering machine and wrote down each message, deleting only those advertising something she knew no one in her family would be interested in or need. The last message caught her interest. It was from Mandy, stating that she'd received Sadie's letter and how much she liked the picture of the blended quilt. Mandy said she agreed with Ellen's suggestion about Sadie creating a book and having it self-published. She even offered to send photos of the quilts on display at her bed-and-breakfast that Sadie could use in the book to compare with Amish quilts. Mandy's obvious enthusiasm made it hard for Sadie to dismiss the idea, but it was unrealistic, or as Mom would call it, "wishful thinking."

Sadie clicked off the answering machine and shook her head. *Don't Mandy and Ellen realize I'm not in any position to be writing a book?* The only thing Sadie had written besides letters were her daily journal entries, and those didn't qualify her to author a book.

But I am an experienced quilter, she reminded herself. *And I do have the journal entries I made during our trip to the Hawaiian Islands. Maybe those could be included in the book.*

Sadie sat quietly, rubbing her forehead. *If I did have enough money to self-publish, I wouldn't begin to know what all would be expected of me, much less find the time to put it all together in the form of a book. I wish Ellen had not suggested the idea, because now I can't stop thinking about it.*

Sadie glanced at the battery-operated clock sitting beside the telephone. It was almost time to leave for Shipshewana, so she needed to take the list of messages up to the house and get out her bike, or she'd be late getting to work.

✳

Shipshewana

Sadie sat at a table inside the Wana-Cup Restaurant, sipping a glass of water while waiting for Wyman to show up. He'd asked if he could meet her during their lunch breaks, but he was ten minutes late.

I hope he didn't forget. Sadie drummed her fingers on the table and glanced at the clock on the wall across the room. *Maybe I should go ahead and order something. Sure don't want to be late getting back to work.*

When the waitress came to check on her a few minutes later, Sadie ordered a taco salad, one of the daily specials.

"Would you like anything else to drink?" the young waitress asked.

"No thanks. I'm fine with water."

"All right, then. I'll be back with your order soon. Maybe by then your friend will be here." The young woman gestured to the empty place setting across from Sadie. When she'd first sat down, Sadie mentioned that she'd be meeting someone for lunch.

"Yes, I'm hoping he'll be here soon, but since I only have an hour for lunch, I need to eat as soon as possible so I can get back to my job."

"You work in the hardware store across the street, right? The last time

I was in the store I saw you."

Sadie nodded. "I've worked there almost six years."

The waitress smiled. "You must enjoy the job."

"I do, but even if I didn't, I would stick with it, because good jobs can be hard to find."

"So true." The young woman glanced over her shoulder then back at Sadie. "I'd better get your order turned in or you'll be late getting back to work." She hurried off, and Sadie reached for her glass of water again.

She looked out the closest window, hoping for some sign of Wyman, but he was nowhere in sight. He'd obviously forgotten about their lunch date.

Sadie struggled with her swirling emotions. *Maybe Wyman doesn't care about me as much as he keeps saying. He should have remembered our plans for lunch and been here on time.*

A short time later, the waitress returned with Sadie's taco salad. Her appetite had diminished, but after a silent prayer, she ate it anyway. No point in letting the meal go to waste.

Sadie was almost finished with the salad and had only ten minutes until she needed to be back at the store when Wyman showed up. His red face and the beads of sweat on his forehead gave indication that he'd probably been running.

"Sorry I'm late," he panted, lowering himself into the seat across from her. "I was stuck in the middle of a big mess at work."

"What happened?" Sadie tipped her head.

"Someone—not sure who, because I didn't see it happen—dumped a bunch of sunflower seeds into the walnut bin." Wyman paused and drank some water from the glass in front of his silverware. "So the boss said I couldn't go to lunch till I cleaned out both bins and started with fresh. That ate up some time, and when I finally got the job done, I realized I was gonna be late meeting up with you."

"It's okay. I understand." Sadie was relieved that he hadn't forgotten about meeting her. She rose from her chair. "Unfortunately I need to get back to work now, so you'll have to eat your meal alone."

His forehead creased as he gave a slow nod. "I'd like to make it up to you, Sadie. Maybe we can go out to supper one evening next week. You can choose whatever restaurant you want."

"All right. We can talk later and decide what day and where we want to eat."

"Before you go, I have a question."

Sadie paused and looked at him. "What is it, Wyman?"

"I wondered if you still need a new horse."

"Jah, but I'm—"

"I know of one that's for sale at a reasonable price."

Sadie glanced at the clock. "Can we talk about it later? I really need to get back to the hardware store now."

"Okay, sure. I'll talk to you soon."

Sadie offered him a brief smile and stepped up to the cash register to pay her bill. She couldn't help feeling disappointed because they'd only had a few minutes together, but it was nice to know that Wyman took his job seriously and hadn't said anything about wanting to quit.

✳

I'd hoped to have a nice lunch with my girl. Instead, due to my ho-hum job, I'm stuck alone to eat my meal here. Wyman stared out the window as Sadie rode off on her bike to the hardware store. *At least she's happy going back to her place of employment.*

After the waitress took Wyman's order, Michael strode up to Wyman's table and sat across from him. "How about this—we're having our breaks at the same time."

"Yep, sure looks like it."

"You seem kind of down today. What's up, little brother?"

"I was supposed to have lunch with Sadie, but I was detained at the bulk food store with a cleanup job I got stuck doing." Wyman paused. "By the time I made it here, she couldn't stay and had to go back to work."

"Oh, I see. That does explain things." Michael reached around to rub an area on his lower back. "Otherwise, how are things going?"

I'd like to come right out and say that I wish Lovina would ease up on me. Wyman collected himself and took a couple calming breaths. "Did your wife give you the money I brought by the other day?"

"Jah, and danki for the payment."

"No problem. I will keep at it till my debt has been paid."

"I don't have any doubts. I can see how you're staying put at that new job of yours." Michael took off his hat and set it aside. "We've been busy at the feed store even more so than usual, and Dad is toying with the possibility of hiring another person."

"Oh? He hasn't mentioned it to me."

"He probably figured there was no point bringing it up, since you've got a job you apparently like."

Wyman wasn't sure how to reply, since the truth was he didn't like the work he did at the bulk food store. So he merely shrugged and drank more water.

The waitress came by and took Michael's order, leaving him also with a glass of water. "This place is sure busy today," he commented.

"I agree, and with the fall weather as warm as it is, any place with AC is going to be favored over being outdoors."

"Here's your order." The woman placed Wyman's roast beef sandwich in front of him and looked at Michael. "Sir, yours should be coming out shortly too, and here's the root beer you asked for."

"Thank you." He picked up the glass and took a good-sized drink then licked some moisture off his lips. "I think you'd like to dig into your sandwich, so we'd better give thanks."

They both closed their eyes to pray silently, even though Michael's order hadn't arrived yet.

"I kinda envy you, Wyman, because on these hotter days you can be inside where it's air-conditioned."

"I get ya. The feed store has only a few fans that run all day to help keep a person cool. With the windows allowing all the sunshine in, it can get pretty warm in there."

"True, and I think I've shed some weight off my middle from sweating and moving bags of feed all day." Michael winced as he rubbed his back again.

"You okay?" Wyman asked.

"Jah. It's just a twinge—nothing to worry about."

Wyman was well aware that moving and hauling heavy bags at the feed store was more intense work, compared to what he did at the bulk food store. But the money he used to make at his father's business was better, not to mention that Dad was a bit more lenient boss than his current employer.

I was selfish in the way I acted when I quit working there. He bit into his sandwich. *But now I'm not so sure my father would risk rehiring me. And how would it affect my relationship with Sadie? Would she think I was job hopping again?*

Wyman figured he'd have to struggle to get through the rest of his day. He was tired of doing such menial, boring tasks and felt trapped in a job he didn't like. He sure wished he could quit and look for something else.

Wyman squeezed his fingers around the glass he held. *If I could find some other place of employment that pays better and is more to my liking, maybe Sadie would be okay with it. After all, what I'm making now, stocking shelves and cleaning up spills, is not enough to support a wife and start a family. Surely Sadie would understand that and give me the go-ahead to work somewhere else if the pay was better.*

He looked back at his plate and picked off a piece of meat. *I'll keep working at the bulk food store until something better comes along, but if I'm going to ask Sadie to marry me, I'll need a better-paying job.*

*

Middlebury

Heading home that afternoon, Sadie passed Ellen and Rueben's bed-and-breakfast. She'd been tempted to stop and say hello but figured if she did, Ellen would bring up the whole book-writing thing again. And if she told her friend what Mandy had said about the idea, it would spur Ellen on even more. That, in turn, would cause Sadie to long for something out of her reach.

In addition to not wanting to be pressured, Sadie was eager to get home and spend some time quilting before helping Mom and her sisters with supper. So she pedaled on past the road she would have turned onto for the B&B, promising herself she'd stop there some other day. In addition to visiting with Ellen, it was always nice to see baby Irene.

As Sadie approached her home, she was surprised to see a white van parked in the driveway. Normally, Sadie's mother didn't go anywhere this time of the day—she ran most of her errands in the morning when it was cooler. Maybe she'd had an appointment she had forgotten to mention and hired a driver to take her there. Either that, or one of their English friends who owned a van had stopped by for a visit.

Sadie put her bike away and went into the house. She found their driver, Sharon, in the living room with Mom. A suitcase sat near Mom's chair.

"Oh good, Sadie, I'm glad you're home." She paused. "Just to remind you, the deep freezer is well stocked with a lot of ready-made entrées. I was going to leave you and your sisters a note if you didn't get here before I left."

"Left for where? What's going on?" Sadie took a seat on the couch next to Sharon.

"Toledo, Ohio. Your daed's going with me. He's upstairs getting packed right now." Mom's chin quivered. "My sister—your aunt Sadie Ruth—was involved in a serious car accident today. She's in the hospital and may not survive."

Sadie stifled a gasp. She'd been named after Sadie Ruth—the aunt who'd left the Amish faith and gone English. It had been several years since they'd seen her, but Sadie had a soft spot in her heart for the lady who'd always been kind to her.

She closed her eyes and lifted a silent prayer. *Dear Lord, please heal my dear aunt, but if it's not meant for her to live, then help Mom and Dad to get there before she dies so they can say their goodbyes.*

Chapter 13

Toledo, Ohio

*G*race sat in a chair beside her sister's hospital bed, head bent in prayer. Sadie Ruth's internal injuries were life threatening, and the doctor said she might not live through the night. She continued to lie there with no movement under the sterile sheets, while her heart monitor gave an ongoing account of how things were going. Little by little, Sadie Ruth's vital signs appeared to be losing ground as her blood pressure and pulse decreased.

How long does my sister have here with us? Grace opened her eyes and placed a hand on Sadie Ruth's arm—one of the few places that looked unscathed by her accident. *If only she would wake up so I could talk to her— make sure she knows I'm here and that I love her. My sister's coloring is so pale, and she seems fragile. I'm glad Sadie Ruth and her husband became Christians before he died.*

Grace's throat felt swollen, making it difficult to swallow. *If the Lord chooses to take you, Sadie Ruth, I'll be sad, but there will also be a sense of peace knowing you'll be rejoicing in heaven in the presence of God.*

With only two years between them, Grace and Sadie Ruth had been close when they were children. But when they grew up and Sadie Ruth decided not to join the church, things changed. Their parents, now deceased, hadn't been happy about their eldest daughter leaving her Plain life behind, and when she'd married a wealthy English man and moved to Ohio, the tension they'd felt increased. At first Sadie Ruth didn't come home for visits, since their parents disapproved of the new life she'd chosen. But later, after Grace had gotten married and children came into the picture, her English sister came to visit and got better acquainted with her nieces and nephews. She'd always favored her namesake, though, often commenting on how much young Sadie reminded her of when she was a girl—not just in looks, but also in personality.

About ten years ago, Grace's sister's visits came less often. When Sadie Ruth's husband, Jim, passed away, without them having children together, Grace had hoped her sister would return to Indiana and live closer to her family. However, Sadie Ruth had chosen to remain at her home in Toledo, seemingly satisfied to fill her time and social life with friends. At least they'd kept in contact via letters and phone calls. Grace realized she should have made more of an effort to visit her sister. *I suppose regret is another part of life we need to give to the Lord.*

Tears seeped out of Grace's eyes and rolled down her cheeks as she looked at her husband sitting quietly beside her. "I've been praying for a miracle, but it doesn't look like it's going to happen."

Calvin placed one hand on her shoulder and gave it a tender squeeze. "We must trust that the Lord's will is done as far as your sister is concerned. You would not want her to remain alive if she has irreversible brain damage and never wakes from her coma, would you?"

"No, but. . . Oh, I do wish her car hadn't been hit. If only God had put His arms of protection around her. . ." Grace's voice broke on the sob escaping her lips, no matter how hard she'd tried to hold it back.

"God's ways are not our ways, and accidents can happen when least expected. When the Lord calls us home, Grace, we go to be with Him." Calvin spoke in a comforting tone.

"This is true." She dabbed at a few escaped tears. "Even so, I can't help the regrets I'm dealing with right now."

"What do you mean?" He looked into her eyes.

"I wonder if we should have brought the rest of our family along so they could say goodbye to my sister."

Calvin cleared his throat, and his eyes misted before he spoke. "She would not know they were here, and there is nothing left to do except pray, which can be done while they wait for us at home. You and I will stay here by Sadie Ruth's side and continue our prayers, while the doctors and nurses do all they can for her."

A nurse they'd met previously stepped into the room and checked Sadie Ruth's vitals, as well as the machines and tubes keeping her alive.

The nurse looked at Grace with a sympathetic expression and handed her a box of tissues. "Your sister's pulse and heart rate are weak. She may not last much longer."

Grace dabbed at her tears before blowing her nose and closing her eyes. "Thy kingdom come, Thy will be done in earth, as it is in heaven," she said, quoting Matthew 6:10.

*

Middlebury

"Were there any messages from Mom or Dad?" Sadie asked when Jana Beth came inside after making a trip to the phone shed.

Jana Beth shook her head. "I'm afraid not—just one from Wyman asking what night you want to go to supper with him next week."

"Okay. When it's my turn to check for messages, I'll return his call." Sadie leaned back against the sofa cushions and tried to relax. It was hard to think of anything other than how her aunt was doing. "Kaylene, you need to leave those cookies alone," she called to her sister, who'd gone out to the kitchen. "I can hear you opening up that container again."

"You've got good ears, Sadie." The sound of two plastic pieces snapping together occurred before Kaylene returned to the living room. "It's hard not to munch when I'm worried. I hope Aunt Sadie Ruth will be all right."

"Me too. I thought we would have had an update by now." Sadie readjusted the soft pillow behind her back and leaned into it. She remembered fondly how much fun she used to have as a girl whenever her aunt came to visit. The fun-loving woman wasn't afraid to get her clothes rumpled or dirty when she played baseball or other outdoor games with Sadie and her siblings. Dressed in a T-shirt, blue jeans, and sneakers, Aunt Sadie Ruth used to climb to the hayloft with them and tell stories about when she was a girl growing up on a farm with her sister. Aunt Sadie Ruth had said she'd always been somewhat of a tomboy and preferred doing outdoor chores over washing dishes, cleaning the house, or helping with the laundry. Yet when she exchanged her jeans and T-shirt for a pretty dress or skirt and blouse, the tomboy aunt looked every bit the proper lady.

I hope she's going to be okay. Sadie squeezed her eyes tightly shut. *Please God, heal Aunt Sadie Ruth's body and allow her to feel Your presence.*

✳

When Wyman stepped into the phone shed and saw the light on the answering machine blinking, he hoped that Sadie had returned his call and left him a message. Wyman had checked his cell phone earlier and found no messages, so maybe she'd called his folks' home number.

He took a seat and clicked the button. Unfortunately there was only a message from his uncle Abner, reminding Wyman's parents of the barbecue he and his wife had planned for Saturday evening. Since he'd made no mention of Wyman coming, he assumed the get-together was only for the two couples. That was fine with Wyman. His uncle was a decent man, but his boisterous voice and the corny jokes he often told got on Wyman's nerves.

Shifting gears, Wyman thought about Michael. If he could get along with his brother's wife well enough, it would be nice to have a game night. But he found Lovina too annoying to be around for any length of time. Wyman wondered if she would be more cordial toward him once he'd paid back every penny he owed. Or was this a side of his sister-in-law that he hadn't observed when she and Michael first got married?

Wyman cringed. Was she curt like this with her husband too? Regardless, spending time with his uncle or Lovina would not be fun.

I'd rather spend the evening by myself than put up with all that unnecessary carrying on, so unless Sadie's free Saturday night, I'll stay home and find something to occupy my time. He released a long breath and mumbled, "I could give my buggy a wash and then clean out the interior if things don't work out so I can be with my girl Saturday evening."

Wyman plucked his cell phone from his pocket and punched in Sadie's number again.

✳

"Think I'll go out and check for messages now." Sadie rose from the chair where she and her sisters had been working on a puzzle. "It's almost eleven o'clock, and we'll need to go to bed soon. Surely Mom or Dad has called with a report on Aunt Sadie Ruth's condition by now."

Kaylene yawned. "You're right. We all have jobs to go to in the morning, and I can hardly stay awake."

"Me neither," Jana Beth agreed, "but I would sleep better if I knew how our mamm's sister is doing."

"Same here, so I'm heading to the phone shed right now."

Kaylene stepped over to her. "I'll go along and keep you company."

"Thanks. I could use some support right now. Besides, it's late and dark out there." Sadie grabbed a flashlight and headed out the door.

Kaylene followed close and crowded into Sadie.

"Ouch, you stepped on my foot."

"Sorry, Sadie, but it's creepy and hard to see out here."

"Jah, well, quit looking around for monsters. Just focus on the light and you should be fine."

Kaylene continued to walk alongside Sadie. "I wish we could've lived closer to our aunt."

"I agree. It's a shame we weren't able to see her more often."

"Sadie, I want us siblings to keep in touch with each other and visit one another often, no matter where we might all live in the future."

"I agree."

After another warm day, the cool night breeze blowing against Sadie's face felt good as she and Kaylene made their way down the path to the phone shed. Upon entering the small building, she turned on the battery-operated light and seated herself in front of the shelf where the answering machine sat. As expected, the light blinked green.

Kaylene stepped inside as well. "Oh good. It looks like we've got some messages. I hope Mom or Dad called to give us an update."

"Me too." Sadie clicked the button and listened to two messages from Wyman. She would call him back and respond to his request, but not until she'd heard the other messages. There was only one more—it was from Dad, stating that Aunt Sadie Ruth's condition was grave and, short of a miracle, she most likely would not make it through the night. Dad ended his communication by saying either he or Mom would call again in the morning.

"Not make it? Did I hear Dad right?" She replayed the message. Listening to it for the second time, she heard exactly what she'd heard the first time.

"This is terrible news. Our poor mother must be suffering to see her only sibling slowly slipping away." Kaylene's voice sounded strained as she placed her hands on Sadie's shoulders. "I wish we were there with Mom and Dad."

"Jah." Sadie's shoulders slumped as she covered her face with both hands. *I wish I had gone with Mom and Dad to see Aunt Sadie Ruth. At least I could have told her how much she was loved and said my goodbyes. Now, short of a miracle, I'll never get the chance to speak to her again—at least not here on this earth.*

As the reality of the situation penetrated her soul, Sadie felt overcome with emotion. She and Kaylene wept together. Then Sadie lifted her face toward the ceiling and shouted, "Dear Lord, haven't You heard our prayers? Won't You please heal our aunt of her injuries and make her well again?"

Sadie felt so depressed she couldn't return Wyman's call. All she wanted to do was spend the rest of the night pleading with God to make Aunt Sadie Ruth well. Was that too much to ask? After all, when Jesus walked the earth, He'd healed many people—making the blind to see, the lame to walk, and the deaf to hear. Jesus had even brought Lazarus back from the dead. Sadie had no doubts that He could restore her aunt if He wanted to.

"I'm going to pray for that," she spoke aloud. "Even if it takes all night."

✳

When they returned to the house, Sadie gave Jana Beth the latest news.

"I am sorry to hear that." Jana Beth slowly shook her head. "I was so hoping—"

"I was too," Kaylene interrupted. "Sure wish we could be there with Mom right now. I'm certain she's taking this pretty hard."

Her throat felt so clogged, all Sadie could manage was a quick nod.

"Did you call our brothers to let them know what's happened?" The question came from Jana Beth.

She shook her head, trying to get control of her emotions. "I was too stunned to think straight, but Saul and Leland should be notified so they can be praying."

Sadie picked up the flashlight again and was almost to the door when Jana Beth called out, "I'll go. You look exhausted and should probably go on up to bed."

"I am, but I doubt I'll get much sleep tonight. I will, however, do a lot of praying."

After her sister went outside and Kaylene went down the hall to the bathroom, Sadie meandered into the kitchen and fixed herself a cup of tea, which she took to her room.

Taking a seat near the foot of her bed, she lifted the cup and took a sip. The warm liquid felt good on her parched throat. *If I pray diligently throughout the night, maybe by morning there'll be a message from Mom or Dad with good news.*

Chapter 14

*W*hen Sadie returned to the phone shed early the following morning, she felt confident that there'd be a message from one of her parents. She hoped all the praying she'd done last night had not been in vain. Although she'd spent the first half of her time in bed, pleading with God to save Aunt Sadie Ruth's life, Sadie had eventually fallen into a fitful, dream-filled sleep. She'd awakened this morning, drenched in sweat.

With anticipation flowing through her veins, Sadie's fingers trembled as she pushed the blinking button on the answering machine. There was another message from Wyman, but responding to it could wait. The next one was from her dad. It was the only message she truly cared about hearing at this moment.

Sadie leaned closer and listened intently.

"Sadie, Kaylene, Jana Beth, or whoever gets this message, I regret to inform you that your mamm's sister passed away at two o'clock this morning. Sadie Ruth never woke up, so there were no verbal goodbyes, but she died with a look of peace on her face. Your mamm and I will be staying here to make arrangements for the funeral, which will take place this Saturday afternoon at three, and we would like as many of our family members to be there as possible. I will call your brothers and give them the news as well. Please make arrangements with one of our drivers to take you all up for the funeral. Since the trip only takes about two and a half hours by car, if you leave early Saturday morning, you should have plenty of time to get here before noon."

As her father's words, spoken so clearly and with a note of regret, penetrated her foggy brain, Sadie hugged herself and rocked back and forth on the folding chair. "No! No! No! How can this be?" With tears streaming down her face, she looked up. "Why, Lord, after all the prayers my sisters and I said last night, did You have to take Aunt Sadie Ruth?"

Sadie covered her face with her hands and cried until no more tears came. Then she left the phone shed and returned to the house to give her sisters the sorrowful news.

While Jana Beth and Kaylene might not take it as hard as she had, she felt certain that they'd be sad, nonetheless.

✼

Sadie didn't know how she had mustered up the strength to get ready for work, but her day off this week wasn't until Saturday, so she felt that she had to show up. With forced determination, she'd taken a cold shower, drunk two cups of coffee, and called a driver to give her a ride to the hardware store. A minivan pulled in the driveway and parked near the house.

"Sadie, your ride is here to take you to work!" Jana Beth called from the living room.

"Jah, I heard the horn toot." Sadie hurried through brushing her teeth and wiping off her mouth.

What a morning! I wish I could crawl back into bed. I'm so tired and depressed about losing my aunt. She looked at her reflection in the mirror. *My eyes are puffy and red from crying, but I need to get to work. Besides, I'm making my driver wait.*

Sadie headed for the kitchen to grab her lunch out of the refrigerator and her purse from the counter. "I'm leaving now. I'll see you this evening."

"All right; we'll be out the door for work soon too." Kaylene came up to Sadie and gave her a hug.

"Take care today, and we'll see you later," Jana Beth called from the hallway.

"Thanks. You too." Sadie hurried out the door to Sharon's van and climbed in. The AC blew strong, and she fiddled with the lever on the dash to control the airflow.

Sharon turned down the cold air. "Good morning, Sadie."

"Morning." Sadie fumbled with the seat belt and secured the buckle.

"I was surprised that you called for a ride to work this morning, what with the weather still being so nice."

Sadie collected herself and spoke in a hushed tone. "Our aunt passed away earlier this morning, and I didn't feel up to riding my bike."

"I'm sorry to hear that. If there's anything I can do for you or your family, let me know." Sharon pulled out of the driveway and headed in the direction of Shipshewana.

"Actually there is." Sadie pulled a tissue from her handbag and dabbed at her eyes. "If you're available this Saturday, my sisters, brothers, and I could use a ride to Toledo."

Sharon scrubbed a hand over her chin as she steered the wheel with her other hand. "I am free on Saturday and can come by as early as you need me. It will take us a couple of hours to get there."

"Yes, we would need to arrive before noon."

"How about I pick you up around seven thirty that morning? Can you all be ready by then?"

"Sure, we can have our bags packed and be waiting for you."

"Okay, I'll write that down in my planner."

They rode the rest of the way in silence, except for the sounds of country music on the radio. Sadie slumped in her seat. Even though she didn't feel up to working today, she hoped keeping busy might help take her mind off the fact that she'd lost someone very dear to her.

*

Sadie went to the cash register and made sure everything was ready, since the manager had just opened the store. When she first arrived, she'd told him about her aunt dying and had received his condolence. He'd also said that if she needed time off from work during the week, he would ask one of the other employees to fill in for her.

Sadie had declined the offer, though, stating that she would work through Friday. She'd also asked her boss if she could have a few days off next week, in case her mother needed help to go through some of her aunt's things. He'd said it wasn't a problem—Sadie could take the whole week off if she needed it.

Sadie felt thankful for her good job and understanding boss and would miss working here if and when she and Wyman got married and their first child came along. Until then, however, she planned to keep working and saving her money toward eventually purchasing a new horse. She'd set aside the idea of writing a book, since it would be too time consuming and expensive.

Thoughts of Wyman caused Sadie to realize she'd never responded to his messages about going out with him Saturday or one evening next week, which, of course, was out of the question now. She felt bad for not calling him back, but after receiving the news of her aunt's death, she hadn't thought of much else.

I'll need to get in touch with him after work today, she told herself. *Or maybe I could go over to the bulk food store during my lunch hour and talk to him then.*

✳

That's odd. . . . I don't see Sadie's bike here this morning. I hope she's inside, because I'd like to touch base with her. Wyman parked and secured his bike then sprinted inside the complex and down the hall toward the hardware store. He'd arrived in town earlier than normal for his job this morning so he could stop and see Sadie. It wasn't like her not to return his calls. Maybe the Kuhnses' voice mail had become full, or maybe for some reason Sadie was put out with him. He couldn't imagine why, however, because to his knowledge he hadn't done anything that might have upset her.

When Wyman entered the hardware store, he found Sadie behind the counter waiting on a customer. *She's a hard worker, and so beautiful. I'm blessed to have her in my life again.* He held back until the English man paid for his purchases and left.

"Hi, Sadie. How's it going? I rode my bike and got to Shipshe a little early this morning and decided to drop by and see if you'd received my messages." Wyman's words were rushed, but he couldn't seem to slow them. He suddenly felt nervous.

"I'm sorry for not returning your calls."

"No problem. By the way—I didn't see your bike locked up outside. How did you get to work this morning?"

"I asked one our drivers to come and get me. I wasn't up to riding my bicycle."

Wyman noticed for the first time that the skin around her eyes appeared to be puffy—as though she hadn't slept much the night before. "Is everything all right? You look mied this morning."

"I'm very tired, because I hardly slept at all last night."

"How come?"

"My aunt was in a car accident yesterday, and this morning we received the sad news that she'd died during the night."

Wyman reached across the counter and placed his hand on her arm. "I'm sorry to hear that. Was it one of your aunts who lives close by?"

Sadie shook her head. "It was the woman my parents named me after—Sadie Ruth." Sadie's chin trembled, and she lowered her voice. "She is—was—my mamm's only sibling."

Wyman's heart went out to Sadie. He wished he could slip around the counter and give her a hug. But there were others in the store who might be watching.

So instead of following his impulse, he patted her arm gently, hoping to offer comfort. "Wasn't Sadie Ruth your aunt who went English?"

"Jah. She married an English man and they lived in Toledo. Uncle Jim died a few years ago, but Aunt Sadie Ruth chose to remain in their home, even though she had no other family living in Ohio."

"Will you be going there for the funeral?"

She gave a nod. "I've already arranged with one of my family's drivers to come by early Saturday morning to take us to Toledo. My siblings will all go, but since my boss said I could have the time off, I'm planning to stay there next week to help my mamm sort through her sister's things and decide what to do with them."

"If she has no other family, then I imagine there will be quite a bit involved in closing her estate."

"Most likely, which could mean Mom might have to stay there for several weeks." Sadie glanced toward the door as two more customers entered the store and began walking toward the front counter. "I can't talk anymore right now, Wyman. In fact, you probably won't be hearing from me until I get back from Ohio."

"I understand."

"Oh, and I have a favor to ask."

"Of course. I'll help in any way I can."

"Would you let my friends Barbara and Ellen know what's happened so they don't wonder why they haven't heard from me in a while?"

"No problem. I'll let 'em both know." Wyman stepped back but then moved up to the counter again. "Before I go, I just want to say that I'll be praying for you and your family during this difficult time."

Tears pooled in Sadie's eyes, and she blinked a couple of times. "Danki, Wyman. We surely will appreciate your prayers."

As Wyman left the store, his shoulders slumped, and his arms hung loosely at his sides. He could almost feel Sadie's pain as though it was his own. *Sure wish there was something more I could have said or done to make her feel better.*

It would be hard to go on to work now and not think about Sadie and her family all day, but Wyman would keep his word and remember to pray for them.

✳

Toledo

Grace entered her sister's house with the key she'd found in Sadie Ruth's purse, which she'd been given at the hospital. Calvin came in behind her. Since their driver had returned to Middlebury and they had no transportation of their own, Grace had called one of Sadie's Ruth's friends to tell her what happened and ask for a ride to the house. Sadie Ruth's longtime friend Brenda had been shocked and saddened by the news and said she would be available if they needed anything while they were here.

Upon entering the house, which felt empty and cold without Sadie Ruth's presence, Grace teared up and sobbed in her husband's arms. "Oh Calvin, I can't believe my sister is gone. It all happened so suddenly, and I'm saddened that we never got to say our goodbyes."

He patted her back gently and spoke tenderly. "Your sister claimed to be a Christian, so we have to believe she's in a better place."

Grace sniffed as she stepped out of his embrace. "You're right, and that's the one thing I cling to right now."

Calvin nodded.

"I could use something warm and soothing to drink. How about you?"

"Sounds good." He looked around for a moment. "It's been awhile since you and I have stayed here."

Grace set aside Sadie Ruth's purse and hers on the hallway bench near the front door. "Jah." Her gaze fell on a familiar doorway. "I'll have to check the guestroom later to see if there are clean sheets on the bed."

They moved into the kitchen, and Grace made some tea. As they sat at the table drinking it, she looked at the desk across the room, where a small wooden box sat. She knew it was where Sadie Ruth kept her friends' and family's addresses and phone numbers.

"I'd better see about calling other people who should be notified about Sadie Ruth."

"Good idea. They'll want to know about the funeral plans too."

Grace took a seat in front of the desk and thumbed through the three-by-five cards in the box. She found several people's names she recognized and pulled those out to call first.

Seeing a large manila envelope on the desk, Grace opened it to see if there might be something important inside. When she pulled a document from the envelope and read the first few pages, Grace gasped. "Ach, my! Calvin, you'll never believe what I've found or what it says!"

Chapter 15

Kapaa

Mandy sat on the blanket with her toes curled in the warm sand. Ken sat beside her, watching his buddy Taavi and other surfers who had come to catch the big waves. Due to injuries he'd sustained a few years ago, Mandy's husband's surfing days were over. Ken had a hard time accepting his limitations after the shark attack, but he'd finally come to grips with it and was able to cheer his friends on.

Although Mandy felt bad about her husband's permanent limp and use of a cane, at least she didn't have to worry about him being out in the treacherous waves anymore. It used to frighten her so much to sit on the beach and watch Ken paddle out to sea and then stand up on that board with no protection from what dangers might lie beneath or around him.

She reached over and clasped his strong hand, giving it a gentle squeeze. "It was nice of your mom to watch Charlie this morning so we could spend a little time by ourselves."

He looked at her and smiled. "Yeah. With the craziness that can go on at the B&B sometimes, we don't always get chances like this."

"That's for sure, but I wouldn't trade what we do for going back to raising organic chickens, would you?"

He rolled his eyes then wrinkled his nose. "Not a chance. I tried that already, and it wasn't nearly as fulfilling as greeting folks from all walks of life and areas of the country." He grinned at her. "Of course, greeting people who come to stay with us is not my only responsibility. I have lots of chores, same as you."

"True." Leaning back and resting her elbows on the blanket, Mandy closed her eyes from the glare of the sun. "I feel guilty sitting here in this peaceful surrounding when Sadie and her family are attending the funeral of her aunt today. I'm sure glad Ellen called and let me know about it so I could be praying."

"It's never easy to lose a loved one." Ken's voice lowered. "Even though it's been a few years, I still miss my dad. I'm sure Mom does even more."

"Yes, which is why she's said many times how much she appreciates having us living together and working with her."

Using his cane for support, Ken stood and pulled Mandy to her feet. "It's not good to be talking about sad things the whole time we're here on the beach today. Let's take a walk along the water's edge, okay?"

Mandy nodded and offered him a smile. "That sounds fine to me." Holding hands firmly, they moved away from the blanket and toward the water. As they plodded through the small waves lapping against the shore, Mandy lifted a silent prayer for Sadie and her loved ones. She couldn't help wanting to be there, supporting her friend and the family today. The situation pulled on Mandy's heartstrings, but she needed to give it to God. *It would be nicer if we could come and go from the island whenever we wanted, but it's out of the question. We can't afford to travel as often as we'd like.*

Mandy splashed at the waves. The warm water on her feet felt pleasant, and it made their stroll even more inviting. She enjoyed holding hands with her husband as they wandered along the shallow waters of the beach.

"After we're done here on the sand I thought we might go out for a bite to eat."

"That would be nice. How about we go someplace we haven't been lately?"

"Sounds good." He lifted her hand and kissed it.

"Maybe we could go to one of the resorts and have a meal."

"Sure, we can do that if you'd like. We don't mind being around tourists, that's for sure." He laughed.

They walked along a few more minutes, and then Mandy noticed a young couple with a baby. She couldn't help staring, and she finally commented to the mother holding her little one. "Hello, I just want to say that I think your baby is adorable."

"Thank you." She smiled.

"How old is your baby?"

"She's a month old now." The young woman shaded the infant from the sun.

"Well, you are blessed."

"Yes we sure are."

"Have a good day." Mandy and Ken continued their walk.

Even though they had their wonderful little boy at home, she was eager to have their second child.

✳

Middlebury

Wyman guided his frisky horse as he came up the driveway to his parents' home. It didn't help that he'd given the animal a good helping of sweet oats before leaving. He'd spent the morning in Topeka watching some of his friends play a game of softball. He'd thought it would be a good diversion for him and a nice way to spend his day off, but he'd been wrong. All he had thought about was Sadie, wondering how her aunt's funeral went and how she and her family were holding up. He wished he could have gone with her to offer his support, but with Sadie planning to stay in Toledo next week to help her mother and him needing to be at work, he hadn't offered to go along. He hoped the time would go quickly until she returned so he could find out how everything went. *If I had stayed working for my daed, maybe Sadie and I could be planning our wedding already. Then I could've gone along and stayed a day or two with my girlfriend's family.*

He pulled up to the rail and got down from the buggy. *Guess I could have gone for the funeral and come back this evening or even tomorrow.* Wyman paused to admire his clean rig. He'd washed it off before going out this morning to see his friends at the ball field. Keeping busy helped some with missing Sadie.

Wyman unhitched his perky horse and led him into the barn. "I almost hate to put you away in your stall since you're so full of energy. How about I turn you loose in the field so you can run for a while?" Wyman took the animal through the corral and undid his halter at the entrance to the wide-open field. The horse pawed in anticipation and let out a whinny before running off.

Wyman closed the gate and walked back through to put the lead rope away. "Guess all I can do for Sadie and her family at this point is to pray for them." He paused and bowed his head. *Lord, please be with the Kuhns family and offer them Your comfort during this difficult time. Protect each one as they travel back to Indiana, and be with Sadie and her mother next week.*

✳

Toledo

When Sadie entered her aunt's house, along with her siblings and parents, an icy cold feeling came over her like a coating of sleet. It didn't seem right to be in this place without Aunt Sadie Ruth here to offer them a pleasant greeting. After attending the solemn funeral this afternoon, Sadie should have been ready for this, but she was not.

She wandered into the kitchen and looked for a glass in one of the cupboards. Sadie needed to get a drink of water since they'd been outdoors in the warmth for the graveside service. Some of her family began to settle into the living room, while others were freshening up in the wash areas. Sadie heard them in the next room chatting about work or projects they had going on at home. For a time their conversations took her away and it was pleasant to hear. *This reprieve is nice. I wish it could go on.* Sadie filled her glass under the running faucet. The days ahead would be busy with sifting and sorting through Aunt Sadie Ruth's many belongings.

Even though her mother said she'd gotten enough rest, the dark circles under her eyes indicated the opposite. *Mom's been doing well under the circumstances. She's been incredible during this whole sad affair. My mother is such an encouraging person.*

Sadie closed her eyes and drank the cool water. She didn't realize how thirsty she'd been until the entire glass was empty. Wiping her mouth, she put the container in the sink and headed in to where most of her family stood around visiting. It seemed strange to her that Aunt Sadie Ruth could have lived alone in such a big house. She found herself looking at the different objects that decorated her home. Her aunt liked oil paintings. Some were of animals and others scenes of places abroad. The house seemed to be a mixture of old and new. The outside was Tudor style, while the inside had been remodeled with newer wood floors throughout and fancy furnishings.

I have to say that Aunt Sadie Ruth had good taste. She ran her fingers over the rigid design on one of the shining crystal dishes on display next to her.

Pushing her thoughts aside, Sadie seated herself between her sisters on the sofa, while Saul, Leland, and Sadie's parents sat in nearby chairs. Saul's wife, Rebecca, excused herself to tend to their baby's needs. Leland's wife, Margaret, had stayed back in Middlebury with their two small children, who were both down with colds.

Mom made a few flighty hand movements and cleared her throat as she looked over at Dad. "Do you want to tell them, Calvin, or should I be the one?"

"You go ahead, Grace. Since you're the one who found your sister's notarized paperwork, you should read it to everyone."

A circle of red erupted on Mom's cheeks as she reached for a manila envelope lying on the coffee table. "This is Sadie's Ruth's last will and testament." She opened the contents and read: " 'To my sister, Grace Kuhns, and her husband, Calvin, I bequeath ten thousand dollars.' "

She paused and cleared her throat once again. " 'To my nephews, Saul Kuhns and Leland Kuhns, and nieces, Jana Beth Kuhns and Kaylene Kuhns, I bequeath five thousand dollars each.'"

Sadie sat very still, wondering why her name had been left out. *Wouldn't Aunt Sadie Ruth want to leave me something too?* She shifted her weight on the couch. *Surely it has to be a mistake.*

Mom looked directly at Sadie and brought a shaky hand to her forehead. " 'The rest of my estate, which includes my home and all of my other assets, and is currently valued at well over two million dollars, I leave to my niece Sadie Kuhns. I entrust this money into her hands. I feel certain that she will be a good steward and use the money at her discretion in the best way possible—for her own benefit as well as for others in need.'"

Sadie sat in stunned silence, barely able to comprehend what her mother had read. She'd had no idea her aunt had that much money, much less that she would leave the bulk of it to her.

What would I even do with all that money, and how do the members of my family feel about this? I don't understand why Aunt Sadie Ruth chose me over them.

Saul whistled. "That's a lot of money! Five thousand dollars is more than I ever expected, but I can't imagine inheriting two million dollars." He looked at Sadie. "How come she chose you?"

Holding her palms up, she shook her head. "I—I have no idea."

Leland spoke up. "Maybe it's a mistake. Or maybe Aunt Sadie Ruth wasn't in her right mind when she wrote her will. It makes no sense that she would play favorites like that and give the rest of us so little while Sadie gets so much."

Sadie looked at each sister, sitting on either side of her, to see if they would say something, but they just sat, staring at her.

Leland said a few more words on the topic; then everyone began to talk at once.

Dad clapped his hands so loud, Sadie nearly jumped off the couch.

"Everyone please be quiet and listen to what I have to say."

All heads turned toward Dad, who now stood in front of the mammoth stone fireplace.

"First of all, I'm sure your mamm's sister was of a sound mind when she made out her will." He looked at Mom, who bobbed her head. "Second, we will have a lawyer look over the paperwork and tell us what all needs to be done and how to proceed." Dad paused and pulled his fingers through the ends of his full beard. "If it's legal, which I believe it is, and Sadie is indeed the recipient of most of your aunt's money, then so be it. Sadie Ruth must have had what she felt was a good reason for choosing her, and the rest of us need to be thankful for what we will receive."

But what was my aunt's reason? Sadie pondered yet again. *Will I ever know why she chose to leave me so much of her estate?* She swallowed hard, attempting to push down the lump that had formed in her throat. *What if this creates problems in the relationship I have with my brothers and sisters? Even Mom and Dad might be affected by Aunt Sadie Ruth's decision.*

Chapter 16

*J*t's so difficult going through my dear aunt's things." Sadie sighed as she placed several sweaters inside a cardboard box. She and Mom had spent the last several days packing up Aunt Sadie Ruth's clothes and personal items. Things that had sentimental value would be taken home to be distributed among those in their family. Others, like the clothing and many household items, would be sent, via one of Aunt Sadie Ruth's friends, to a local charity. It didn't take long for Sadie to realize that this process would take more than a week. Since Sadie needed to get back to work or risk losing her job, Jana Beth had volunteered to take a week off from the trailer factory and return to Toledo to help Mom continue clearing things out of the house so it could be put on the market. If more time was needed to get the job done, Kaylene would take off the week after that to help out.

When the topic of Sadie needing to return home and to her job at the hardware store was first brought up, Mom had looked at Sadie and rolled her eyes, saying, "With all that money you'll be inheriting soon, you really don't need to work anymore." To that, Sadie had replied: "But I enjoy my job at the hardware store. Besides, it could be some time before I receive my inheritance."

Stopping in the middle of her work, she thought, *I'm used to the way my life has been and don't want it to change. I hope having a lot of money won't alter who I am.* She shook her head. *No, I can't let it happen. I need to put God first and then place others before my selfish needs. That is what the Bible teaches.*

Sadie stepped back through the door that opened into the large walk-in closet. She still couldn't get over the vast amount of clothing her aunt had accumulated. The room was well organized with storage areas for shoes, handbags, and other accessories. *Why, she had enough skirts and blouses to wear a different outfit every day for several months. I'm not sure if I could ever feel the need to live like her in a big house such as this and have so many clothes in my closet.*

Sadie had to admit, though, that she'd eyed the big fancy canopy bed that stood between two french windows in the master bedroom. It looked so comfortable, inviting her to curl up and take a nap. But there was no time for resting right now, with so much work to be done.

She carried more clothes out of the closest and piled them on the bed to sort. Instead of continuing to go through the clothes, however, Sadie stood staring at the bed.

"What are you thinking about?" Mom tapped Sadie's shoulder.

"I can't help admiring Aunt Sadie Ruth's canopy bed. Do you think it would fit in my bedroom at home?"

"Jah, I believe so." Mom bent down to look at the places the bed joints connected. "We should be able to take this apart and get it ready to bring home when the time comes."

Sadie smiled, relieved that her mother had no objections.

Some of the other select pieces of furniture in the house would be sold during the estate sale. Mom had set some furniture and other items aside in another room. Those would be trucked home to disperse among the family members.

Sadie thought back to her mother's comment about her not needing to work anymore. She pursed her lips while tucking a strand of loose hair back under her head covering. *I'm sure Mom, the rest of the family, and soon others, will feel the same way once the word gets about my good fortune. I bet everyone I know will tell me to quit my job at the hardware store.*

They had met with Aunt Sadie Ruth's lawyer yesterday and learned that the will was legally binding. They'd also been to the bank and discovered that Sadie had been listed on her aunt's bank accounts as the beneficiary. Mom was named as the executor of her sister's will, but she had the option of letting the lawyer take care of that. Of course, it would mean he would charge them a fee to do it, but Sadie could afford it, if that's the way Mom wanted to go. The estate would also have to be processed through probate before the funds could be distributed.

Sadie still couldn't come to grips with the fact that her aunt had so much money or that she'd indicated in her will that Sadie would receive such a large portion of it. *Why did my aunt choose me? What did she expect me to do with all that money?* These questions kept rolling around in her head. *I would think she would have given more to Mom than anyone else. I did nothing to deserve any of Aunt Sadie Ruth's money, let alone receiving more than the others.*

Forcing her thoughts aside, Sadie moved over to the dresser and opened the bottom drawer. She was surprised to discover two photo albums cushioned by several colorful silky scarves. Curious to see what pictures these books held, she lifted each one out and placed them on the other side of the enormous bed.

"What have you got there?" Mom moved closer to Sadie.

"They're photo albums." Sadie took a seat on the bed and opened the first one. She drew in a quick breath as her gaze came to rest on familiar faces. "Look, Mom, these are pictures Aunt Sadie Ruth took of me and my siblings when we were young and she came to visit us."

Sadie's mother took a seat beside her and pointed at one of the photos. "Well, for goodness' sakes—a few of these pictures have your daed and me in them. That sneaky sister of mine took these without us even knowing. I wonder what possessed her to do such a thing."

"I bet she took the pictures so she could remember what we all looked like."

Mom folded her arms and gave a little huff. "I don't see how Sadie

Ruth could forget what her only sister looked like."

"Maybe it wasn't just for her benefit. She may have taken the photos so that we, your kinner, would have pictures to remember you by when you join her in heaven someday."

Mom sat quietly, staring at the photos with tears in her eyes. Then she turned to Sadie and spoke. "I suppose that could be the case. She might have also wanted you to see how you looked when you were young children." She drew in a breath and blew it out slowly. "I suppose it doesn't really matter why she took photos of us and put them in albums. The question now is what should we do with them?"

"I think we ought to take the photos home so the rest of our family can see them."

"All right, then, but no one outside of our immediate family should see them. We wouldn't want the ministers or anyone else in our church district to think we'd posed or allowed someone to take our pictures."

Sadie thought her mother was worried about nothing, but she kept quiet. She was glad Mom had agreed that the albums could go home with them. In fact, Sadie planned to take them along when she returned to Middlebury next week.

They looked through the rest of the albums, commenting from time to time on the pictures that were mostly of their family. Sadie looked over at Mom. "I don't think it is right that I should get more inheritance from Aunt Sadie Ruth's estate than you or my siblings. Since you're her only sister, the money should all go to you." Sadie paused for a breath then rushed on. "So after the will goes through probate and the money is released to me, I'll take the same amount my sisters and brothers are getting and turn the rest over to you and Dad to do with as you choose."

✳

With her mouth gaping open, Grace stared at Sadie. She could hardly believe the words her daughter had spoken. If she were being honest, she'd have to admit that ever since the will had been found and read, she'd struggled with envy and a sense of confusion as to why her sister had chosen Sadie over her to receive such a large sum of money.

Now with Sadie offering to give it all to her, Grace's envy was replaced with guilt. She swallowed hard and put both hands against Sadie's flushed cheeks. "I must admit that I don't understand why Sadie Ruth chose you as the one to receive the most money, but she must have had her reasons. Perhaps it was because she knew you have such a generous heart. Or maybe she felt that you would spend the money wisely."

Sadie opened her mouth as if to say something, but lowering her hands, Grace shook her head. "Please allow me to finish. Your offer to give me and your daed the money you are supposed to receive is most generous, but it's not what my sister wanted," Grace continued. "So despite your willingness to make that sacrifice, I insist that you keep the inheritance your aunt wanted you to have and put it to good use."

Tears pooled in Sadie's eyes. "Oh Mom, I wish you would reconsider."

Grace shook her head determinedly. "You must abide by your aunt's wishes and be grateful."

*

Middlebury

"A quarter for your thoughts." Jana Beth bumped her sister's arm as they stood at the kitchen counter, cutting vegetables for a tossed green salad.

Kaylene pursed her lips. "I was thinking about Sadie and wondering why our aunt left so much money to her, while the rest of us get so little."

"Five thousand dollars is nothing to sneeze at, you know."

Kaylene wrinkled her nose. "Humph! Compared to what our sister's getting, the money our aunt left us is like a drop in the bucket."

"True." Jana Beth hated to speak the words out loud, but she too felt cheated and hurt by their aunt's favoritism. *She must have liked Sadie better than us. Why else would she leave her most of the estate?*

It was Kaylene's turn to bump Jana Beth's arm. "You haven't said much since we found out how much money we would all be getting. What are your thoughts on the matter?"

Jana Beth stiffened. "How come you're asking me this? Why don't you ask Saul and Leland for their opinions?"

"I brought the topic up to you because you're here right now, and our *brieder* are not."

"But have you talked to our brothers about it—asked if they feel envious of Sadie?"

"No, but I could see by their expressions when Mom read Aunt Sadie Ruth's will that neither of them was too pleased. There were some comments made, if you'll recall."

Jana Beth chopped another carrot as she tried to remember how either of her brothers had reacted that day. She'd been so stunned herself that she hadn't paid much attention to Leland's and Saul's expressions. As she thought more about it, Jana Beth remembered that her brothers had been pretty quiet on the trip home the day after Aunt Sadie Ruth's funeral. For that matter, no one in the van said a lot on the return trip to Middlebury—not even Saul's wife, who was normally quite talkative. Perhaps everyone, including Mom and Dad, felt confused and hurt by their aunt's decision to leave Sadie such a huge chunk of money, while the rest of them got so little in comparison.

Kaylene cleared her throat. "So tell me, Jana Beth, what are your thoughts on this? Don't you feel envious of Sadie?"

Jana Beth looked directly at Kaylene. "Okay, I admit it—*Ich duh's* Sadie *vergunne.*"

Kaylene gave a nod. "I'm glad to know that you envy Sadie too. I sure wouldn't want to be the only one feeling jealous right now."

Jana Beth gave no response as she tried to focus on cutting up the last of the carrots. There was really no point in having this discussion, since there was nothing they could do about it anyway.

*

Kapaa

Mandy moved about one of the guest rooms, tidying things up and trying to ignore the sharp pain in her belly that had started soon after she'd awakened this morning. Assuming it was from something disagreeable that she'd eaten last night, Mandy had chosen to ignore the cramping. She'd tried a hot water bottle against her stomach earlier, but that had done nothing to squelch the pain.

Should I say something to Ken or Vickie? Do I need to call the doctor and be checked out—to be sure nothing's wrong with my pregnancy? Mandy placed both hands against her stomach as another spasm came. *I shouldn't take any chances.*

She turned off the light in the guest room and headed down the hall. Passing through the living room, she spotted her son sitting on the floor with some toys, while one of their guests—a middle-aged woman who'd arrived yesterday afternoon—sat reading a book on Hawaiian culture. It was one they kept on the coffee table, along with several pamphlets so their B&B guests who were new to the island could learn about many of the things they could see and do.

The woman, whose name was Robyn, looked up and smiled at Mandy. "Your little boy is sure a sweetie. He's been keeping me entertained."

"Well, if he gets too loud or disturbs your reading, let me know. I'm sure you came here for some peace and quiet, not to be entertained by a youngster."

Robyn chuckled. "I don't mind at all. I have a granddaughter about his age, so I'm used to young children, and I enjoy their cute antics."

Mandy forced a smile as another spasm of pain took hold in her abdomen. "If you'll excuse me, I need to go to the kitchen, but someone will be back soon with some refreshments for you."

"Sounds good. When I'm done with that, I may go out for a while and do a little exploring. I'll probably do some shopping too."

Mandy nodded and hurried from the room. When she stepped into the kitchen, she found Vickie taking a tray of macadamia nut cookies from the oven.

"Where's Ken? I thought he was in here with you." Mandy placed both hands against her belly and grimaced.

"He was, but he went outside to pick up some branches that blew off the trees in the yard last night when that hefty wind came up unexpectedly." Vickie placed the cookie sheet on the cooling rack set out and turned to face Mandy. "What's wrong? Why are you holding your stomach?"

"I'm having some cramping, and I'm worried that—" Another contraction came, and Mandy almost doubled over from the pain. "I think I may be having a miscarriage."

Vickie's eyebrows pulled inward, and she gave a little gasp. "Take a seat at the table. I'll go get Ken."

As her mother-in-law rushed out the back door, Mandy sank into a chair. "Dear Lord," she whispered, "please don't let me lose this baby."

Chapter 17

*H*ot tears rolled down Mandy's cheeks as she lay in the hospital bed with Ken sitting beside her, holding her hand. A short time ago, she'd lost their baby, and her throat ached from crying so hard. Ken offered words of encouragement, but he hurt too. She saw his grave expression and the look of sadness in his blue eyes.

"The Lord will see us through this ordeal, just like He did when I had my accident." He leaned over and kissed her cheek. "If it's His will for us to have more children, you'll get pregnant again when the time is right."

Mandy stared out the window into the low-lying clouds. It was a gloomy, rainy day. Her mood was at rock bottom, and no amount of positive talk could change that. A sob rose in her throat as she clutched the sheet covering her trembling body. "I can't talk about that right now. I just need to sleep."

"Of course you do. I'm going down the hall for a cup of coffee and to call our pastor." Mandy's folks and his mother had already been notified. Ken kissed her forehead. "Try to get some rest. I'll be back soon."

After her husband left the room, Mandy closed her eyes, but sleep would not come. She had wanted this baby so much.

While kneading her chest with the heel of her hand, salty tears kept flowing as troubling thoughts swirled through her mind. *What if I can never conceive again? What if I do get pregnant and lose that baby too?* An uncontrollable moan escaped her lips. *I don't think I could bear it.*

Mandy's thoughts switched to a heartfelt prayer. *Heavenly Father, please help me deal with this horrible, all-consuming grief. I know my little boy needs me, and my help is needed to run the B&B, but right now I don't feel like I'll ever be able to function normally again.*

✳

Ken stood in the hallway outside of Mandy's door. He ran shaky fingers through his thick, wavy hair. *I wonder what happened to make this sort of thing occur. Mandy had no issues with our first child—everything went well throughout the entire pregnancy.* Ken pulled out his phone and looked to see how much charge was left on it. *I wonder if Mom called my brother Dan and his wife to let them know about our loss. I'd like to make sure I've covered all the bases while Mandy is trying to recoup from this trauma.*

His cell phone battery ran low, and the charging cord Ken needed was at the house, where he'd left it behind in a flurry to get Mandy the help she needed. If his cell phone died, he would ask to use a phone at the nurses' station.

Ken closed his eyes as the scene before they'd left home replayed in his mind. Mom running out of the B&B, calling to him with a shocked expression. Ken hearing the news with disbelief that his wife was in trouble and thinking she might lose their baby. Seeing Mandy crying in pain as she cradled her stomach.

Ken could barely maintain composure. *Lord, keep me strong for Mandy, no matter what,* he prayed. *Also, please give us a sense of hope and peace that You are still in control.*

Ken opened his eyes and swiped at the hot tears. He couldn't help being worried about his wife and kept asking himself if there was something he could do to help ease the pain of her grief. Of course, Ken felt a great loss too, but he hadn't grieved as uncontrollably as she had when the doctor gave them the heartbreaking news.

Ken had not said anything to Mandy at this point, unsure of how she would respond, but he wondered, had the baby been carried to full term, if it may have been born with some sort of birth defect that would have affected the quality of the child's life. Or if Mandy had carried their baby to full term and it had been born with acute physical complications, it might have died soon after Mandy gave birth. This would have made it even harder for them to accept.

The veins on top of Ken's hands protruded as he gripped his cell phone. It had been difficult telling his mother that Mandy had lost the baby— especially when she'd begun to cry when he'd called to give her the sad news. Mom was a wonderful, caring grandma to little Charlie, and she had said several times how much she looked forward to the addition of another grandchild in their family.

But it was not meant to be, he told himself yet again. *So we must learn to accept it and move on with our lives, looking to God for emotional healing.*

When Ken had called Mandy's parents, he'd gotten their voice mail and left a message. He felt sure that Miriam and Isaac as well as Mandy's four brothers would be disappointed when they heard what had occurred. What would probably make it even harder for his in-laws was knowing they couldn't be here to offer their only daughter love and support. They too were caring grandparents.

At times such as this, Ken felt guilty for his role in influencing Mandy to leave her home in Middlebury, Indiana, and move to Kauai in order to take on the job of helping him and his mom run the bed-and-breakfast. But he hadn't pressured her to do it. In fact, Mandy had been excited about their new venture, and Ken felt sure she loved living on this beautiful tropical island as much as he did. Even so, it had to be difficult for her to live so far from her family and all the friends she had made in Amish country.

Ken headed down the hall to get a cup of much-needed coffee. *Hopefully, once Mandy has regained her strength and is feeling better emotionally, we'll be able to make a trip to the mainland so she can spend some time with friends and family. That in itself should cheer her up.*

✳

Shipshewana

As Wyman carried two empty cardboard boxes to one of the back rooms in the bulk food store, his thoughts went to Sadie. He'd talked to her only twice since her aunt's death and wondered how things were going as she helped her mother clean and sort things in Sadie Ruth's house. He had been taken by surprise when she'd told him about her aunt's will and the large sum of money she would be inheriting. Even now, several days later, Wyman's mind hadn't fully digested the fact. How could a person have so little money that they couldn't afford to buy a new horse one day, and the next day become wealthy, with two million dollars in their bank account?

Of course, Wyman reasoned, *Sadie doesn't have possession of the money yet. It could be several weeks or even months before she acquires those funds. How fortunate she is, though, to have had such a generous aunt.*

Wyman had trouble admitting it, even to himself, but he couldn't help feeling envious of Sadie and her good fortune. If he had even a fourth of Sadie's inheritance, he could pay off his debt to Michael and still have money left to buy an adequate home for him and his bride to live in after they were married.

Wyman didn't know anyone with the kind of money Sadie would soon have. Even if he did, it wasn't likely that they'd leave any of their fortune to him.

What am I doing? I'm in the middle of working right now. I don't have time to be preoccupied about Sadie's money, he chided himself.

He set the boxes in place near some others that had been stacked up and wiped a trickle of sweat from his forehead. It was another warm day for October, and this storage room had no air-conditioning vent, like the main part of the store.

I wonder if Sadie becoming rich overnight will change the way she thinks or acts toward me, her other friends, and her family members. Will Sadie's large inheritance change anything in our personal relationship? If we should ever get married, would Sadie be worried that I might want to spend her money foolishly? She may still think I'm irresponsible and might not fully trust me yet.

Wyman continued to wipe his damp forehead. *Maybe she won't want to marry me at all. With so much money, Sadie might decide to travel or leave the Amish way of life, like her aunt did. This windfall could change everything between me and the woman I love.*

Wyman's fingers curled tightly, causing his nails to bite into his palms. *Don't think I could stand it if I lost Sadie. This whole matter has me deeply concerned. Should I question Sadie about her intentions or keep quiet and see what happens after she returns home and gets the money?*

"Say, what are ya doin' in here when there's work to be done out there? The boss has been looking for you."

Wyman whirled around to face one of his fellow employees. "I came in to put some empty boxes away."

"That's good, but you're needed out there in the main part of the store now." The young man squinted as he stared at Wyman. "You okay? The way you were standin' there, rubbing your forehead when I first came in, made me wonder if you might be sick or something."

Wyman shook his head. "I'm fine. Just paused a few minutes to wipe the sweat away and do a bit of thinking."

"Well, there's no time for that right now, unless you were thinkin' about what the boss has next for you to do."

"Nope, but I'll head there right now and talk to him." Wyman hurried past the young man and into the other room, stopping for a few seconds to enjoy the cooler air. *There's probably some big mess for me to clean off the floor or maybe more boxes to unload.*

A muscle on the side of his face quivered. *Sure wish it was me who'd come into a large sum of money. Then I wouldn't have to keep working at a job I don't like—or anyplace else, for that matter.*

*

Middlebury

Michael grimaced as a sharp pain shot through the middle of his back. *Ye-ow—that hurt!* He froze in his tracks. *I've had some pain in my back before, but this is the first time it's been this bad.*

Michael closed his eyes as he tried to relax. His back had bothered him yesterday too but not nearly as bad as right now, after loading several bags of chicken feed into a customer's market buggy. "This is not what I need right now." He reached around to rub the spot hurting him the most.

Thankfully, his workday was almost over, with just another hour to go. Michael looked forward to going home, where he could either lie down on the couch or sit in his easy chair and give his aching back some relief. If it still hurt in the morning he might make an appointment with one of the chiropractors in their area. It would most certainly be what his wife would suggest that he do. Lovina saw a chiropractor regularly to keep her spine in good shape.

Gritting his teeth with determination, Michael loaded the rest of the man's order. Each one he lifted and sat inside the back of the Amish rig was more difficult than the last.

Once the feed bags were in the market buggy, Michael said goodbye to the driver—one of the ministers in their church district—then made his way back to the store. He'd no more than stepped inside when his back went into a horrible spasm, causing him to drop to his knees. *What is happening to me?* Michael's jaw clenched, and his fingers closed into tight fists.

"What's wrong, Son?" Within seconds, his father came around from behind the counter and knelt beside him.

Michael winced as he fought against the debilitating pain. He could barely speak through his rigid jaw. "M–my back hurts something awful, and I'm not sure I can get up. This is the worst pain I've ever felt, Dad. It's crippling."

"I don't think I can lift you." Dad's brows drew together as he leaned toward Michael and looked him in the eye. "Think I'd better call 911."

"Huh-uh—no—I don't wanna go to the hospital. I just need to go home and rest, but I don't think I can get there on my own."

"Here then, let me try to get you to your feet." Dad put his hands under Michael's arms and attempted to pull him up, but it was no use. Michael couldn't aid in the process.

A deep moan escaped his lips as the stabbing pain in his back worsened. "I—I can't do it. The pain's too great—there's no way I can stand right now."

"I wish Ira weren't home sick today. If he were here, he could help me stand you up. Better stay still, Son. I'll be back as soon as I've made the call."

Michael knew what that meant—Dad was going to call 911, and there was nothing he could do about it. *What did I do wrong? I've never had any serious back issues before—just some occasional spasms.* He squeezed his eyes shut. *Oh Lord, I just want to stand up straight again. I have no time for this kind of suffering.*

The tension in Michael's neck, shoulders, and arms increased as he tried to hold himself in place without making his back any worse. *I'm stuck going to the hospital, whether I like it or not.*

Tears sprang to Michael's eyes. He felt like a boppli—a baby who couldn't walk or stand on his own. He remained there the whole time, waiting on his hands and knees. Michael felt so needy and humbled being stuck on the floor, relying on the mercy of others for help. He hoped the problem with his back was something the doctor could fix with a shot or some pills to make him feel better. He couldn't afford to take any time off work. Michael had a family to support and bills to pay, so he had to keep working no matter what—even if it meant crawling on his hands and knees.

Chapter 18

*W*hen Wyman arrived home from work that evening, he was surprised to find Mom in the living room with his brother and sister-in-law's children. Priscilla sat on the floor, playing with a doll, while Mom, seated on the couch, held Aaron on her lap.

"I see you're babysitting tonight." Wyman hung his straw hat on a wall peg near the door. "Did Michael and Lovina go out for supper somewhere?"

Mom shook her head. "Michael's in the hospital. Your daed and Lovina are there with him, so I'm taking care of the kinner."

Wyman clutched his fists to his chest. "Wh–what happened? Is my bruder *grank*, or was he involved in an *unglick*?"

"He's not sick, and there was no accident. His back went out at the feed store this afternoon, and he couldn't walk or stand." Mom paused for a few seconds then rushed on. "Your daed called for help, and when the emergency squad arrived, they took Michael out on a stretcher and loaded him into the ambulance before heading to the hospital in Goshen. Then a driver was called to take your daed and Lovina to the hospital, but they brought the kinner here first so they could be with me."

Wyman sank into the nearest chair. "Have you heard anything since— an update on Michael's condition?"

"No, but what with having these two little ones to watch, I have not made it out to the phone shed." Mom gestured toward the kitchen door. "And I haven't even started supper yet."

"How about this—I'll go out and check for messages, and when I come back in, I will keep an eye on the little ones so you can fix something for us to eat."

"That would be most appreciated, but to tell you the truth, I'm not all that hungry." She looked at Priscilla, still playing happily on the floor. "She has to eat, though, and I imagine after a day of work, you do too. I'll also need to fix the boppli a bottle."

"I can fend for myself with just a sandwich, so don't worry about me."

Mom looked at him. "Danki for your consideration. I must admit I'm feeling a little *iwwerheifle*, not to mention full of *baddere*. What if there's something seriously wrong with your brother's back?"

"It makes sense that you'd feel overwhelmed and full of worry, but let's try to think positive. It might only be a pulled muscle that can be eased with medication, rest, and ice packs."

She put the baby over her shoulder and patted his back. "From the way your daed talked, it sounded much worse than a pulled muscle. He said Michael was in such pain, there were *draene* rolling down his cheeks."

Wyman winced at the thought of his brother being reduced to tears. "I'll head out to the phone shed now and see if there are any messages from Dad. Maybe it'll be good news, which will put both of our minds at ease."

"Danki." Mom held up a hand. "Before you go, I need to fix a bottle for your nephew. Could you please hold him for a moment?"

"Uh, sure, let me have the little guy." Wyman held out his hands while his mother passed Aaron to him. He watched her disappear into the kitchen, and Priscilla jumped up from her play to follow. It wasn't long before Mom returned with the bottle, and his niece scampered into the room behind her with a couple of cookies in her hands.

"It looks like the grandkids will be happier soon." Wyman grinned.

"Jah. Thanks for holding him for me." His mother picked up the baby and took a seat in the rocking chair, cradling him with a satisfied expression. No doubt Mom would be eager to have more grandchildren in the future.

Wyman rose to his feet and went out the door. As he walked down the path leading to the small wooden building that housed their phone, troubling thoughts swirled through his head. *What if Michael's back is so bad that he can't continue working at the feed store? What would Dad do then?* For the umpteenth time, Wyman regretted having quit working for his dad. *If Michael's out of the picture, even for a short while, at least I can be there to help out.*

He raked his fingers through the ends of his hair. *But no, I'm stuck at the bulk food store doing chores I don't like.*

He stepped into the shed, took a seat, and clicked on the answering machine. Sure enough, there was a message from Dad, letting them know that Michael had been admitted and tests were being run. His father's final words were that he'd call again when they knew something definite.

Wyman's forehead wrinkled. *Think I'll give Sadie a call to tell her what happened and ask her to pray for my brother.*

Using his cell phone, he called her aunt's number, which Sadie had given him earlier in the week. It rang several times, but no one answered. Since there was no voice mail service, Wyman clicked off his phone. Apparently Sadie and her mother had gone out somewhere, so he'd have to try again later.

✳

Alma remained in the living room, waiting for her son to return from the phone shed. She hoped there was a message from her husband, Ernest, letting them know how things were going.

She held on to Aaron while feeding him from his bottle. *Sure wish I could be at the hospital right now, giving support for my son and his wife, but I'm needed here with my grandchildren.*

Alma tried not to worry as she continued to feed the baby. She attempted to focus on something else, yet what popped into her mind next was Wyman, and the news he'd shared with them the other evening about Sadie's aunt leaving her a large inheritance and how much she would be getting. She'd been shocked by her son's announcement. Ernest seemed stunned too as he shook his head and let out a hefty breath before asking if he'd heard Wyman correctly.

Wyman assured them it was true and stated that he too had a hard time comprehending such a turn of events for Sadie.

I don't think I'd know how to handle so much money, Alma thought. She hoped if Wyman and Sadie got married that they'd be responsible with all the money she'd been blessed with. To be young and have access to such a large sum could be a good thing or could cause some serious issues.

Alma had noticed a change in her son's behavior lately. When Wyman first went to work at the bulk food store, he'd had no complaints about his day, and there seemed to be a spring in his step. Alma had a feeling it was because of his renewed relationship with Sadie. But for the last several days she'd noticed Wyman's demeanor was less than enthusiastic. No doubt he missed Sadie.

She set Aaron's bottle aside after he finished it. The little guy fussed in her arms until she put him up to her shoulder and patted his back. It wasn't long before a burp erupted. Alma glanced at her granddaughter playing on the large area rug nearby. It pleased her to see Priscilla engaged in a happy way—smiling and talking in Pennsylvania Dutch to one of her favorite dolls.

"I need to thank the Lord for the good things too," Alma whispered before praying silently. *Lord, please help Michael through this difficult time, and be with his wife and children. I am grateful for my grandchildren and happy that Wyman is back with Sadie. She's a sweet young woman.*

Alma nuzzled her grandson and continued. *Lord, I'm thankful for my loving family and pleased that we all care for one another through the good times and bad. We look to You for guidance in all that we say and do.*

✳

Toledo

"It's nice that the three of us can spend a little time together before Sadie goes back home tomorrow." Sadie's mother smiled at Sadie and Jana Beth, sitting across the table from her at the Italian restaurant where they'd chosen to eat supper this evening after Jana Beth arrived to take over for Sadie.

Jana Beth nodded. "Have you two accomplished much this past week?"

"Yes, we have, but my sister accumulated a lot of things, and there's still much to be done."

"Mom's right," Sadie put in. "It could be several weeks before the house is ready to be sold, so it's nice you could get time off work to come help out."

Jana Beth looked over at Sadie. "Speaking of work, are you sure you want to keep working at the hardware store now that you've come into such a large sum of money?"

I had a feeling that topic would come up again. First Mom and now my sister. I wonder who else will ask about it. Sadie picked up her glass of iced tea and took a drink. "Of course I'm sure. I have to keep working because I don't have the money yet. Even if I did, I wouldn't want to sit around all day and do nothing."

"That's understandable," Mom responded. "But perhaps once you receive your inheritance, you'll change your mind and decide to leave the hardware store."

Sadie shrugged her shoulders. "I suppose it's possible, but for now at least, I am definitely going to keep working."

✳

Middlebury

Wyman's mother had put the little ones to bed, and he sat with her in the living room, waiting for some word on Michael. He'd checked for messages about an hour ago and found one from his father, stating that the doctor had decided to keep Michael overnight, and that he and Lovina would be coming home soon.

Mom kept busy mending a pair of Dad's trousers, while Wyman thumbed through the latest issue of *The Connection* magazine. Waiting for further news on his brother's condition made it hard to concentrate. He'd also been thinking about Sadie and wondering why he hadn't been able to get ahold of her this evening.

He set the magazine down and glanced at the clock above the fireplace. It was almost ten thirty—probably too late to be calling her now. It would have to wait until morning. *I should have tried calling her again sooner,* Wyman berated himself. *Maybe I would have if Mom hadn't been discussing her concerns about Michael.* He couldn't fault her, though, for he too was worried about his brother. If Michael's back was too bad, he might not be able to work for several days, weeks, or even months. That would put their dad in a bind—especially since Ira Yoder, the young man he'd hired to help out after Wyman left, had made plans to move to Perry County, where his wife's family lived. They'd be making the move next week. There was no way Dad could run the store by himself. He needed at least one other able-bodied man.

Wyman's thoughts switched gears when he heard a vehicle pull into the yard. Mom was on her feet and heading for the door before Wyman could rise from his chair.

"Your daed is back," she announced, flinging open the front door.

Wyman joined her in the entryway and waited until his father got out of the van. He was surprised to see that Lovina was not with him. Didn't she plan to pick up her children and take them home?

When Dad entered the house, Mom gave him a hug. "How's Michael doing? Was he in any less pain when you left the hospital?"

"Jah, but only because of the medication they gave him." He glanced at Wyman then back at Mom. "Let's go into the living room, and I'll fill you both in."

Once they were all seated, Dad explained that Lovina had decided to spend the night in Michael's room, sleeping in a chair that reclined. She'd asked if it would be okay to leave the children overnight, and Dad had said it would be fine.

Mom bobbed her head. "I have no problem with it. I understand why Lovina would want to be there with her husband. She's worried about him, as we all are. Please, Ernest, tell us everything you know about our son's condition."

"Well, after several tests had been run, the doctor said it appears that Michael has one ruptured disk, as well as some other disks in his back that are bulging. He has the option of surgery or perhaps undergoing decompression treatments by a local chiropractor who specializes in that type of treatment. For now, he's been given something for the pain and inflammation, in addition to putting ice packs on his back periodically."

"What a shame. So he obviously won't be able to return to work at the feed store anytime soon." Mom pursed her lips. "How are you going to manage without him, Ernest?"

"I can't—not without Ira's help, and since he'll be moving. . ." Dad paused and looked at Wyman. "It's a lot to ask, but would it be possible for you to speak to your boss and see if he would let you take off a couple of days a week to work for me?" He leaned slightly forward. "I really need you, Son—you know the business, and I wouldn't have to train you like I would if I had to hire a new man."

Wyman placed both hands on his knees and gave them a tight squeeze. *I figured this was coming, and I can't really say no. For my brother's sake, as well as Dad's, I need to help in any way I can.* "Sure, Dad," Wyman responded. "Since tomorrow is Saturday—my day off—I'll go to the bulk food store in the morning and talk to my boss. From there, I'll come to the feed store and help you the rest of the day."

Dad sagged against the back of the couch. "Danki, Son. I appreciate your willingness to help out."

"Same here," Mom said. "During a time such as this, we all need to pull together and do whatever we can to make things a little easier. This is going to be a difficult trial for Michael and Lovina, so we must pray for both of them."

Wyman nodded.

Dad lifted his arms over his head in a stretch as he released a noisy yawn. "I don't know about you two, but I'm more than ready for bed."

"Jah," Mom agreed. "I'll check on the kinner then head for bed too."

After his parents left the room, Wyman sat quietly for a while, mulling things over. If his boss wouldn't give him time off to help dad, he might have to quit his job at the bulk food store. Then he'd either need to keep working at the feed store full-time or look for some other job if and when Michael's back was healed enough that he could return to work.

As Wyman rose to his feet, another thought came to mind. *If my brother won't be able to work at the feed store for the time being, he can't do chores at his place either. Someone will need to go over there and help out, and that someone should be me.*

Chapter 19

"How'd it go with your boss?" Wyman's father asked when Wyman entered the feed store the following day.

"It went well. He said I could take a few weeks off to work for you and that my job would still be there if I want to come back once you don't need me anymore."

Dad's forehead wrinkled a bit. "That was nice of him, but the thing is. . ." He paused and pulled his fingers through the ends of his full beard.

"What is it, Dad? Is something else wrong?"

"Not wrong exactly, but there is a problem. Since the new fellow I hired when you quit working for me will be moving with his wife to Perry County next week, that's going to put me in a bind." He heaved a hefty sigh. "And with Michael being laid up for who knows how long, I'm going to need full-time help beyond just a few weeks."

"I understand, Dad, and I'll help as long as you need me." Truthfully, Wyman didn't care for his job at the bulk food store, but working for his dad on a full-time basis wasn't his first choice either. Trouble was, Wyman had no idea what kind of work he wanted to do for the rest of his life.

He looked across the room at some feed sacks waiting for customers to pick up. *If I were in Sadie's shoes, I'd never have to work another day. I could spend all my time doing things I enjoy, like fishing, hunting, playing ball, and—*

An English man Wyman had never met before entered the store, halting his thoughts. The gray-haired man approached Dad, who had stepped behind the front counter, and said a few words. The next thing

Wyman knew, he was asked to haul three large bags of dog food out to the man's vehicle.

"They're right over there." Dad pointed to the sacks closest to the door. "You can take them out to Mr. Green's truck while I write up the bill."

Without a word of protest, Wyman picked up the first bag and went out the door. Since there was only one truck parked in front of the store, he had no trouble identifying the man's vehicle. Once it had been placed in the bed of the truck, he went back for the second bag of feed. As he placed it into the truck, he saw Sadie's dad drive by with his horse and buggy. Wyman waved, but he wasn't sure whether Calvin had seen him or not.

I need to try calling Sadie again, Wyman reminded himself. *I want to tell her about Michael's situation and find out when she'll be coming home.*

✳

As Sadie's driver approached her home late Saturday afternoon, a multitude of thoughts swirled through her head. She looked forward to seeing her friends at church and wondered how many of them had heard about her coming inheritance. Of course, Wyman already knew, but she hadn't spoken to Ellen, Barbara, or Mandy about it yet. For that matter, Sadie had not talked to Wyman for a few days and wondered how he was doing.

Sharon drove up the driveway and parked her car near the house. Sadie paid her and then opened the passenger's door and got out. She'd taken her suitcase from the trunk when Dad and Kaylene came out of the house. They rushed toward Sadie to greet her.

After the three had hugged, Dad said a few words to Sadie's driver before picking up the suitcase and starting toward the house. Sadie and her sister followed.

"It sure feels good to be home." Sadie paused on the porch and looked at the pots filled with chrysanthemums sitting in various places. She'd missed sitting out here in the mornings, enjoying the sights and sounds of the birds that often visited their yard. Since Aunt Sadie Ruth's house was close to the city, there weren't nearly as many birds, trees, or flowers to look at. Although her aunt's home was lovely, the yard seemed barren compared to what Sadie had become used to here on her parents' farm.

"How's our mamm doing, and how are things coming along with all the sorting at Aunt Sadie Ruth's?" Kaylene asked as they entered the living room, where Dad had seated himself after placing Sadie's suitcase in the hallway near the stairs leading to her room.

"Mom's fine, although she's been working too hard." Sadie took a seat on the couch beside her sister. "She'll appreciate Jana Beth's help next week, I'm sure." She grimaced. "When Sharon and I left this morning, they were already hard at work."

"It'll be my turn the following week," Kaylene responded. "Hopefully most everything will be done by the time I need to return home."

"If not, I'll be going there to help out till she's done with everything," Dad added. "It'll be good to get your aunt's house sold and everything involving her estate wrapped up." His brows squished together. "Your mamm's place is here with her family, and I miss her so much."

Sadie looked at him with a curious expression. "It could end up to be several more weeks. Can you take that much time off from the trailer factory, Dad?"

He nodded. "I have some vacation time coming, so I'll spend it in Toledo if your mother needs me."

"I'm sure she'll appreciate it. Oh, by the way. . .I brought something back from Toledo with me. Mom and I discovered these photo albums in Aunt Sadie Ruth's dresser." She held them in her hands.

Kaylene and Dad stepped over to her with curious expressions. Sadie's sister smiled. "Can I take a look at one?"

"Sure." Sadie opened the other album and looked at the first page of photos.

Dad leaned in for a closer look. "I didn't realize my sister-in-law had taken these pictures of us." He pointed at one. "Look how little you girls were, and look at how much younger I was too. I used to have more hair back then."

Sadie passed the album to him. "I've looked through these already, but be careful, because there are some loose photos that tend to fall out."

Kaylene held up one of the pictures that had slid out from the page. "Here's a loose one, and it's of you, Sadie." She flipped it over. "Apparently our aunt wrote something on the back of this picture."

"What's it say?" Dad asked.

Also curious to know, Sadie turned toward Kaylene.

"It says, 'Cute little Sadie, playing with her doll. She's a special child—always willing to do for others. If I had a daughter, I'd want her to be like Sadie.'"

Sadie froze as her father looked up from the photo album he'd been studying. "Let me see that, please."

Kaylene went over and showed it to him. Sadie joined them. She was surprised to discover that it was true—their aunt had written that note on the back side of Sadie's picture. Mom and she hadn't discovered it before or seen any writing on the other loose pictures prior to this. Could what Aunt Sadie Ruth wrote on this picture of Sadie explain her will? Her aunt had favored Sadie, pure and simple, and wished she could have had a daughter like her.

Dad handed the photo back to Kaylene. "Your aunt shouldn't have chosen one of you children over the others—that wasn't a good thing. But she did, and we'll need to keep working through this, one day at a time."

Kaylene slipped the photo back into place and continued to scan through the pages, while Dad did the same with the other album. He made a few comments about family members he saw in the photos, the way Mom had done a week ago.

Kaylene commented on how in one of the photos, the three sisters' dresses all matched and she remembered the day that picture had been taken. Every once in a while, she would glance at Sadie.

Although Kaylene did not come right out and say it, Sadie felt tension and hurt feelings from her sister. She hadn't considered that the photo albums would bring additional problems, but apparently they'd stirred up more hard feelings.

Sadie felt awkward as she watched them look through the photos. "I'd like to say, I wish Aunt Sadie Ruth hadn't favored me like she did. It doesn't feel good in my heart, and I'm sorry for the hurt it has brought to our family."

Dad closed the book and set it aside. "It's not your fault, Daughter. Your aunt had the right to choose, and she apparently saw something in you that caused her to make the decision to give you more than the rest of us. Envy is not pleasing to God, and we will honor her wishes."

"Would anyone like a glass of iced tea or some lemonade?" Kaylene interjected. Sadie figured her sister was ready to drop this subject.

Dad bobbed his head. "That sounds good."

"That would be refreshing." Sadie appreciated the topic change. "Would you like me to help you?"

Kaylene shook her head. "I can manage. Why don't you sit and relax while you visit with Dad?"

"Okay." Sadie's back rested against the sofa cushions as she looked over at her father. "How have things been going here? Anything new to report?"

"Not around here, but I did see something interesting this morning while I was out running errands."

She tipped her head. "What was that?"

Dad leaned forward with one hand on his knee. "I saw Wyman outside the feed store loading bags into someone's rig. What's up with that boy? Has he switched jobs yet again?"

Sadie's spine stiffened. "I have no clue." *But I plan to find out.*

✳

Sunday after church ended and the noon meal was over, Sadie joined Ellen and Barbara, who sat in the yard with a group of other young mothers.

"It's good to see you." Ellen rose from her chair to give Sadie a hug, and Barbara did the same. "We heard you were coming home this weekend."

"I am glad to be back, and it's good to see you all too." She stood close to her friends.

Ellen's happy expression soon faded. "First I've got some sad news to share with you. I was asked to tell you and Barbara, so I've picked today, while we're here together, to fill you in on what's happened."

Sadie looked deeply at Ellen. "What's going on?"

"I got a call from Ken about Mandy the other day." Ellen lowered her gaze to the ground.

Sadie's muscles tensed as she waited. Her friend seemed to be deeply affected about something, for her eyes filled with tears. "He informed me that Mandy lost the baby."

"Oh no. I'm so sorry to hear this. It must be such a sad time for them, as well as Ken's mother and Mandy's parents." Barbara gave a distant stare. "I'm sure it makes things all the harder having her mom and dad living so far away and unable to offer comfort in person."

"We'll need to keep Mandy, Ken, and their families in our prayers." Sadie spoke from her heart, even though she couldn't fully relate to her friend's suffering, as she had not experienced motherhood, much less the loss of a child.

Ellen shook her head. "I can't even imagine being in Mandy's position right now."

"Me neither. I've had no problems with either of my pregnancies," Barbara chimed in.

Sadie sat quietly, listening as her friends talked more about the matter.

"It would be nice if we all sent Mandy and Ken sympathy cards," Sadie suggested.

"Yes definitely. We should do it right away," Barbara agreed.

Ellen nodded while she dabbed at her tears.

Sadie realized that Mandy and Ellen had formed a strong bond during the time they'd been stranded on the island of Kauai. Then working at the B&B for many months had drawn them even closer.

When Sadie and Barbara had finished the cruise without their friends, they too had become close. However that faded some after Barbara got married.

"On a happier note. . ." Ellen's voice pushed Sadie's thoughts aside. "We heard you might soon be looking for a new horse to replace Daisy."

"Oh come on, Ellen. That's not all we heard." Barbara's smile widened. "How's it feel to have two million dollars?"

A warm flush crept across Sadie's cheeks. "I don't have the money yet."

"But you will as soon as your aunt's estate is settled, right?" Barbara questioned.

Sadie bobbed her head. "I haven't gotten used to the idea yet, and I probably never will. I knew my aunt was well off, but I had no idea she had so much money."

"I'm excited for you." Ellen clasped Sadie's arm. "Just think, now you will have more than enough money to self-publish a book, buy a new horse, or do anything else you may have been thinking of."

Sadie's hand dropped to her side. Caught up in the craziness of all this, she hadn't even thought of the possibilities Ellen suggested. *Could I really put a book together, comparing Amish and Hawaiian quilts, in addition to some other information? Would anyone buy such a book? It certainly is a nice thought.*

✳

Wyman stood in one area of the yard, watching Sadie talk to her friends and hoping he might catch her attention. It wouldn't be right to barge in—especially when the women had gathered on one side of the yard and the men on the other. *If she would just look this way, I could signal that I want to talk to her.*

He reached under his jacket to fiddle with his suspenders. He needed something to do with his hands. *Come on, Sadie, please glance my way. I can't stay here much longer. I need to be on my way.*

Wyman kicked at a small stone with the toe of his shoe. He'd already hitched his horse to his buggy, and it stood waiting for him at the hitching rail, but he didn't want to leave without talking to Sadie.

Finally, when he thought she was never going to look his way, Sadie glanced in Wyman's direction and waved. He waved back and gestured for her to come over to where he stood. Wyman felt relieved when she obliged.

"I'll be leaving for the hospital in Goshen soon. Will you walk with me to my buggy?" he asked.

Sadie's eyes widened. "Why are you going there? Is someone in your family grank?"

"No one is sick. Michael injured his back on Friday." Wyman began walking toward the line of carriages parked in the yard, and Sadie walked beside him. When they reached his buggy, he turned to her and explained what had happened. "Mom and I are going to the hospital to see how Michael is doing, while Dad takes his turn watching Michael and Lovina's kinner."

Sadie blinked rapidly. "I had no idea. I'm sorry to hear that."

"I tried calling you Friday evening, but no one answered, and there was no voice mail to leave a message."

"Sorry about that. Jana Beth arrived Friday to take over for me, and the three of us went to a restaurant for supper."

Wyman struggled with the desire to take Sadie into his arms and kiss her, but that was out of the question with so many people around. "I was gonna try calling you yesterday, but things got really hectic at the feed store, so I figured I'd wait and hopefully talk to you today."

"Now I understand why my daed saw you outside the feed store yesterday. You were filling in for Michael, right?"

"Jah, and depending on how things go for my brother, I may end up helping out there for some time."

"What about your job at the bulk food store? Are you planning to quit and work for your daed full-time again?"

He shrugged. "I don't know—it could come to that. For now, I'm going to take one day at a time."

Sadie dropped her gaze to the ground. "Tell Michael I hope he feels better soon."

"You're not angry with me, are ya, Sadie?" He lifted her chin so he could look in her eyes.

"Course not. Why would I be?"

"Thought maybe you were thinkin' I was job hopping again."

Sadie shook her head. "You're just doing what's expected of you, and if it turns out that you end up working at the feed store full-time, then I have no problem with it."

Wyman moved a little closer and clasped her hand. "I'm glad. I wouldn't want you thinkin' that I'm acting irresponsibly."

"There is nothing irresponsible about helping a family member when there's a need. Quite the contrary—it proves that you're a mature, responsible person who puts others' needs ahead of his own."

He drew a deep breath, feeling a release of all tension. "I'd best be on my way now, but we'll talk again soon. I want to find out how things are going with you."

Sadie gave him a radiant smile. "I've missed you, Wyman, and it's good to be home."

"I've missed you too."

Wyman got into his buggy, and as he backed his horse up, a sense of calm and happiness filled his soul. It didn't matter that he might end up working at a job he wasn't fond of or that Sadie was on the brink of becoming a multimillionaire. The only thing he cared about was that everything was all right between them and they could soon begin planning for a future together.

Chapter 20

The following Saturday after Wyman finished working at the feed store, he headed over to his brother's place to help with outside chores and any other things Lovina wanted to have done. He'd been so busy and exhausted the past week that he'd only had one brief phone conversation with Sadie. He hoped she understood how busy he was. He certainly wasn't avoiding her intentionally.

Wyman loosened his grip on the reins as he guided his horse up his brother's driveway. *How much longer should I wait till I ask Sadie to marry me? Would she say yes if I asked her now, or do I need to wait a little longer— until she's confident that I'm no longer irresponsible?*

After Wyman pulled his horse and buggy to the hitching rail and got out, he set his questions aside. He'd come here to work, not fret about his future with Sadie. He would deal with that later, when they had time to spend together.

When Wyman approached Michael and Lovina's house, prepared to knock on the front door, he heard angry voices through the screen door.

"Stop hovering over me, would you? I'm not an invalid, you know."

His brother's sharp tone of voice let Wyman know that Michael was either in a lot of pain or had reached the end of his rope with his wife's nagging and sharp tongue. And boy, was Lovina ever good at pestering until she got her own way. Wyman had dealt with it himself whenever she'd brought up the topic about him needing to repay the money Michael had loaned him. Two evenings ago, when Wyman came by to feed the livestock, Lovina jumped him about it, saying things were even tighter for them now that her husband was laid up and couldn't work. Michael had begun decompression treatments, but so far there'd been no improvement. It didn't look like he'd be returning to the feed store to work anytime soon. Maybe never, since one of the many duties at the store was lifting heavy sacks of feed.

Wyman lowered his hand and stood off to one side of the open door. *Maybe if I wait a few minutes, they'll quit arguing and then I can make myself known.*

Instead of things quieting down, though, Lovina's voice rose as she shouted: "You're not helping yourself by trying to move around. You need to rest like the *dokder* said—otherwise you'll never get back to work again."

"I'm not overdoing it. I need to walk a bit, which the doctor also told me to do."

"You don't need to be so snippy with me. I'm just worried about you."

"Worried about me, or concerned about the money I'm not able to make right now?"

"Both." Lovina's tone softened a bit. "We don't have much in our savings, and if you're not able to return to work soon, we could end up using it all to pay bills."

"Dad said he'd help us financially, so you needn't worry about that." Michael's voice was a bit quieter too.

Wyman figured this was a good time to let them know he was here. He knocked on the side of the screen door then opened it a crack. "Hello! I'm here to do some chores!"

A few seconds later, Lovina came to the door. She said nothing, barely making eye contact with Wyman.

"I came by to see what chores need to be done." He shuffled his feet against the wooden boards on the porch.

"Oh yes. . .I forgot you were coming."

Wyman couldn't help noticing Lovina's pinched expression and the dark circles beneath her eyes. Several strands of her hair had come loose from her white head covering. No doubt she was stressed and not getting much sleep.

"How's my bruder doing today?" he asked. "Is he still in a lot of pain?"

She nodded. "He's in the living room on his recliner, in case you'd like to talk to him before you go out to the barn to take care of the animals."

"Sure, I'd like to find out how he's feeling."

Wyman followed Lovina into the living room. She glanced at Michael and then quickly left the room.

Michael looked up at Wyman and groaned. "I suppose you heard us arguing?"

"Jah." Wyman took a seat in the other recliner. "I'm sure this is a stressful time for both of you."

"You've got that right. Even with decompression treatments, my back is still not right." Michael grimaced. "I can't sit around forever when bills are waiting to be paid. I need to get back to work."

"We're managing okay, and I've decided to quit my job at the bulk food store so I can work full-time at the feed store. Ira moved this week, and there's too much for Dad to do by himself five days a week."

"I know. That's why I—"

Wyman held up his hand. "You need to quit worrying about it, brother." He reached into his pocket and pulled out the money he'd brought along. "Here's another payment on what I owe. I should be able to pay you the balance of the loan by next month." Wyman placed the bills on the small table beside his brother's chair.

Michael's eyes teared up. "I appreciate that, but it's not enough to keep us going, and our saving's account is running low."

"Dad's gonna help you, and I'll chip in too if it's needed."

"You're already doing so much by coming over here every evening to do chores that I should be doing."

"It's okay. I don't mind. Besides, that's what family is for—to help each other whenever there's a need."

Michael glanced in the direction of the kitchen door. "Things have been strained between me and Lovina for several months, but they've gotten worse since my back started acting up. I think she's afraid I may never be able to work again." He clutched the arm of the chair until the veins on top of his hands stuck out. "I'm scared of that happening too."

Wyman got up and put a hand on his brother's shoulder. "Lots of prayers are being said on your behalf—not just from family, but those in our church district. Keep looking up and remember that God will provide as needed."

"Danki for the pep talk and for doing all you've done so far to help out. Maybe someday I can return the favor."

Wyman gave Michael's shoulder a squeeze. "I'd better get busy with those chores now. I'll check back with you before I leave."

✳

"I think you're gonna be happy with that gaul we just bought for you, Sadie. She's a nice young mare, full of energy, but with what appears to be a good temperament."

Sadie looked over at her father as they headed home in his open buggy. He'd talked her into looking at the horse he had mentioned previously and then convinced her to let him loan her the money, since she didn't have her inheritance yet. She had to admit it would be nice to have her own horse again, especially with the cooler fall weather that had finally arrived. With winter on the horizon, she wouldn't want to ride her bike anyway. Besides, Sadie had borrowed her mother's horse for long enough.

Of course, Sadie thought, *if I were to quit my job in Shipshewana, I wouldn't have to go anywhere unless I really needed to. I could stay home all day and work on the book I've decided to write.*

Yesterday, during her lunch break, Sadie had called a few places about self-publishing and decided to go with a printing company in Ohio. They would send her some information in the mail about the cost to self-publish, along with all the details concerning what was expected of her. She was eager for the packet to arrive and couldn't wait to get started on the project.

Sadie's foot bounced on the floorboard, keeping time with the rhythm of the horse's hooves. She still felt like pinching herself to make sure this wasn't a dream.

She looked at her father. "There's something I haven't told you."

He adjusted his hat and glanced at her. "Oh, what's that?"

"Back in Toledo when I was still helping Mom sort and organize things, I mentioned that I'd be willing to give my inheritance to her. She wouldn't hear of it, but I am wondering how you feel about that."

"She mentioned it to me during one of our recent phone conversations, and I agree with your mamm. Sadie Ruth felt that you should have the bulk of the money, and we will stand behind that decision."

"All right, but those photo albums I brought back with me have turned out to be a sore spot too."

"Yes, Jana Beth and your brothers didn't take it so well, but they'll work through this—you'll see."

"I've been praying about the money, and I'd like to give something back to my family."

"You would? In what way?"

"My sisters could use horses of their own, so I'd like to make it happen." Sadie smiled.

"That would be nice."

"I'll talk to my brothers and see what I might do for them as well."

Dad nodded.

"And for you and Mom, whenever you decide it's time to build a daadi haus, I'd like to pay for that."

His reached over and patted Sadie's arm. "You're such a thoughtful daughter. I'm beginning to understand why your aunt chose you."

✳

Kapaa

Mandy straightened a few pillows on the couch then took a seat. A lump formed in her throat as she placed one hand on her stomach. *Will I ever get past the heartache of losing my child?* She had been doing okay physically since her miscarriage, but emotionally Mandy was a wreck. *I wish I could talk to someone who's dealt with the same kind of loss. It might help me learn how to cope.*

Her phone rang, pushing Mandy's thoughts aside. Since Ken had gone out to run some errands and Vickie was outside with Charlie, Mandy rose from the couch and went to the kitchen to answer it.

"The Palms Bed-and-Breakfast. This is Mandy speaking."

"Hey friend, it's Ellen. I'm calling to see how you're doing."

Mandy sank into the chair at the desk, where all the paperwork regarding the B&B was kept. "Okay, I guess." Mandy hoped the sullen tone of her voice would not give her away. She didn't want Ellen's pity.

"I've been praying for you—and Ken too."

"Thanks." Mandy could barely squeak out the word.

"Although I've never been in your situation, I understand to some degree how you must feel emotionally."

"Oh?"

"My mamm had a miscarriage two years after my sister, Lenore, was born. She struggled with depression for several weeks."

Mandy swallowed hard, hoping she wouldn't break down. "I—I can certainly relate to that."

"As time goes on, it'll get better. It did for Mom."

"I hope so." Mandy couldn't imagine what her life would be like if she kept grieving like this. It wouldn't be fair to Ken, Charlie, or Vickie if all she did was mope around. All of them had plenty of work to do here at the B&B, and she needed to concentrate on that, as well as taking time out to spend with her and Ken's precious boy.

"How are you doing, Ellen?" Mandy asked. "Anything new or exciting at your bed-and-breakfast?"

"Not really, but Sadie's life is about to change in a very exciting way."

"Oh, how's that?"

Mandy listened with interest as Ellen told her about Sadie's aunt dying and making Sadie a wealthy young woman.

"Wow, that's incredible. I'll bet Sadie was surprised to learn of her inheritance."

"Yes, it took the whole family by surprise."

"I can imagine."

"I'm a little concerned about Sadie's boyfriend, though."

"In what way?"

"Well, now that Sadie will be getting all that money, I hope Wyman won't quit working if he marries her, and then rely on Sadie to support him."

"Do you think he would do something like that?"

"I wouldn't be surprised. After all, Wyman's never been happy with any of the jobs he's had, and now he is back working for his dad, doing work he has never liked."

"Then why did he start working for him again?" Mandy shifted in the hard-back chair, trying to find a more comfortable position.

"His brother suffered a back injury recently, so Wyman quit working at the bulk food store to help his father at the feed store. He may have to stay there permanently if Michael can't do heavy lifting anymore."

"But if he and Sadie get married, Wyman may not have to work anywhere."

"Exactly. He'll be living off her money and can kick back and do whatever he wants."

Mandy couldn't imagine her husband doing such a thing, even if she suddenly came into a lot of money. Ken would want to do something constructive, not just loaf around. Even though he couldn't do all the things he used to, her husband was not a slacker.

The sound of boyish chatter broke into Mandy's thoughts, and she looked toward the door leading to the lanai. "I'm sorry to end this conversation, Ellen, but I think Charlie and his grandma are coming back inside, so I should probably hang up now and see if they want some fresh pineapple juice that Vickie made up this morning."

"Okay, I'll let you go. Keep looking to God for emotional healing, and remember that many people are praying for you and your family."

Mandy hung up feeling a bit better. She needed the reminder that prayers were being said on her and Ken's behalf. She bowed her head and whispered a prayer. "Lord, help me feel better emotionally so I can be a good wife and mother once again."

✳

Ken left the house and went to fill his gas tank. The sun shone brightly, and the warmth of it felt good. It had been cloudy and raining earlier this morning. The wonderful thing about living on the island was that the rain didn't usually last long, and it left the plants looking refreshed.

Ken stopped at the station and pulled up to the pump. He got out of his camouflage-colored rig and filled his tank with the gas he needed then paid. Getting back into his vehicle, he had a thought. *While I'm out today, I'll see about getting Mandy something she might like. She's been having such a hard time bouncing back from the miscarriage.*

Ken put the key into the ignition and started it up. He glanced toward the entrance and saw Taavi Kumar pull in next to him. "Aloha, Ken. How's it going today?" He spoke through the open window of his car door.

"Hey Taavi." Ken paused then spoke with a feeling of regret. "It's going as good as it can, under the circumstances."

Taavi got out and proceeded to fuel up his rig while speaking to Ken. "It's gonna take some time, and don't forget our church members are praying for you and Mandy. I hope things will keep improving. You both deserve to be happy."

"Thanks, my friend. I better pull out of this spot now. Looks like someone else is needing the pump. I'll see you at church Sunday." He gave a quick wave.

"Okay, *mahalo*—many thanks."

Ken drove out of the lot and on to the store. In less than ten minutes he reached the market and parked; then he went inside to get a couple of items.

Walking down one of the aisles with a basket in hand, he spotted something for Mandy. *She likes those toffee-coated macadamia nuts. I'm definitely getting them for her. Think I'll grab two packages.* Ken placed them into his basket. He then headed toward the meat department to look for something to grill for supper and found ready-made shish kebabs, which would be easy to fix. Tonight they had no guests staying at the Palms, so Ken would give Mandy and his mother a night off. He'd also picked out some rice pilaf to go with their meal.

When he was through shopping, Ken went up an aisle toward the checkout. He saw a young mother with a tiny infant in her arms. Ken tried not to envy her, but the scene tugged at his heartstrings. Every day, he saw the endearing bond between Mandy and their son and appreciated it. *I'm thankful for the family we do have. But if one day, Lord willing, Mandy and I are blessed with another child, I'll be thankful for that too.*

Chapter 21

Shipshewana

Sadie couldn't believe how quickly the last two months had gone by, but here they were at the beginning of December and her life had changed in more ways than she could imagine. She'd received her inheritance from Aunt Sadie Ruth's estate, and the rest of the family had gotten theirs as well. The house had sold, and she would be receiving the money for that when the deal closed next week. Sadie had also received her aunt's four-poster bed when it was trucked to Middlebury several weeks ago, along with some things other family members wanted.

Sadie had paid her father back the money he'd loaned her to get a new horse, and she'd given Kaylene and Jana Beth enough money so they could each have a horse of their own. Sadie still felt that she didn't deserve to get so much more than the others, so she'd offered to help her brothers with anything they might need financially. However, Saul and Leland had turned her down, saying they were doing fine on their own but would remember her offer should the need arise.

Her parents still refused to take any of Sadie's money, so she promised them that when the time came for them to add on a grandparents' house, she would pay for the addition.

In her free hours, Sadie had been working hard on her book. It seemed to be on her mind a good deal of the time, even at the hardware store when she was supposed to be working, like she was now.

Since there were no customers approaching the front counter at the moment, Sadie lowered her head and let her mind wander as thoughts of

Hawaii and some things she might include in the book about the beautiful islands took over. Now that Sadie had more than enough money, she could visit the islands again if she wanted to. Of course, it wouldn't be much fun if she went alone. *Maybe after Wyman and I are married,* she thought. *That is, if he ever asks me to marry him.*

The fact was, Sadie wasn't seeing much of her boyfriend these days— mostly because she kept so busy between her job at the hardware store and the work on her new quilt book. Wyman was busy too—at the feed store and helping out at his brother's place. Poor Michael still had trouble with his back, although he'd gone back to work part-time, waiting on customers and taking over the books. The doctor had said Michael's days of heavy lifting were over, which put that responsibility on Wyman and his dad.

Tonight, however, Sadie and Wyman would be going out for supper, and she looked forward to spending some time with him, if only for a few hours.

"Excuse me, miss, but did you hear my question?"

Sadie jerked her head up when she realized an English woman stood on the other side of the counter, looking at her with wrinkled brows.

"Oh, I'm so sorry," Sadie apologized. "What was your question?"

"My husband sent me here to buy some nails for a project he's working on, but I don't know where they are located. Can you direct me to them?"

"Yes, of course." Sadie explained which area of the store the nails were kept and stated the aisle number.

"Thank you." The woman turned and walked away.

Sadie grimaced. This was not the first time she'd been daydreaming when a customer needed her attention. Ever since she'd begun working on her book, she'd had a hard time focusing on other things.

Maybe I need to quit my job, like others have suggested, since I don't need the money anymore. That way I can put all my focus on finishing my new project, and someone who needs a job can fill my spot here. Sadie bit the inside of her cheek. *At the end of my shift, I'll give the boss my two weeks' notice.*

✽

Middlebury

"You've barely touched what's on your plate." Wyman gestured to Sadie's plate. "The food's really good here at Das Dutchman Essenhaus. Aren't you hungerich?"

Sadie didn't respond as she wrote something on the notebook she'd taken from her purse a short time after they'd been seated.

"Did ya hear what I said?" Wyman snapped his fingers, causing Sadie to jerk her head.

"Umm. . .what was that?"

"I wondered why you haven't eaten much and asked if you aren't hungry."

Sadie's cheeks flushed pink. "Guess I've been too busy to eat." She pointed at her notebook.

"I've noticed you've been writing something on it." He scrunched up his nose. "Are ya taking notes on how well our conversation's been going since we arrived at this restaurant?" Wyman couldn't keep the sarcasm out of his tone.

The color on her cheeks deepened. "Sorry, Wyman. I needed to get my thoughts down on paper before I forgot them."

"Thoughts about what?"

"My book. New ideas have been coming to mind about things I might include in it besides quilt patterns and information on the similarity between Amish and Hawaiian quilts."

"I see." Wyman wadded his napkin into a ball then pressed it against the table. "Correct me if I'm wrong, but I thought the purpose of us having supper together this evening was so we could visit and spend some quality time, which is something we haven't done in a while." This whole thing with Sadie writing a book was getting in the way of their relationship, and he wasn't happy about it.

"Sorry, Wyman." Sadie slipped the notebook back into her purse. "How are things going at the feed store these days? Are you and your daed managing to keep up, since it's just the two of you doing the manual labor?"

"So far, but I think it's hard for Michael to sit behind the counter or at Dad's desk all day and watch us do the jobs he used to take care of."

"I can understand that, but at least he's back working again so he can provide for his family." Sadie forked a piece of chicken into her mouth.

Wyman nodded. He was tempted to tell Sadie that he'd overheard Michael and Lovina quarreling a few times when he'd gone to their house to help with chores. But he decided the less said, the better. If he mentioned it, she might repeat what he said, which could lead to some gossip going around their community. And that would not be a good thing.

She drank some water and set her glass down. "I put in my two weeks' notice at the hardware store this afternoon."

Wyman blinked. "You did?"

"Jah. I figured there was no point in working there anymore, since I have my inheritance. Besides, it'll give me more time to get my book ready to send to the place that will be printing it for me."

"I see. Guess that's a good thing, then." Wyman envied Sadie for being able to quit working. He wished he were in a position to do that too. It would give him more time to pursue other things—like fishing, hunting, and taking long hikes. Despite the jealousy he felt for Sadie's good fortune, Wyman looked forward to the day when her book would be finished so they could get their courtship back on track. He was still waiting for the right time to ask her to marry him. Maybe once the book was done.

They talked about a few other things as they finished their meal. When the check came, Sadie snatched it up before Wyman could reach his hand out for it.

"I was planning to get that," he said.

She shook her head. "I'd like it to be my treat this time. I'm sure you need your money for other things."

Wyman pulled his hand back and gave a nod. Although he wasn't happy about her paying the check, he didn't want to make an issue of it—especially not here in a public place. But if Sadie thought she had to pay every time they went out on a date, he would say something. Didn't she realize how it made him feel to be courting a woman who wouldn't allow him to pay the bill after he'd invited her on a date?

✳

Kapaa

I can't believe it's the first of December already. Mandy carried the dirty dishes from the dining room into the kitchen. Breakfast was over, and their B&B guests had taken off to do some sightseeing.

Mandy and her mother-in-law worked like a well-oiled machine putting leftovers away and cleaning up the kitchen. Ken had stepped out on the lanai to enjoy his coffee and a bowl of yogurt with fruit and granola. Mandy liked to make them up as an option to offer their guests. They'd also had the breakfast casserole she'd made, and Vickie baked two different sweet breads to eat with whipped butter or tropical jams.

"What are you going to do with your free time this morning, Vickie?" Mandy watched Charlie wander out to the living room and climb up on the sofa to watch his favorite kid show on the television.

"I'm thinking about going for a walk when we're done in here. My doctor said I should be getting exercise every day, and other than my work around here, I've not been doing that."

"Sounds like a smart idea. It's a good day for walking outdoors."

"After I return, I'll most likely head out to the garden to do some weeding."

Mandy filled the sink with warm water and added the dish soap to it. "You're right. It could use some attention. The weeds seem to grow overnight, don't they?"

"They sure do, and we need to keep ahead of them." Ken's mom had finished putting the food away and wiped off all the dirty surfaces on the table and counter. "I'm going to get ready for my walk now. With the sun so bright, I'll need my sunglasses."

"All right. Thanks for your help, and have a nice walk."

"No problem."

After Vickie left the room, Mandy washed the dishes by hand. Some of the Amish ways of doing things seemed to stick in her day-to-day life, although for sanitizing reasons, the dishes they used to serve their guests were always put in the dishwasher.

In addition to sometimes washing dishes by hand, Mandy had allowed her hair to grow long again. She felt more like her old self and had even used the sewing machine to make a new maxiskirt to wear for church. It had inspired her to buy more material to make another one. Ken had shown approval the day she'd modeled it for him and Vickie. Mandy couldn't help feeling a bit of pride in her ability, which she hadn't lost from the training she'd received from her mother during her childhood.

As she continued to clean the dishes, she thought about the approaching holiday. *I sure would like to make a trip back to Middlebury to see my family. We've been keeping busy here, and I'm thinking a getaway is in order. Besides, we've been saving funds for a while, so there ought to be enough money in our savings account to make the trip.*

Ken shuffled into the kitchen and slid in next to her. "Sorry, but here's another dirty dish."

"No problem. I'm still washing our breakfast dishes anyway." Mandy turned her head to look at him directly. "I'm really missing everyone back home. I'd like us to get away and take a trip to see them."

Ken smiled. "I'd like to see your family too, and I believe it's time. I'm sure Charlie should do fine on the trip."

"We'll need to get some things set up here for your mother—like some help while we're away—unless we can close the Palms for a week to ten days."

"Don't worry. We'll come up with an answer." Ken reached around his wife's waist and pulled her close. "It's good to hear you sounding more like your old self again. I've missed her, to be honest."

"It's good to feel better again and have a more hopeful outlook. The Lord can work in our lives if we allow Him to. It also helps to have people who care enough to be praying for you."

Ken kissed her. "Let's plan our trip for Christmas. Would you like that?"

She leaned into his embrace. "Absolutely!"

✳

Middlebury

Michael drove his buggy while clenching his hands around the reins. "I can't wait to get to Mom and Dad's place," he mumbled. "That fraa of mine can sure make it tough on me."

Earlier, Lovina and Michael had exchanged harsh words. He had thought it best for both of them to get away from each other for a while.

Michael winced as he remembered their parting. . .

✳

Michael hurried to grab a few things to take along with him, and then put on his straw hat to head out.

Lovina met him near the front door. "What are you doing? Are you leaving?"

"What's it look like?" He waited a moment, holding a bag with some of his things. "I don't want to fight with you, but you're being ridiculous!"

"I'm not either!" Her voice grew louder. "You're the one who is leaving."

"You've left me no choice." His voice was strained.

"Go ahead and leave, then, but where will you sleep?"

"At my parents' place. I'm going there to get away from your negative attitude!"

"Fine, then, be my guest!" Lovina turned and stomped off. Soon, he heard their bedroom door slam shut.

✳

Reliving the scene cause Michael to feel more stressed, and his back began to spasm. He'd had it with all of his wife's nonsense and needed a break. His folks' place offered comfort and a quiet refuge. Later, when he felt like talking to them, they'd sit and listen while he poured out his heart. This was a bold move and wasn't something he took lightly. Truth was, Michael had never done this kind of thing before. Admitting he didn't have a handle on his marriage and needed to leave their home in order to cope with their sad situation was a humbling experience.

When Michael pulled into his parents' yard, he saw his father outside, chopping a stack of wood—no doubt for the fireplace, since the temperatures had dropped.

"Hey, Son, what brings you by here this evening?" Dad asked after he set the ax aside and stepped up to Michael's buggy.

Heat flooded Michael's face in spite of the chilly weather. "I'd like to stay here tonight if that's okay."

"Oh, really? How come?"

"Something happened with me and Lovina, but I'd rather not discuss it right now." Michael winced as he began his descent from the buggy.

"Here, let me help you." Dad grabbed Michael's arm and steadied him until his feet touched the ground.

"Thank you. My back isn't feeling so great right now."

"I can tell by the way you're moving. Why don't we head into the house and let your mom know you'll be staying with us?"

"What about my horse? I need to take care of him first."

Dad flicked his hand. "Don't worry about it, Michael. I'll come back out here soon and put this fella away for you. Come on now. Let's head in so you can take a load off your feet. I'm here for you."

"Thanks, Dad."

As they entered the house, Michael felt a bit better on an emotional level. At least he didn't have to go another round with Lovina or deal with her admonishing look and sharp tongue tonight.

"Hello, Michael. What's in the bag?" Mom stood with a hand on her hip and smiled.

"It's a few of my things I brought over. I'd like to stay here tonight."

Mom's smile faded. "What's going on, Michael? Did you and Lovina have a disagreement?"

He sighed. "We had a heated argument, and I'd rather not be around her right now."

"I'm sorry to hear that." Mom moved closer and gave him a hug. "Seeing the way you're standing, your back must be hurting."

"Yep, his back is giving him some trouble this evening." Dad spoke before Michael had a chance to reply.

"Why don't you two take a seat in the living room while I check on the guest room to be sure the bed is made up? I made a chocolate cream pie that we can have if you'd both like some."

Dad smiled and motioned to the door. "First, I need to go outside and put Michael's horse away, and then I'll take you up on the offer."

"Okay." Mom readjusted her apron.

"Thanks for letting me stay here tonight." Michael swallowed against the constriction in his throat.

He shuffled at a slow pace into the living room and settled into one of the recliners. But his mind wouldn't let go of the stressful events that had brought him here this evening. *I can't stay here indefinitely, but how can I make things better with my wife?*

Chapter 22

*M*ichael woke up the next morning feeling as though he were in a fog. The bed he'd slept in seemed familiar, but it didn't feel right. He rubbed his eyes and glanced around. *Oh, right. . . I'm at Mom and Dad's, and this is my old room.*

He pulled himself up and sat on the edge of the bed, reflecting on the events of the night before. Lovina's constant nagging had become too much to bear, and Michael struggled to control his temper. He figured it would be best to put some distance between them for one night—and maybe longer. It could be that some time apart would give them both a better perspective on things. Michael hoped that was the case, because he didn't know what to do anymore—it seemed like everything he said or did was never good enough for her.

He walked over to the window and stood looking out while rubbing his back. Although it hurt less than it had two months ago, there was still some pain. Michael figured his back would never be the same, even with the treatments he'd been getting. He hoped Lovina would understand and accept the fact that physically he wasn't the same man she'd married. How thankful he felt for friends and family members, like Wyman and Dad, who stepped in to help out when something needed to be done that he could no longer do for himself. In that respect, he truly was blessed.

Last night during dessert, he'd explained to his parents about the disagreement he and Lovina had and said it had become a regular occurrence. Both Mom and Dad suggested that Michael and Lovina get some marriage counseling.

We probably need it, he thought, *but would my fraa agree to such a thing?*

✳

"You have a visitor," Mom announced when she entered the sewing room where Sadie sat, typing a section in her manuscript about the history of Hawaiian quilts. The yummy aroma of Mom's fresh-baked, spiced cookies permeated the room. The cinnamon fragrance lingering in the air tickled Sadie's nose. *I could use a little pick-me-up from one of my favorite fall treats.*

Before she even asked if the cookies were frosted, Sadie noticed a couple of frosting smears on her mother's brown apron. *I can't wait to sample a few. I hope Mom offers me some.*

Sadie lifted her fingers off the keyboard of the old-fashioned typewriter she'd purchased to help with her project and smiled when she saw Ellen come in behind her mother.

Engrossed in her work, she hadn't heard a horse and buggy pull in, much less a knock on the door.

Sadie got up and went over to hug her friend. "It's good to see you. What brings you here this chilly afternoon?"

"I was in the area, and since Rueben is watching Irene, I decided to drop by and see how your book is coming along."

"Come on over to my worktable and I'll show you what I've accomplished so far." Sadie moved back across the room.

Ellen followed. "I'm eager to see what kind of progress you've made. I find the ins and outs of putting this kind of thing together intriguing."

It pleased Sadie that her friend showed such an interest. No one else seemed to care that much—although everyone in the family had busy lives of their own, so perhaps that was the reason.

"I'm heading back to the kitchen to finish the cookies I started baking, but I have a batch cooling on the racks right now," Mom said. "Would

"I'm fine." Tears welled in Mandy's eyes as she turned to look at him. "Okay, I'll admit that it sort of got to me when that couple showed up with their children."

"I figured as much. It made you think about the baby we lost, right?"

"Yes. Oh Ken, I so want for us to have another child. It would be nice for Charlie to have a sibling." She placed the pitcher of juice on the table. "My arms ache to hold another baby and teach him or her about the love of God and all the wonderful things He's created."

Ken pulled Mandy into his arms. "I want that too, and if it's the Lord's will for us to have another child, it will happen in His time. Let's try not to fret over it. We need to remember to take one day at a time and be thankful for the opportunity we have to live on this island and raise our son."

She leaned her head against his shoulder. "You're right. I shouldn't complain or want more. I'll try harder to be content and enjoy what's right here before me."

Ken gently patted Mandy's back. Contentment was an area he'd been weak in himself—sometimes feeling envious of others, like Taavi, who could surf and do many other things Ken used to do before the shark attack. He'd been bitter, full of self-pity, and angry at God after the accident, but none of those feelings had gotten him anywhere except deeper into depression. Although Ken had come a long way since then, at times a feeling of discontentment still crept in. Perhaps because he'd dealt with it and learned to live with his disability without complaint, he could help others going through a similar situation. If nothing else, Ken could pray for Mandy and offer encouragement whenever he saw that she might be feeling sorry for herself.

✳

Middlebury

Wyman arrived at work a short time after his father and brother did. The jaunt between the business and their home wasn't far, which made the travel quick and convenient. The feed store hadn't opened up, yet already a couple of customers were parked outside. *I'm thinking we're going to be busy today. At least Mom packed me a good-sized lunch. It looks like I'll need it.* He pulled into the back, set the brake of his rig, and put his horse away in the corral out behind the store.

When Wyman entered the building, Dad had a cardboard box open and was busy unloading salt blocks onto the floor. "Son, after you've set your lunch aside, would you put these on the shelf for me? I will need to open the store soon."

"Sure, Dad."

As Wyman was putting his lunch away in the refrigerator, Michael came into the break room. "Could you please grab me a bottle of water?"

"Sure. Here you go."

"Thanks." Michael unscrewed the lid and took a drink. "I have some horses' bits to unpack and bridles to add to the displays out there. It's light work so it shouldn't bother my back."

"Be careful, now. If your back acts up, let me know, and I'll take over the job."

"Thanks."

"Will you be going over to your house to see Lovina and the kinner after work?" Wyman asked.

"Most likely. I want to see my kids, and I need to talk to my fraa." Michael moved toward the door. "Guess we'd best head out there and get busy now."

Wyman nodded and followed his brother out of the room. While he worked at putting the salt blocks on the shelves, Wyman's mind wandered. *This is boring, and carrying the sacks of animal feed is backbreaking. I wanted to drive forklifts at the other place, but that never happened.*

Wyman carried the empty boxes out to where they kept the recycling bin. *At least the pay is better here. Also, my daed is more lenient than my employer at the bulk food store. Guess I really can't complain.*

After he finished outside, Wyman returned to the counter where his dad stood. The OPEN sign had been turned over, and several customers had come in. Wyman noticed a few English folks browsing the aisles and saw Michael go over to see if they needed help finding what they'd come for.

Wyman figured he'd better get busy setting out merchandise from the boxes stacked up by the office. Before heading in that direction, he saw the front door open and watched as an elderly Amish man came into the store and walked over to Dad. "Hey, Ernest. How's it going?"

"Good. How about for you, Thomas?"

Wyman listened as the two men bantered in Pennsylvania Dutch about what had been going on in the area lately, before Thomas said what he needed.

Dad asked Wyman to carry out the bags of dog and horse food for Thomas. Wyman rolled out the cart to load up the man's order and pushed it out to the market buggy. Despite the chilly day, the sun glowing against the blue sky urged Wyman to be away from his job.

He loaded the order and looked up. *What a gorgeous day. I'd sure like to be out by the lake fishing right now.* Wyman wiped some sweat off his forehead and watched a couple of buggies pull into the lot.

He chatted briefly with the customers before following them into the store. Dad greeted the clientele from behind the counter while he filled another order.

When things slowed down around noon, Dad told Wyman and Michael to go ahead and eat.

They headed for the break room and got out the lunches their mother had made them that morning. Then Wyman and his brother took seats at the table and offered a silent prayer.

Michael opened his bottle of lemon tea and dug into his lunch box, and Wyman took a sip from his can of root beer. "I haven't seen Sadie for a while, and it really annoys me," he commented. "It seems she's constantly working on that book of hers. I've tried several times to set up a day for us to go out together, but she's either too tired or has to get back to her obsession—the book."

Michael raised his eyebrows. "Is that so?"

"Jah. The last time we went out together, Sadie talked on and on about that quilt book. It was frustrating to sit there and listen to her obsess over it." Wyman huffed.

Michael leaned back in his seat. "If it's really that bad, maybe you should break up with her. You don't want to end up marrying Sadie only to discover that you're not well suited and she cares more about her own needs than yours."

"I hear you. I've been mulling over that very thing in my mind." Wyman reached for his sandwich and unwrapped it. "It's not easy being in a relationship."

"I can relate. As you know, I'm having my own situation to deal with."

"What are you planning to do about your problem?"

"I want us to seek marriage counseling, and of course we need a lot of prayer."

As Wyman ate his sandwich, he listened to his brother talk more about the troubles with his marriage. The fact was, when he'd heard them arguing, he'd felt discouraged. It wasn't as if they could run out and get a divorce, believing it would solve their problems. That was not an acceptable alternative in the Amish faith. But Michael's situation caused Wyman to do more thinking about his relationship with Sadie. *I don't want to be miserable in my marriage someday. Do I want to take that chance with her?*

Chapter 23

Lovina sat at the kitchen table, unable to make out her grocery list. All she could think about was that Michael had stayed at his folks' house last night and didn't come back in the morning. The quarrel they'd had must have put him over the edge, but she'd never expected he would retreat to his parents' place.

No doubt he gave them an earful—probably said I was the one at fault. I wonder how Michael would feel if every time we had a spat, I went running to my folks' house. Her fingers curled into the palms of her hands. *Alma and Ernest and most likely Wyman must think I'm a terrible wife. But they don't realize that not everything's my fault. Michael can be hard to live with—especially since he started having severe problems with his back.*

In an effort to relax and think about something else, Lovina picked up her daughter's coloring book and crayons. Opening to a page with a puppy on it, she began coloring in the details. This was something she'd done as a child when things weren't going her way. It usually took Lovina's mind off her troubles, so maybe it would do the same thing for her now.

Lovina jumped when her daughter howled from the other room. Then the baby began to wail. So much for trying to calm herself. Now she had two little ones who needed her attention.

Lovina hurried from the room. She found Priscilla crouched by the couch, pointing at a little brown spider crawling across the floor in her direction.

Lovina grabbed a tissue, picked up the insect, and took it outside. When she returned to the living room, Priscilla was still crying, so she swept the child into her arms and took her out to the kitchen. Fortunately, Aaron had settled down and, for the moment at least, seemed content to be in his playpen.

"Would you like to color a picture with me?" Lovina asked her daughter in Pennsylvania Dutch as she placed the child into a booster seat at the table.

Priscilla bobbed her head and grabbed a red crayon. As they sat side by side, each working on their picture, Priscilla began to giggle.

"What's so funny, little one?"

The child pointed to Lovina's picture. "*Der hundli is en danser.*"

Lovina smiled. The puppy she had been coloring was leaping in the air, pawing at a leaf, so was it any wonder her daughter thought the pup was a dancer?

She pointed to the cat Priscilla was coloring. "You're doing a good job with the *katz.*" Even though she'd never seen a red cat before, Lovina wanted to say something encouraging to her daughter.

If my husband spoke encouraging words to me, I might be willing to speak nicely to him, she thought. *But I suppose anything I said, Michael would take the wrong way. He's been doing a lot of that lately. Hopefully Michael will return home for supper this evening, and we can work things out.* She picked up a green crayon, clenching her fingers around it. *Or maybe I'll give him the silent treatment. That's what he deserves.*

✳

Grace turned the propane burner beneath the kettle of stew down and faced her youngest daughters. "Supper's almost ready, so if you two will set the table, we can eat as soon as your daed comes in from the barn. I'm sure he's hungry as a horse and is glad to be home from work."

"I'm sure glad to be done for the day and can't wait to eat your hearty stew." Kaylene grabbed the plates from the cupboard.

"Where's Sadie?" Jana Beth asked. "Why isn't she in here helping?"

"She's finishing a chapter in her book, but she should be joining us for supper."

Kaylene's brows furrowed. "Sadie hasn't helped with much of anything around here lately, and she hardly ever goes anywhere nowadays, even though she has a nice horse. All she seems to care about is that book she's working on. It's like nothing else matters to her anymore."

Jana Beth bobbed her head. "Kaylene's right, Mom. Sadie's the one with all the money, and now she doesn't have to do much around here except work on the book. It's not fair."

Grace was about to respond when Kaylene spoke again. "I'm surprised our sister hasn't moved out of this house by now. After all, she has more than enough money to buy a place of her own." She shook her head. "The rest of us hardly got anything."

With both hands on her hips, Grace looked at her daughters. "Have you two forgotten your sister's generosity in buying you both horses?"

Kaylene and Jana Beth lowered their heads. "Sorry, Mom," they mumbled in unison.

Grace had never said it out loud to anyone, not even her husband, but she wished her sister hadn't singled out Sadie to receive so much of her estate. In addition to the dissension it had caused among the girls, Sadie almost seemed like a different person now.

✳

Michael had gone to his folks' place after work, to clean up and sort out his thoughts before heading to his own house to see his wife and the children. Wyman would be coming by later to take care of some heavier chores, so hopefully Lovina would be on her best behavior, which would help Michael feel less apprehensive about being there.

Michael took it easy as he rolled the buggy to a suitable spot to hook up the horse then got into the rig. He couldn't help stressing over how this would all play out. It hurt him when his daughter cried anytime she heard him and Lovina argue. No doubt it frightened Priscilla to hear her parents' raised voices.

Michael backed up his buggy and jiggled the reins to get the horse moving. It wasn't a long drive, and a short time later, his horse picked up speed as it neared home. He pulled in and parked the rig near the barn. When Michael got out, a chill in the air made him shiver. He wondered how long it would be before they'd have snow covering the ground.

Michael unhooked the horse and took off the harness. He hung the gear on its hook and led the animal to the corral. Their other horse made joyful whinnies over seeing his buddy. Michael wished he felt as excited about seeing Lovina right now. He figured he'd have to walk on eggshells when he spoke to her.

Michael left the barn and stepped up to the front door. He paused and waited for a moment before opening it. "It's Daadi!" Priscilla shouted when he stepped inside.

He hugged his little girl and followed her into the kitchen, where he took off his hat. The smell of chicken was unmistakable. The succulent aroma made his mouth water.

Lovina came in. "It's nice to see you."

"Thank you." He looked toward the living room. "Is Aaron in his playpen?"

"Jah."

Michael headed there and scooped up his son. "How ya doin', little guy? Have you done some growing these last few days?"

Traipsing into the room, his daughter giggled. "Daadi, you're *schpassich*."

"I am, huh?" Michael kissed his son's soft cheek. "Your sister thinks I'm funny." It felt good to be with his children.

Lovina stepped up to him. "Have you eaten supper yet?"

"No, I haven't."

"I've made fried chicken. You're welcome to eat with us."

Continuing to hold the baby, Michael looked at her and smiled. "That would be nice." So far things were going fairly well.

"I made dessert too. It's the German chocolate cake with the pecan frosting you like."

"That sounds good."

"Let me get things finished in the kitchen and set one more plate at the table." She turned and left the room.

With Aaron on his lap and Priscilla by his side, Michael sat on the couch, soaking up this special time with his children. He'd felt anxious when he spoke to Lovina—like he needed to carefully choose his words for fear of saying the wrong thing. His wife could be overly sensitive at times, and Michael didn't want to say or do anything that might set her off. They hadn't made up or taken care of the issues that had brought them to this point, so the longer Michael was in the same room with Lovina, the riskier things could get.

His wife called him and the children to the dining-room table. He put Aaron in his carrier near Lovina, so she could feed him his baby food. Priscilla climbed into her booster chair, while Lovina and Michael took their seats.

After their silent prayer, she passed the platter of meat to him.

"Everything looks good." He forked a couple pieces of chicken onto his plate and put a drumstick on Priscilla's dish before handing the platter back to Lovina.

"Here are the mashed potatoes."

With a quick nod he took a good serving and helped his daughter with hers.

The meal was quiet at first. Michael thought Aaron looked cute as he opened his little mouth wide to receive the soft food Lovina spooned him.

She took a bite of her food and gazed out the dining-room window. Michael wanted to ask what was on her mind, but he thought better of it. After a drink of water, he looked at her. "Wyman should be by in a while to take care of the heavier chores."

"That'll be good. Maybe he can move the refrigerator out from the wall for me. I'd like to clean behind it."

"I'm sure he wouldn't mind." Michael picked up his ear of corn and worked on it.

"*Mammi* made *kuche* for later." Priscilla licked her lips.

Michael nodded. "I'm looking forward to that."

The meal went along with mostly small talk between him and his wife. When they finished eating, he cleared the table while she took Aaron to be cleaned up and have his diaper changed.

When Lovina reappeared without the baby, she came up to him. "Would you like some cake now?"

"Sounds good." Michael followed her into the kitchen. She took out three small dishes and placed them beside the cake. Lovina picked up a butter knife, cut a few thin slices of the dessert, and then plated them. "Priscilla," she called. "It's time for kuche."

Their daughter headed back to her spot at the table.

Soon the sound of a horse and buggy was heard. "I think Wyman's here." Lovina looked out the window. "I'm glad he's been helping us out."

"Me too."

"By the way—more bills came today. They're over there." She pointed to a stack of mail on the counter.

"I'll take care of them after I get paid."

"We're behind on most of the bills, you know." Her tone had an edge to it, and Michael cringed.

"I am well aware. Now that I'm working again, we'll get caught up. You need to be patient."

"Oh really? Well, that's easy for you to say." Lovina carried two of the plates out to the table and returned to pick up his.

"I think it's time for us to see a marriage counselor. I'm doing the best I can, and things between us aren't improving." Michael took a seat next to his daughter.

Lovina stepped over to Michael with the cake in her hand. "So now you're saying we need marriage counseling? With our tight finances, we can't afford it, and who wants some stranger listening to our problems and telling us what to do?"

"Are you hearing yourself, fraa? You're being lecherich."

Wyman entered the dining room just then.

"So I'm ridiculous, huh?" Her tone hardened, and her hand shook as she dropped the plate of cake into his lap.

Michael's face warmed as he looked at the cake and then back at Lovina. He wasn't sure if it had been an accident or she'd done it on purpose, but with his brother standing there, this was most embarrassing. For him, it was the last straw.

Michael scooped up the cake and dropped it on his napkin. "I'm done here. It's time for me to go."

Lovina's chin trembled as she sat the plate down and took a seat across from her daughter.

With tears dribbling down her cheeks, Priscilla slipped off her chair and ran out to the living room.

Michael stood up and wiped some frosting off his pant leg. "I'm leaving, and let me make myself clear—I'm not coming back until you're ready to see a counselor with me."

❋

"This meal is sure tasty, Mom. You're such a good cook." Sadie licked her lips.

Her mother smiled. "Danki, but I can't take all the credit. Your sisters helped me prepare the meal."

"Jah, and it would have been nice if we'd had your help making it." Kaylene looked at Sadie through narrowed eyes.

"Sorry. When I get busy working on my book, I lose track of time. I didn't even realize it was time to eat until Mom called me and said supper was ready." Sadie handed her father the bowl of stew then reached for a buttermilk biscuit and slathered it with butter.

"That project of yours seems to be taking up a lot of your time," Dad commented. "How much longer till it's done?"

Sadie shrugged. "I'm not sure, but hopefully soon. I'm eager to get all the pages I've typed sent off to the printer, as well as the photos that will be included."

"Not to change the subject or anything, but shouldn't we be making plans for Christmas?" Jana Beth asked. "The holiday's only a few weeks away, and we should figure out our menu." She turned in her seat to look at Mom. "Don't you agree?"

"Most definitely. We need to make a list of everything we want to fix and what we'll ask your brothers' wives to bring. Maybe after the dishes are done this evening we can begin working on that. And speaking of Christmas..." Mom paused and drank some water. "I saw Mandy's mother this morning, and she mentioned that Mandy and her family are planning to join them for Christmas. They will be closing their B&B in Kauai for the week of Christmas, and while they're visiting Mandy's folks, Ken's mother will be in California with her son Dan and his family."

Sadie gave a wide grin. "That's exciting. I can hardly wait to see Mandy and tell her about everything I've included in my book."

They continued to talk about Christmas throughout the rest of the meal. Once everyone finished eating, Dad reached for his Bible. "It's time for our scripture reading and devotions."

This time of reading the Bible and talking about whatever passage Dad read had been a regular occurrence since Sadie could remember.

Dad opened the Bible. "The verse I'll be reading this evening is Proverbs 15:16. Here's what it says: 'Better is little with the fear of the Lord than great treasure and trouble therewith.' " He glanced over at Sadie, making her wonder if the verse he had chosen was directed at her.

Does my daed think I'm too focused on the money I inherited? Sadie squirmed in her chair. *I know one thing: I should have helped my mother and sisters with supper. I'll try to be more considerate from now on.*

Chapter 24

*M*ichael followed Wyman and their folks across the yard in the direction of Freeman Yoder's buggy shop, where church would be held this morning. He spotted a group of women who had gathered on one side of the building but saw no sign of Lovina among them.

He scanned another part of the yard where more women had gathered, but she wasn't there either. *I wonder if my wife decided not to come here today. It might be an embarrassment for her to show up without me.*

Michael gave his earlobe a tug. *I wonder if anyone's noticed that I came with my parents and brother, instead of with my fraa and kinner. If so, they probably think it's a bit odd, although so far no one has asked me about it.* His face heated, despite the cool outdoor temperature. *Don't know what I'll say if they do. Admitting that I spent the last two nights at my parents' house could raise a few eyebrows, not to mention the possibility of being asked a lot of questions I'd rather not answer.*

After everyone entered the building and took their seats, Michael glanced at the women's side of the room and felt relieved when he saw Lovina, looking somber as she held their son. Priscilla sat on the bench beside her.

Whew! That's a relief. I may not have to answer any questions now. Anyone who saw me walking toward Freeman's shop with my folks may not have realized I had ridden to church in my daed's carriage.

Michael tried to connect with Lovina, but she didn't so much as glance his way. *I need to talk to her after church is over. We can't keep going on like this.*

It's not good for Lovina, me, or the kinner for us to be living separately. Sooner or later the news will get out that we're having marital problems, and then we'll both face a lot of questions.

✳

Sadie followed her friends into the buggy shop. She'd thought about sitting by her mother and sisters when they came in but chose to be seated by her friends instead.

"I can't believe how tired I am this morning." Sadie yawned.

"You do look a little beat. Did you stay up last night working hard on your book?" Ellen whispered.

Sadie nodded.

Barbara slid in with her children. Placing her tote on the bench, she grabbed a tissue in time to catch a sneeze.

"Bless you," Sadie and a few women close by responded.

"I'll give you a nudge if you start to doze off." Ellen spoke quietly as she held her precious baby. "Would you mind holding Irene while I take off my jacket?"

Sadie didn't hesitate as she took the sweet child and placed the little girl in her lap. She hoped that one day she'd be holding a child of her own.

As Sadie studied the little girl's features, she toyed with the idea of her and Wyman someday being parents with their first baby. *I wonder if we'd be nervous as new parents.*

She looked across the room where the men had begun filling up the benches. She hadn't noticed Wyman come in, but there he sat between his dad and brother.

Sadie's gentle rocking movements caused the child's eyes to close. The longer she held Irene, the more her arms felt the strain. *How does Ellen do this through a three-hour church service?*

"All right, I'm ready to take her now." Ellen held out her arms.

"Irene is such a good baby. You and Rueben are so blessed."

Ellen smiled. "We certainly are."

Sadie's mother sat with some women her age, while Jana Beth and Kaylene were seated on the bench in front of Sadie and her friends.

It wasn't long before the song leader announced the first song. Sadie grabbed the *Ausbund* and turned to the correct page in the hymnal. She did well for a time, stifling yawns as she continued to sing. *I don't think I'll stay up late on a Saturday night again. All I want to do is close my eyes and sleep.*

By the time the first sermon began, Sadie's eyes felt heavy as she struggled to stay awake while the words were spoken in High German. They seemed to drone on and on, although in a soothing manner. Sadie's lids closed and her breathing deepened as she faded off in near slumber.

In a flash, an elbow met up with her side. Sadie's eyes popped open, and she looked at her friend. *Oh great. I must've dozed off for a bit.*

Ellen gave a brief smile before looking back at the minister.

It wouldn't be easy to keep awake throughout the sermons. Sadie fought the urge to sleep as she focused on any action available. If she could watch someone coming in or going out of the building, it helped. Fussy babies or children were another thing to distract her, but when things slowed, and all was still, Sadie's sleep-deprived eyes took over.

Again, Ellen gave Sadie's side a needed nudge, and she responded with a jolt. *Oh no, not again. I hope I don't keep doing this.*

Ellen patted Sadie's hand and whispered, "Hang in there. You'll make it. Our service is almost over."

Sadie grimaced. *Mom wouldn't be happy if she caught me dozing during church. I'm thankful I chose to sit by Ellen and Barbara today. Sure hope no one else noticed me nodding off.*

✳

Wyman had been surprised to see Sadie sitting with her eyes closed and her head leaning to one side. She'd seemed to be dozing on the backless bench despite the boisterous voice of the minister giving his sermon.

Wyman couldn't help watching her. *I don't want to stare. Someone might catch me and wonder what's going on.*

Ellen bumped Sadie again, and she came awake. He hoped that would hold his girlfriend for the rest of the church service, but after a while her eyes seemed to grow heavy again.

I need to keep my focus on the sermon, Wyman reminded himself. But his mind kept racing as he tapped his chin a few times. *I bet Sadie stayed up late last night working on her book. No wonder she keeps nodding off. I believe she cares more about it than she does me these days.*

His stomach tightened. Then he glanced at Michael, remembering the spat between his brother and Lovina yesterday evening. It wasn't a pleasant experience, witnessing them go at it like that. But at least Michael had made it clear that he wanted them both to seek counseling to help their situation.

Wyman glanced down at his hands. *I hope things work out for my brother and his wife, but I'm not too sure about Sadie and me. I want to propose marriage, but not until I'm certain that she's ready to commit and is willing to put our relationship ahead of her all-important book.*

✳

Lovina didn't know how she'd made it through the three-hour church service, or the noon meal that followed, but she was glad they were over and it was time to go home. First, however, she needed to speak to her husband before he headed back to his folks' house, which she felt sure was where he'd end up going. It wasn't fair that he'd given her an ultimatum, but if she wanted Michael to return to their house, Lovina had no choice but to agree to counseling.

Looking out from the buggy shop window and scanning the area where many of the men had gathered outside after they'd eaten, Lovina saw Michael heading for the barn. *I don't see how talking to a counselor about our issues will do either of us any good, but I suppose it's worth a try. We have to do something about our situation, because we're both miserable and divorce is not an option.*

Lovina asked her friend Abby to watch the children, saying she needed to take care of something before going home.

"No problem." The woman extended her arms, and Lovina passed Aaron to her. Then she instructed Priscilla to sit beside Abby and said she'd be back soon. Fortunately, Lovina's friend had not asked any questions. If Lovina's mother or one of her sisters were in this church district or had been visiting, she would have asked them to watch the children.

Drawing a deep breath, Lovina headed across the yard, until she reached the barn where her husband had gone. Upon entering the building, she spotted him talking with Wyman. She stood off to one side until their conversation lulled and then stepped up to Michael. "May I speak with you for a few minutes?"

"Of course, I also wanted to talk to you before you left for home." Michael led the way to another part of the barn that was out of earshot from the other men talking in the barn.

"I've been thinking things over." Lovina moistened her lips with the tip of her tongue. "I want you to come home, and I'm willing to see a counselor if you still want to."

He drew in a deep breath and nodded. "My daed knows of a Christian marriage counselor, so tomorrow I'll call and make an appointment."

Lovina reached under her shawl to rub her cold arms. "Does that mean you'll be returning to our house this evening?"

"Jah. I'll need to get the clothes I took to my folks' place first, and then I'll head for home."

With quivering fingers, she touched his arm. "I'll see you later, then."

✳

Since Michael was busy talking to Lovina, Wyman decided this was a good time to seek out Sadie. He figured she might still be in the buggy shop, visiting with some of the ladies.

Poking his head inside the door, he spotted her sitting at a table beside Ellen. They appeared to be deep in conversation, so he didn't want to interrupt.

Wyman remained near the door, hoping she might look his way. *How am I supposed to let Sadie know I want to talk to her if I don't go over there and say something?*

Wyman batted the idea around awhile as he tried to drum up the courage to march right over there and say what was on his mind. Common sense won out, however, so he continued to stand where he was and waited. He was almost ready to give up when Jana Beth entered the barn and stepped up to him.

"Did you come in here to talk to Sadie?" she asked.

He nodded.

"Then why don't you?"

He shuffled his feet against the concrete floor. "She's busy talking to Ellen, and I didn't want to interrupt."

"I'm sure she'd rather talk to you." Jana Beth smiled up at him. "I'll let her know that you're here waiting."

Before Wyman could form a response, Sadie's sister hurried off. He watched as she walked up to Sadie and leaned close to her ear, and he held his breath, waiting to see how Sadie would respond. After a few seconds, she came over to him.

"Hello, Wyman. Jana Beth said you wanted to talk to me."

"Jah. I was wondering if you'd like to go for a buggy ride this afternoon."

"That sounds nice, but I'm feeling kind of mied, so I think I ought to go home and take a nap."

"I guess you are tired today. I saw you nodding off a couple of times during church."

"I never actually fell sound asleep, but I have to admit, I was close to it a couple of times." Sadie yawned. "I worked on my book until late last night and didn't get much sleep."

Wyman frowned. "I figured that might be the case. It's always the book, isn't it?"

"What do you mean?"

"Seems like it consumes your life these days, Sadie."

"You don't understand, Wyman. It's important that I get it done and sent off to the printer soon so I can start promoting."

His brows lifted. "Why would you have to do that?"

"I'll need to let people know about the book and see if any of the bookstores in our area would be interested in selling it in their stores."

"Won't the printing company take care of the promotion?"

Sadie shook her head. "In the method I chose for self-publishing, it falls on me to get the word out and promote the book."

"I see."

A cold wind blew in when the door opened, and Kaylene entered the building. "Mom and Dad are ready to go home, and they were wondering if you're ready too."

"Jah. I'm quite tired and in need of a nap." Sadie looked at Wyman. "I may not be able to see you much till I get the book done and sent off to the printer."

He nodded. "I get that, Sadie. You've made it pretty clear that you don't have time for me anymore." Without waiting for her response, Wyman whirled around and rushed out the door. He'd been taken by surprise when Sadie said she would have to promote her book once it was done. Wyman wondered what all would be expected of her and hoped whatever it turned out to be that it wouldn't take up too much of her time. Their courtship had already been slowed to a near standstill, and as time went on, it seemed to be only getting worse. At the rate things were going, Sadie might never slow down long enough for him to propose.

Wyman's shoulders hunched as he trudged back to the barn. *It pains me to even think such a thought, but if Sadie doesn't believe our relationship is more important than that book of hers, it might be best if we go our separate ways. But before I make up my mind about this, the smart thing is to wait till the book is finished and see how things go. Maybe by the time the book is done, Sadie will have come to her senses.*

Chapter 25

Christmas morning dawned with a blanket of snow covering the ground. Sadie's heart swelled with excitement as she stood at her bedroom window looking out. Her book was done and at the printer's; she had plenty of money in the bank; and in addition to Wyman coming by sometime today to exchange gifts, they had special guests coming over this evening. As well as the pies Mom had baked earlier this week, Sadie had made a coconut carrot cake from a special recipe she'd included in her new book. She'd eaten something similar during her visit to the Hawaiian Islands and wanted to surprise Mandy with it this evening.

"I have everything that I need and more," Sadie murmured as she stood with her nose pressed against the cold glass of the window. "What more could I possibly ask for?" *Well, there is one thing I still don't have. I want to become Wyman's wife.*

She reflected on that Sunday when Wyman had been upset with her for being too tired to go on a buggy ride. She'd been concerned that he might break up with her if she couldn't find the time to spend with him. But things were better between them now that the book was done, and Sadie hoped their relationship was back on track. Of course, she wasn't sure how Wyman would respond once it was time for her to begin promoting the book. Hopefully, he would be understanding and supportive.

After slipping out of her nightgown and into her dress, Sadie headed for the bathroom to wash up and put her hair in a tight bun. No doubt

Mom and her sisters were in the kitchen by now, and she wanted to be there to help them.

✳

As Michael sat at his parents' table Christmas Day, he recalled earlier that morning how he, Lovina, and the children had received their gifts. Lovina had presented him with a new vest and trousers that she'd made. He planned to wear them to church on Sunday. Michael had received a raise plus a bonus check from his dad and used the extra money to buy Lovina a sturdy bookcase for their bedroom, since she liked to read novels in her spare time. The baby had received a couple of new outfits, and Priscilla got a new dress, along with a few toys.

Michael was happy they could spend the rest of the day celebrating Christmas with Mom, Dad, and his brother. Tomorrow they would be with Lovina's folks and her siblings to celebrate the holiday.

The food had been fully prepared and now sat on the table ready to eat. They'd prayed and were beginning to enjoy a lovely meal. Michael hoped he wouldn't eat too much, because Mom's cooking was always a treat.

From his seat at the head of the table, Dad cleared his throat. "It's a blessing to have our family here together."

"I agree, and I'm happy for the pretty snow we got last night," Mom added.

Priscilla looked at her grandma and grinned. *"Schnee!"*

"Jah, snow." Mom tweaked her granddaughter's nose.

Wyman smiled. "I'm thankful for this family, and also my job, as well as the bonus check I got from Dad. I look forward to going to the Kuhnses' place later to celebrate Christmas with Sadie's family too."

Michael glanced at his wife. "I thank God for my family and am grateful that my fraa and I have been working through things better these days."

Lovina smiled. "I've learned a lot since Michael and I decided to see a

Christian counselor. I'm also thankful for everyone at this table."

Baby Aaron sat next to his mother, holding his mouth open while staring at his bowl.

"The boppli's hungerich." Priscilla pointed at her baby brother.

All eyes seemed to be on the little guy as his mother brought the spoon up to his open mouth. Aaron bounced in his high chair and squealed seconds before he got a taste of his food.

Everyone laughed. The day would be filled with moments like this and shared memories of days gone by. Michael hoped that someday there might be another little Kaufman on the way. They had a lot of love to give their children, but for now it was best to take one day at a time.

After two helpings of nearly everything, Michael pushed himself away from the table. "That was delicious, Mom. I'm glad I don't eat that much every day."

Dad chuckled as he rose to his feet. "I don't dare eat like you do, Son, or my clothes would soon become too tight."

"You've never had a problem with your weight," Mom chimed in. "I'm the one who can just look at food and gain a few pounds." She shook her head. "It's terrible."

"You look fine." Dad patted her arm. "I think I might go into the kitchen and grab a hot cup of your good *kaffi* to follow supper."

Michael thumped his stomach. "I'll join you. How about you, Wyman? Care to have a cup of coffee before you head out to see Sadie?"

"Why not? I have some time yet before I need to leave."

Mom and Lovina came into the kitchen with the dishes and began to clean up, while Michael, Dad, and Wyman got their coffee and hung out in the kitchen to talk.

Mom worked around them as they stood chatting, until she finally interrupted. "If you three want to stay in here, you'll be put to work."

Dad chucked. "Okay, okay. We'll get out of your way."

They strolled into the living room, and Wyman and Michael took their seats, while Dad went to the glass-fronted hutch and opened a drawer to take out some board games for later.

"I hope we'll have a chance to play some games at Sadie's," Wyman said.

"Aw, you'll be too busy hanging out with your aldi to play any games," Michael teased.

"Leave your brother alone." Dad took a sip of his coffee before easing into his recliner.

"I hope she likes my gift." Wyman looked over at Michael. "Lovina gave me some ideas and so did Mom."

"How's your back doing today?" Dad tugged at his suspenders, looking over at Michael.

"Not bad. I just wish it were completely healed."

"Don't forget, I'm available to help out whenever I'm needed."

"I appreciate it, Wyman."

Lovina came in and took a seat with Aaron in her lap. Priscilla followed. Then Mom walked in carrying two hot beverages and set one of them by her daughter-in-law. "We're taking a short break, so we thought we'd sit out here with you to visit before Wyman leaves. I see the games are sitting out. That will be fun." Mom patted her granddaughter's shoulder. "And Priscilla is spending the night with us too."

Michael looked over at his daughter's grinning face. It would be nice for her to spend some one-on-one time with her grandparents.

Michael noticed Wyman looking up at the battery clock on the far wall. A few minutes later, he left his seat and gave Mom a hug. "I'd better head to Sadie's." He wished them all a nice evening, slipped into his jacket, and moved toward the door with his hat in his hand.

"Don't rush off too quick," Mom called, "or you'll forget Sadie's gift."

Wyman's face flushed a bright pink. "Oh yeah, that's right. I'll get it now."

Michael looked at Mom and winked. There was no doubt about it—

his brother had been bitten by the love bug.

✳

I can't wait to get over to Sadie's place. Wyman felt the cold evening air seep into the buggy and chill his clean-shaven face as he guided his horse through the fresh snow that stuck to the roads. Once the Kuhnses' house came into view, he slowed his horse and guided him up the driveway.

Wyman pulled up by the corral and set the brake. He worked quickly to get the horse unhitched and put in the barn and then headed to the house. Before he laid a fist to the door, Sadie opened it.

"*En hallicher Grischtdaag,* Wyman. I saw your buggy pull in and waited for you to come up to the door."

He smiled and removed his hat then presented her with his gift. "A merry Christmas to you. I hope you like this present."

"Hang on, I've got yours right here." She picked it up off the hall table and handed it to him.

Sadie opened her gift first. "Oh my—it's a thousand-piece puzzle of a sunset with palm trees."

He leaned in close to her. "It reminds me of how you described your journey to Hawaii—one I would like to take myself someday." *Maybe with you, Sadie, after we're married.*

"Danki, Wyman. I'm eager to begin putting it together. It looks difficult, but I'm up to the challenge."

He opened his gift and grinned. "A new *backebuch*! I can't wait to switch out my old wallet for this nice leather one. Danki, Sadie."

"You're welcome. By the way—a little later I'll bring out the special dessert I made. I waited to serve it until you arrived. Earlier my brothers, along with their wives and children, joined us for a scrumptious Christmas meal." Sadie paused and took a breath before rushing on. "Afterward, my mamm served us the pumpkin and apple pies she'd made with the help of Jana Beth and Kaylene. You're welcome to have a piece of those pies, in addition to a slice of my cake."

"That sounds nice." He slid off his heavy jacket and hung it on the coatrack by the front door.

"Let's go to the living room so we can get comfortable." Sadie led the way, carrying her new puzzle.

Wyman was glad she liked his gift and seemed happy to show it to her family. It was good to be with Sadie and celebrate Christmas together. Maybe before the day was out, he'd get the opportunity to offer her a marriage proposal.

✳

Sitting beside Ken in the front seat of their rental car, Mandy reached over and placed her hand on his arm. "Thank you for planning this trip. It was wonderful to spend Christmas with my family today."

He glanced over at her and smiled. "I'm glad we were able to get a good fare on our plane tickets."

"Same here. Now are you sure you don't mind us stopping by the Kuhnses' place this evening so I can say hello to Sadie and her family?"

"It's not a problem. I enjoyed the time we spent visiting with Ellen and Rueben earlier this evening, so I'm sure our next stop will be enjoyable too."

Mandy turned her head to look back at Charlie, asleep in his safety seat. He'd been such a good boy all day—"a real trouper," her father had said. It was a shame her mom and dad couldn't see him more often. They were missing so much of his childhood. Mandy hoped she and Ken would be able to make yearly trips to the mainland so their son could know his grandparents, aunts, and uncles and develop a bond with them. The relationship Charlie had with Ken's mother was strong, and Mandy felt grateful for that. It was good for their little boy to have the influence and nurturing of at least one grandparent on a regular basis.

When Ken drove up the Kuhnses' driveway and stopped near the

house, Mandy noticed only one buggy parked in the yard. She figured
it must belong to one of Sadie's relatives but had expected to see more
Amish carriages, since Sadie had two brothers, plus some other relatives in
the area. But maybe they'd been here earlier and gone home already. Well,
they'd know soon enough, because Ken had turned off the engine and
gotten out of the car.

✳

Sadie had been about to suggest that she and Wyman work on the puzzle
he'd given her and have their dessert when a knock sounded on the front
door. "I bet that's Mandy." Before anyone else could make a move, she
hurried to answer it.

"Merry Christmas! It's so good to see you." Sadie hugged Mandy and
shook Ken's hand. Bending down, she tousled Charlie's hair. The little guy
looked up at her with a big grin.

She smiled, looking back at Mandy. "I'm surprised he's not shy, since
he was too little on your last trip home to remember me."

"Since we have so many people coming and going at our B&B,
Charlie's used to strangers," Mandy explained. "Sometimes he pesters our
guests by jabbering and showing them his toys."

Ken nodded. "Yeah, our son can be overly social, so we have to keep an
eye on him and make sure it's not an annoyance to our guests."

"Well, he can jabber all he wants and it won't be an annoyance to me.
I'm eager to get to know your son better." Sadie motioned to the coatrack.
"Why don't you hang up your outer garments? Then we'll go into the living
room and join Wyman and the rest of my family. I am sure they're all eager
to greet you."

"We've been looking forward to seeing them too." Mandy removed
Charlie's coat, as well as her own. Once their wraps had been hung, they
followed Sadie to the living room, where Mom, Dad, Wyman, and Sadie's
sisters greeted them. Then everyone took a seat.

After they visited awhile and got caught up on each other's lives, Sadie brought out the coconut carrot cake she'd made for the occasion.

"Yum." Mandy grinned at Sadie after she'd eaten her first bite. "This cake is delicious. It reminds me of something we might eat in Hawaii."

"You're right. It sure does," Ken agreed. "Mandy has made something similar, but yours tastes a little different. Maybe you could share the recipe with her."

"No problem. I was hoping you would like it." Sadie glanced at Wyman. He hadn't said anything, but since he ate his piece of cake eagerly, she figured he liked it too.

While everyone ate dessert, Mandy and Ken answered some questions about their bed-and-breakfast, as well as ones about what it was like living on a tropical island.

"How's that book of yours coming along?" Mandy asked, taking their conversation in another direction. "Are you getting close to having it done?"

"Oh, it's been completed and is at the printer's now, getting put together." Sadie's words were rushed as she sat forward in her chair. "I can hardly wait till they send my copies to me."

"That's wonderful news." Mandy gave Sadie's shoulder a pat.

"What comes after you get the books?" The question came from Ken. "Will you be the one responsible for getting copies into stores and on the internet?"

Sadie's eyes opened wide. "The internet?"

He nodded. "There are several online bookstores where people can order books if they prefer to shop that way rather than having to leave their home and go to a store."

Wyman spoke up. "Sadie can't do anything with the internet. We Amish are not allowed to have computers in our homes."

"I realize that, but she could ask someone who isn't Amish to manage that end of promotion for her. Of course, the person would have to be experienced," Ken added.

Sadie hadn't thought about trying to sell her books via online bookstores, nor did she know anyone who might be able or willing to do that for her. "When my books arrive, I'll start by visiting all the bookstores, gift stores, and quilt shops in the area to see if they'd be willing to take some of my books on consignment."

More comments came from Mandy and Ken, and Sadie appreciated their enthusiasm. Mom, Dad, and her sisters chimed in a few times too, also mentioning how busy Sadie would be once it was time to start her promotion.

She glanced over at Wyman and noticed his look of disapproval. At least that was how she interpreted his folded arms and drooped shoulders as he sagged in his chair. Could he be jealous because she'd been talking more to Mandy and Ken than him? Or did the real problem stem from the fact that Wyman did not share their interest in her book? Sadie had felt from the beginning that her boyfriend wasn't supportive of her endeavors, and as time went on, it had become more obvious. She couldn't help wondering how things would go between them once she became busy trying to get the books into stores.

Chapter 26

Shipshewana

*T*his is a nice way to celebrate Valentine's Day," Lovina commented as she and Michael entered the Blue Gate Restaurant with Wyman and Sadie. "Thanks for including us in your plans this evening."

"We're glad you could join us." Sadie looked over at Wyman and gave his arm a little bump. "Isn't that right?"

He nodded. What else could he do? It would be impolite to admit that he would have preferred to celebrate Valentine's Day with Sadie alone—especially when he'd planned to ask her to marry him after they'd eaten supper. Wyman had wanted to ask his girl back in December on Christmas Day, thinking it would be a memorable day, but too many things had been happening, so it didn't work out. Now he'd have to wait again for a more suitable time, since he wasn't about to propose with his brother and sister-in-law sitting at a table with them. Wyman had put off proposing marriage too long, and since he planned to join the church in the spring, now was the time to see if Sadie would be willing to become his wife. He figured if she wanted to make that commitment, she would give up the notion of putting all her time and energy into promoting her book in order to gain back what she had paid to have a number of copies printed. As far as Wyman was concerned, getting her book published was a waste of time. A young woman Sadie's age, who had said more than once that she cared deeply for him, should be concentrating on preparing for marriage.

Wyman clenched his fingers. *Instead, all I'm probably going to get from this goofy endeavor of hers is an autographed copy of her book.*

Once they were seated at a table and the waitress had taken their orders, Michael looked across at Sadie and Wyman and smiled. "Lovina and I are glad that my folks were willing to watch the kinner for us tonight. It's been quite some time since we've had an evening away from the house without our little ones along."

Lovina bobbed her head before taking a drink from her glass of water. She looked content—more so than before she and Michael had gone for marriage counseling.

Wyman was glad things were going better between his brother and sister-in-law. They seemed much happier now. Of course most of it stemmed from seeing the counselor and working harder on their marriage, but Michael had been noticeably happier since their father had given him a raise. Wyman figured he should have gotten one too, since he did so much heavy lifting and difficult tasks, but Dad hadn't said a word about increasing his wages.

Maybe he's waiting to see if I'm going to stick it out this time and not run off looking for some other job I might enjoy more. Wyman shifted in his chair. *Well, he needn't worry, because I'm not going anywhere. My daed needs me more than ever now that Michael can no longer do any of the heavy work, and I won't run out on either of them.*

Wyman jumped when an elbow connected to his ribs. He turned and looked at Sadie. "What'd ya do that for?"

"I tried to get your attention, but you didn't seem to be listening."

"Sorry. Guess I was deep in thought. What were you saying?"

"I mentioned seeing Ellen and her family across the room, and since our meal isn't here yet, I thought I'd go over and say hello. Would you like to come with me?"

Wyman hesitated; then he nodded and pushed back his chair. It would be impolite not to go with her, and it would give Michael and Lovina a few minutes to themselves. *Which is more than I'm gonna get with Sadie this evening,* he thought with regret.

✳

Sadie made her way across the room and stood next to the table where Ellen and Rueben sat by themselves.

Ellen looked up at her and smiled. "Happy Valentine's Day." She pointed to the two empty chairs at their table. "Would you and Wyman like to join us?"

"That'd be nice," Sadie replied, "but we're with Michael and Lovina. Our table's over there." She gestured toward it.

"So you're double-dating tonight, huh?" Rueben grinned and shook Wyman's hand. "It's nice to see you. How are things going at the feed store?"

"Okay. We're keeping plenty busy. No free time to do much else, that's for sure."

As Wyman and Rueben launched into a discussion, Ellen started a conversation with Sadie.

"Any news on when copies of your book will be sent to you?"

"No, but it could be another month or two."

"That'll go by quickly, and then you can start contacting some stores in the area. I'm sure with you being a local author, they'll want to carry your book."

Sadie snickered. "I've never thought of myself as an author."

"You'd better get used to the title, because I bet others in our community will think of you that way."

Sadie lifted her gaze to the ceiling. "I doubt it."

"Have you made any plans to do some book signings?"

"No, I haven't really thought about it."

"You'll need to do some strong promotion in order for the book to sell."

"Jah, I'm aware of that."

"You could see if some of the quilt shops in the area would carry the book, and then there's gift stores, bookstores. . ."

"Where's your daughter tonight?" Sadie steered their conversation in another direction in case Wyman's ears were tuned more to her and Ellen's conversation than to what Rueben was saying. She didn't want him to think all she ever talked about was her book.

"We left Irene with my parents," Ellen replied. "They were quite open to the idea, and I can only imagine how much they will spoil her this evening."

Sadie chuckled. "She's such a sweetheart. It would be easy to spoil her. I hope someday I'll be blessed with a special baby like her."

"Speaking of babies. . .I heard from Mandy yesterday. She shared the good news that she's expecting another boppli. The baby will be born in September."

"That's exciting. I hope everything goes well for her this time."

Ellen nodded. "Jah, Mandy was so depressed when she had a miscarriage last fall. I hope she has an uncomplicated pregnancy this time."

✳

Kapaa

Mandy had made Ken and her a picnic lunch to celebrate Valentine's Day together. She'd packed the cooler with fried chicken, potato salad, sweet rolls, and two hefty slices of triple chocolate cake with strawberries for dessert. They'd loaded up a couple of beach chairs, a small folding table, and an umbrella to sit under if they wanted to get out of the sun and driven to one of their favorite spots that wasn't too busy today. On Kauai that was rare, what with the number of tourists the island got during the winter months.

After Ken parked his SUV, they unloaded the rig and found a spot to set everything up. Mandy adjusted her wide-brimmed hat as she rested in her seat. "This is the life, huh?"

"I agree, and we're sitting in a beautiful spot." Ken scooted his beach chair next to Mandy's.

Mandy thought he looked more handsome than ever in his blue shorts and white tank top, with a pair of sunglasses perched on top of his head.

"I might take a dip in the water in a while. It's a great day even though it is overcast."

"Sounds like a nice idea." Mandy was pleased that Ken had arranged for his mother to watch Charlie today so the two of them could have some time alone.

While they relaxed and watched the waves, Mandy felt a weight on her heart she hadn't dealt with yet. She turned to face Ken. "There's something I want to tell you."

"What's that?"

"I'm nervous about being pregnant again. I—I fear that I may have another miscarriage."

Ken reached over and clasped her hand. "I understand how you might feel that way, and it's a normal reaction, but we'll get through this together and trust the Lord for the best. We need to remember that God doesn't want us to worry. John 14:1 says, 'Let not your heart be troubled: ye believe in God, believe also in me.'"

"I like that verse. Thank you for the reminder."

"You're welcome." His stomach emitted a noisy growl. "Oops!"

She snickered. "Sounds like you're getting hungry."

"Yeah, I guess so. Actually, I can't wait to enjoy all that food you packed in our cooler."

"Did we grab the green-and-white-striped bag? That has the paper plates, plus the things we'll need to serve and eat with."

"I'm sure it's there." Ken jumped up and checked. "Yep, it's right here."

"Okay, I'll open up the cooler then set out the food." As she was doing that, Ken's cell phone rang. Based on what he said, Mandy figured it was Vickie. Ken's puckered brows and serious tone caused Mandy to feel concern. She hoped Charlie was okay. She continued to listen while getting out the bowl of potato salad but couldn't decipher the reason for his mother's call.

After Ken put his phone away, he turned to face Mandy. "That was my mom. She had a call from my brother Dan."

"Is there a problem?"

"Apparently Dan's wife fell and broke her leg, so Mom would like to go there and help out while Rita is healing."

"Oh dear, that's too bad. Of course she'd want to go. How long will she be gone?"

"Three weeks, and then Rita's mother, who is currently on a cruise with Rita's dad, will go and help out until Rita's leg is healed enough that she can take over her regular chores and caring for the children again."

Mandy opened the bag containing the plates. "She should definitely go. We can manage without her."

Ken nodded. "That's what I told her. Mom apologized for interrupting our picnic, but she needed to call Dan back right away and let him know if she's able to come to California."

"That's understandable." Mandy passed him a plate of food.

After saying grace, Ken took his first bite of potato salad. "Yum...this is sure good."

She smiled. "My mom's recipe is always a winner."

As they ate, Mandy watched the waves roll onto the beach. She drew a deep breath of the fresh island breeze, enjoying this special time with her husband. Her mood changed, however, when she noticed his furrowed brows. "What's wrong, Ken?"

"I don't want to stand in the way of my mother going to help out family, but I'm worried about you doing too much while she's gone."

"I will not overdo it, and like I said before, I'm sure we can manage. If necessary, we can hire someone to come in and help out."

Ken leaned toward Mandy and kissed her. "All right, we'll keep that in mind, but I'm gonna keep an eye on you and make sure you don't do too much."

"Whatever you say, husband." Mandy nibbled on a sweet roll. She appreciated Ken and how much he cared about her and their unborn baby's welfare. She placed her hand on her stomach and promised herself that in Vickie's absence, she would not overdo it.

✳

Shipshewana

Toward the end of their meal, as they were finishing their desserts, Sadie was taken by surprise when the same woman whose purse she had retrieved from a thief in the parking lot some months ago stepped up to their table. "Well, hello there. I don't believe we ever introduced ourselves, but do you remember me?" the woman asked.

Sadie nodded. "Yes, I certainly do. My name is Sadie Kuhns."

"I'm Clara Williams." The woman extended her hand.

"How have you been?"

"Very well, dear, and you?"

"I'm fine." Sadie introduced the woman to Wyman, Michael, and Lovina.

Clara put her hand on Sadie's shoulder. "This young woman is quite the heroine. She rescued my handbag from a purse snatcher."

Sadie's face warmed. "I just did what I would want someone to do for me if I were in that situation."

"I'll always be indebted to you, dear, and I still wish there was something more you would let me do for you."

"Do you know any way to help Sadie promote her new book?" Lovina joined in.

The woman's mouth opened slightly. "You've written a book?"

"Yes." Sadie explained a little about it and ended by saying that in a few months she would have copies of the book and would need to begin promoting.

Clara tapped a finger against her chin. "You know, I believe I could help you with that. I have developed a blog page with a good many followers. I also have access to several social media sites." She reached into her purse and pulled out a business card. "Here's my phone number. As soon as you have some copies of the book, let me know and I will do everything in my power to promote it. It'll be my way of saying thank you for your good deed." She tapped Sadie's shoulder. "Will you let me do that for you?"

Sadie felt kind of funny accepting the woman's offer, but she agreed to let her know once copies of the book had been delivered.

Even if she does promote the book on her blog, Sadie thought after Clara said goodbye and walked away, *I doubt it will do much to sell my book. After all, how many Amish people will read someone's blog on the internet, when they don't even own a computer? I appreciate the kind offer, but I doubt anything will come of it.*

Chapter 27

Middlebury

On the first day of April, a delivery truck pulled in front of the Kuhnses' home, and Sadie went out to greet the driver. The wait was over—copies of her book were finally here. She'd known they were coming today because the printer had called and left a message, saying she could expect them to be delivered on April 1. Sadie was beyond excited as she waited on the front porch while the driver loaded twelve large cardboard boxes on a hand truck and pulled them up the stairs.

"Oh my—I didn't think there'd be so many."

"That's only half of 'em." The driver gestured to the truck. "There's twelve more boxes I've yet to unload."

Sadie sucked in a breath of air. "I don't know where we're going to put them."

"That'll be your problem, miss. I'll just stack the boxes on the porch, and you can take it from there."

Sadie stood off to one side as the boxes stacked up, nearly covering the porch. Her sisters and father were still working at the factory. Mom had gone shopping, so Sadie was here by herself and didn't have a clue what to do with all the boxes. The only thing she was sure of was that every box contained copies of her book and she couldn't wait to tear one open and take a look.

The idea of holding her very own book sent shivers of excitement up Sadie's spine.

As soon as the truck pulled out of the yard, she raced into the house, got a small knife from the kitchen, and returned to the porch. Carefully slicing open the nearest box, she reached inside. "*The Blended Quilt* by Sadie Kuhns," she murmured, sliding her fingers across the embossed title and her name. "I can't believe my copies are finally here." *I'll have to make up a list of who I'll be giving books to. That will need to be done soon, but for the moment I just want to relax and look over my book.*

Sadie took a seat on the porch swing and thumbed through every page, stopping long enough to read each heading and look at every photo.

The first chapter gave an account of the trip she'd taken to Hawaii with three of her closest friends, explaining how they had stopped at each of the four main islands—Oahu, the Big Island, Maui, and Kauai. She'd highlighted some of the things they'd seen on each island and given a bit of history about them. In subsequent chapters Sadie had written about the similarities she'd seen between the Hawaiian people and the Plain communities on the mainland. She'd also included information on Hawaiian quilts, including their beginnings. Then she'd compared Hawaiian quilt patterns to the Amish ones she'd grown up knowing about and had created since the first nine-patch quilt she'd made as a young girl.

Sadie's final chapter told how she'd come up with a pattern that blended some of the Hawaiian culture with that of the Amish. It also included directions to make a blended quilt in case anyone reading the book wished to try making one of their own.

Sadie smiled with satisfaction as she closed the book, overcome by the reality that all the hard work she'd done putting everything together had finally come to fruition. She could hardly wait to send Mandy an autographed copy and give one in person to Ellen, Barbara, and the rest of her friends. Sadie would also make sure that every member of her family got a book, as well as Wyman and anyone in his family who showed an interest. Completing this book and now holding it in her hands brought Sadie a sense of deep satisfaction and pride. Of course she wouldn't express that to anyone in her family, for she'd surely be accused of having hochmut and would probably get a lecture on the importance of humility and learning to be content.

Sadie lifted the book, stretching her arms over her head. "I am content now that my copies of the book are here, and I can't wait to see how many bookstores might be willing to sell it for me."

✳

When Grace approached the house after putting her horse and buggy away, she was surprised to see numerous stacks of boxes on the front porch. She spotted Sadie sitting on the porch swing, holding a book.

"Ach, my! What is all this?" Grace moved closer to a stack of boxes.

"My books arrived from the printer." Sadie held up the book in her hand. "Isn't it exciting, Mom?"

"Yes it is, but what are you going to do with all these *kaschde*? They certainly can't be left here on the porch."

"I know, and it's a lot more boxes than I had expected." Sadie got up from the swing and handed Grace the book she'd been holding. "See how nice it turned out? I'm quite pleased with the cover, and the pictures inside the book have such vivid colors."

Grace studied the picture of Sadie's blended quilt on the cover, which had been draped over a quilt rack. The mixture of the ocean waves pattern combined with pineapples in the gentle hues of beige and green made it look quite tropical but familiar at the same time.

She opened the book and turned several pages. "You're right, Daughter, it's been put together quite well."

Sadie grinned. "I'm glad you like it, and as soon as I sign it, this copy will be yours. While I'm at it, I'll autograph copies for my sisters and my brothers' wives."

"Danki, Sadie. I look forward to reading it, and I'm sure the others will too."

"Now I need to figure out where to store all these boxes until I can find some stores that are willing to try to sell the books."

Grace massaged her forehead, feeling as though a headache might be coming. In addition to the issue of where to store all of Sadie's books, there was the problem of who would buy them. The reality of it was that this type of book might not be something most people would be interested in, unless they'd either visited Hawaii or planned to make a trip there.

Grace continued to rub her forehead as she gazed out into the yard. *I wish things could go back to the way they were before my sister died and left Sadie such a large sum of money. If not for my daughter's inheritance, she wouldn't have been able to pay to have all these books printed. And who knows—she may have been engaged to marry Wyman by now.*

✳

Since there were still a few hours before it was time to start supper, Sadie had decided to take an autographed copy of her new book to some of her friends. She'd already stopped to see Barbara, but since she wasn't home, Sadie left the book in a plastic bag, hanging on the doorknob. Her next stop was to see Ellen.

After pulling her horse and buggy around the back of the bed-and-breakfast, Sadie guided the horse to the hitching rail, got out, and secured the mare. Reaching into the buggy, she took out the book and headed for the back door, which was the part of the home where Ellen and Rueben lived. There was no electricity in this area of the building, but the rest of the B&B had most of the basic conveniences that travelers and locals who weren't Amish would expect. This included electricity, a telephone, and even air-conditioning to use during the hot summer months. Ellen and Rueben had gotten permission from the church to offer these modern conveniences to their guests since the area their family occupied was not part of the rooms that comprised the bed-and-breakfast.

Sadie rapped on the door. A few seconds later, it opened and Rueben greeted her.

"Well hello, Sadie. Was Ellen expecting you to come by today?"

"No, it was a spur-of-the-moment decision, but if she's busy. . ."

Rueben shook his head. "Ellen's not here. She took Irene to a doctor's appointment."

"Oh dear. Is that sweet little girl grank?"

"She's had a cold for the last two weeks, and her cough is lingering. We decided it would be best to have the doctor take a look at her to be sure it's nothing serious." Rueben leaned against the door opening. "I would have gone with them, but we're expecting two couples to arrive at the B&B this afternoon, so someone needs to be here to greet them."

"That makes sense." Sadie held out her book. "Would you please give this to Ellen when she gets home? It's an autographed copy of my new book."

His eyebrows rose slightly. "Wow, that's great, Sadie. Ellen will be excited when she sees this."

"She's the one who first encouraged me to write the book."

He smiled. "Maybe I'll look through it while I'm waiting for our guests to arrive."

"I hope you like it."

"If there's information about Hawaii in it, I'm bound to enjoy reading it. It was fun living there for a time, and I kinda miss Kauai."

"Jah, there's lots of information about the islands, along with some photos Mandy sent me of Hawaiian quilts."

"Sounds like the kind of book our B&B guests would enjoy too. If you have an extra copy we could buy, we'll put one out on the coffee table in the living room where our guests like to sit and relax."

"That's a good idea, but you don't have to pay me for the book. I'll gladly donate one and will drop it by sometime soon. Maybe Ellen will be home when I come by and I can find out what she thinks of the book."

The front doorbell rang, interrupting their conversation. "Guess that must be some of our guests."

"I'll let you see to them and be on my way. I still want to stop and see Wyman before heading back home."

"Good to see you, Sadie, and danki for this." Rueben lifted the book and said goodbye.

Sadie felt a bit disappointed that she hadn't connected with either Barbara or Ellen, but at least the books had been delivered. Now on to see Wyman and find out what his reaction would be when she handed him his own autographed copy.

✳

Wyman swiped at the perspiration that had formed on his brow. He'd loaded many bags of feed so far today. Dad's business sat in the heart of the Amish community, which made it a convenient source for a lot of farms in the area.

I need to get a drink—think I'll go snatch a bottle of water from the break room.

Wyman had barely taken a sip when the front door bell tinkled again. *I'd better get to the counter since Dad stepped out to talk to a customer and Michael went home for lunch.*

Two middle-aged Amish sisters entered the store. Neither were married, and they usually came in to buy items for their cats. The oldest wore metal-framed glasses and was the most talkative. The other woman seemed more soft spoken and often carried a handkerchief.

"How are you ladies doing today?" Wyman asked.

"We're doing all right. We wondered if you had any other cat toys besides those over there." The more talkative woman pointed toward the feline section.

Wyman scooted out from behind the counter and went with them to look. "I'm afraid this is all we have. But I can take a look in the back room just to be sure."

The woman with the hankie nodded as she blotted her nose.

"That would be nice. My sister and I will look around while we wait to hear if there's something else," the other sister said.

Wyman went to the back room and checked, but he was right. Even though the sisters were a tad eccentric, he couldn't help liking them.

When Wyman returned, he told them he hadn't seen anything else back there. They seemed content with the news and continued gathering some other items in their baskets, while Wyman went back to the counter and took a seat on the stool.

A few seconds later, Dad came in and spoke in a quiet voice to Wyman. "Guess who I saw pulling up in her buggy?"

He shrugged. "I have no idea."

"Sadie. Did you have any idea she'd be stopping by today?"

"Nope, I sure didn't." Wyman's brows knitted together. *I wonder what brought her. She has to know I can't visit with her and do my job.*

Sadie sauntered in holding something in a plastic bag. Wyman wasn't sure what this was about as she stepped up to him by the counter.

"Hi, Wyman. How are you doing today?"

"Not too bad—keeping busy as usual."

The bell sounded again when an English woman came in with a boy. They headed quickly down one of the aisles to shop.

"What brings you by today?" Wyman asked, turning his attention to Sadie again.

"I'll show you in a minute." She stepped aside when the sisters came up to the counter with their baskets full of canned cat food and some other items. "Hello, Ernest. We'll need a bag of the adult cat food and a bag of the kitten food too." The talkative sister pointed toward the two sacks at the end of the aisle.

Wyman's dad tugged on his long beard. "Doing some stocking up, huh?"

"Oh yes, because one of our mama cats just had a healthy litter of babies, and they're so cute. Sister and I want to be prepared in the weeks to come."

"It's good to plan ahead. Wyman will take those sacks out to your rig, and I'll make out your bill while he does that."

Wyman looked at Sadie. "I'll be back in a few minutes. If you don't have to rush off, that is."

"I can wait." Sadie held on to the bag she'd brought in and glanced off at the goods in the store.

He grabbed the cart and loaded the women's order. *I wonder what's inside the bag Sadie's holding. Maybe she made my favorite kind of cookies.*

Wyman toted the bags out to the buggy and quickly returned. Sadie stood there waiting while his dad took care of the English woman and the boy who came in earlier.

Wyman motioned to Sadie. "Let's go into the break room."

"I can't wait for you to see what I've brought." Sadie handed him the bag.

"What did you bring me? Oh, it's your quilt book. How nice is that?" He forced a smile. *I would rather it was cookies.*

"I wanted you to have a copy, and I signed it too. I've got a couple of extras out in my rig for you to give your mom and Lovina."

"It was nice of you to bring this by, and I'm sure they'll like their copies."

"I also need to ask you a favor."

"Okay, what is it?" He slid the book back inside the bag.

"I'd like to use your cell phone for a few days—no more than a week."

Wyman's eyebrows shot up. "Really? What for?"

"I need to make some calls to a few bookstores in the area, and when they return my call with their answer, they won't have to leave a message and I'll be able to answer on your cell phone right away."

"Guess that makes sense." He removed the phone from his pocket and handed it to her. The bell on the door tinkled again as he quickly gave her the password to access the phone. Wyman looked out from the break room and saw it was getting busier. "I need to get back to work, Sadie. I hope things work out for you."

"It's looking better now that I can use your phone. I'll see you later. Oh, and I'll bring in the other books before I leave."

Wyman followed her back out to the main part of the store. Then he went to check on one of the customers to see if he needed any help. The man said he was fine and went on with his shopping. Michael had returned and stood talking to Dad.

Sadie came back in with the other books and showed them to his dad and brother. They seemed pleased about giving them to their spouses and thanked her.

"I'll talk to you soon, Wyman, and thanks again." She held up his phone and headed out the door.

Even though he'd done a good deed to help out his girlfriend, Wyman couldn't help feeling upset. *Am I only fueling Sadie's obsession with that book of hers?* He continued to stew about this while watching Michael wait on a customer. *I can only imagine how busy Sadie will be once she begins to get orders for her book. Anyways, why couldn't she have waited for a better time to come by and give me the books? Sadie could have at least waited till I was done working for the day. It's obvious where her priorities are these days.*

Wyman scratched his head. *Sure hope she doesn't keep my phone too long. She's a church member and might get called out if one of our church leaders should find out she has a cell phone in her possession. I should've thought about that before agreeing to let her borrow the phone.*

Chapter 28

A week later, when the boxes of books were piled in several places around the house, Sadie decided it was time to put an ad in *The Connection* magazine, as well as *The Budget* newspaper. Hopefully she could get some individual sales that way. She'd spent the last few days calling and visiting many bookstores and gift shops in the area and had managed to get a few of her books placed, but it barely dented the supply still in the house.

I wish I could have received my books before Christmas, Sadie thought as she sat at the supper table with her family. *Some folks might have bought copies of the book to give as Christmas presents.*

"Can't some of those boxes of books be hauled out the barn to be stored?" Mom asked, looking at Dad from across the table.

"No way! There are too many other things stored in my barn." He looked at Sadie and squinted his eyes. "You need to find more places to sell those books."

"Jah, Dad. I plan to run a few ads, so maybe. . ."

"I'm tired of dodging those boxes that are in the hallway outside our bedrooms upstairs," Jana Beth put in.

"Same here. The other day I came out of my room and nearly ran right into that stack of boxes sitting closest to my door." Kaylene turned to face Sadie. "Maybe you should rent one of those storage units in town. With all your money, you can certainly afford it."

Sadie folded her arms. "I'm doing the best that I can."

"What about the woman whose purse you rescued some time ago?" Mom asked. "Didn't she say when you saw her at the Blue Gate Restaurant that she'd be willing to help promote your books?"

"Jah, but I've misplaced her phone number." Sadie sighed. "Besides, selling the books is my problem, not hers."

Mom passed Sadie the bowl of mashed potatoes. "Would you like another helping?"

"No thanks." Sadie passed it on to Jana Beth. She felt so discouraged. If there were something more she could do to generate interest in her books, she certainly would. Even after all the phone calls she'd made using Wyman's cell phone, she'd gotten few responses. The worst part of all was that no one in her family seemed that supportive, and neither did Wyman. The day Sadie returned his phone, he hadn't said much when she'd mentioned the lack of interest she had received so far.

"Sister, did you hear what I said?"

Sadie jerked her head when Kaylene spoke and gave her a nudge. "Umm, no. . . What did you say?"

"I asked if you had considered trying to sell your book in other places— like stores that cater to the tourists in Pennsylvania and Ohio."

"No, I haven't."

"It's worth a try, don't you think?"

"Well, maybe. . ."

"If I were in your shoes, I'd make a trip to some other states and visit as many bookstores and gift stores as you can."

"Kaylene has a point," Jana Beth added. "With summer only a few months away, lots of tourists will be flocking to Lancaster and Holmes Counties, just like we get here."

Sadie clasped both hands under her chin. "That's not a bad idea. I'd have to hire a driver to take me there, and I might be gone for a few weeks, but it could be worth the time and money I'd have to spend on the trip."

Mom's gaze flitted to Sadie and then over to Dad. "If our daughter's going to make such a trip, I should go with her, don't you agree, Calvin?"

He tipped his head to one side, as though weighing his response. "That all depends."

"On what?" Mom asked.

"On whether our other two daughters are willing to chip in while you're gone and do all the cooking and household chores."

Mom looked at Jana Beth and then Kaylene. "I'm aware that you two and Sadie filled in during my stay in Toledo after your aunt passed away. It's a lot to ask, I know, but your sister needs me to go along on this trip. Well, girls, what's your response to that?"

They nodded simultaneously. "Sure, we can manage while you're gone," Jana Beth said.

Sadie was on the verge of telling her mother that she would be okay making the trip on her own, but the determined set of Mom's jaw let Sadie know that her mother had made up her mind.

Sadie sipped some iced tea as she collected her thoughts. "I'll start making some calls in the morning about hiring a driver and making hotel reservations."

✳

Kapaa

Mandy pulled out the sausages from the package and put each one in the hot skillet. Not long after, the strong scent of the sizzling meats made her morning sickness intensify. She'd downed a few saltine crackers a few minutes earlier and left the box nearby. This morning they had a few guests to attend to, and with Vickie still in California, Mandy had been trying to make the best of it. She put the lid on the pan. *If it weren't for the nausea, I could breeze right through this. My poor husband has filled in for me at times, but I feel bad to be adding more responsibilities on him.* Mandy lifted the lid and quickly worked at turning all the links over. It wasn't as if Ken didn't have his own chores to do around the Palms Bed-and-Breakfast.

Mandy figured Vickie's daughter-in-law must be going through her own rough time. It was good for Ken's mother to be there to help and offer support.

All Mandy could hope for was that her morning sickness would taper off in the days to come. After that, their lives would get back to normal, but for now it was going to be tough.

Ken entered the kitchen with a more pronounced limp than usual. No doubt his old injury had reared its ugly head, which happened whenever he'd done too much walking or stayed on his feet too long. "How's it going in here?" he asked. "The food you're making for breakfast sure smells good."

Mandy nearly gagged but staved it off by drawing a quick breath. "I–I'm afraid I won't be able to finish frying these links. The smell of them cooking is grossing me out."

"I'd better take over for you, then. Is there anything else that needs to be done?"

"I've already scrambled some eggs, and they're keeping warm in the oven." Mandy backed away from the stove and moved closer to the open window. "The fresh air coming in helps some, but maybe I should take these crackers and go lie down in the other room for a while."

"I'm sorry you're going through this. It has to be rough." Ken checked on the sausages. "We have plenty of juice and grapes to serve. I'll make up some toast when I'm done cooking here."

"Will you be able to watch Charlie while I'm lying down?"

"Sure thing. Please don't worry. I'll make certain that everything's under control. Now go on, honey, and take it easy."

"Thanks, I will." Mandy went out of the kitchen and to their room. She reclined on the bed and nibbled on a cracker, determined to get through this round of nausea that had gone on too long. Mandy stayed there awhile, hoping her stomach would settle down, but it didn't help at all. *I should go outside, because the smell of that sausage has filtered in here.*

She rolled off the bed and hurried out the front door. The fresh outside air felt like a tonic against the waves of nausea. *While I'm out here, maybe I'll check on the mail.*

At the mailbox, she slid out a package and looked on the front. *It's from Sadie. I wonder what's inside.* She grabbed the rest of the mail and seated herself at the picnic table in the side yard.

Mandy's breath caught when she tore open the package and saw an autographed book by Sadie Kuhns. *It's her quilt book. How exciting! And what a beautiful cover.* She turned it over to read the back. *I think I'll stay out here awhile and look through the book.*

As Mandy observed Sadie's work, she was impressed with how well it had turned out and hoped the book would do well for her friend. With the type of information Sadie had included, anyone who read it might be enticed to visit Hawaii.

Mandy looked up from the last page. *I should give her a call and ask if I can buy a few more copies to put in each of the guest rooms here at our B&B. I'm sure this quilt book would be of interest to a good many of our guests.*

✳

Middlebury

Wyman had finished working for the day and had gone to the break room to get his empty lunch pail when his cell phone rang. He looked at the caller ID but didn't recognize the number. Normally, he would have ignored a call like this, but he decided to answer.

"Hello."

"Good afternoon. May I speak to Sadie Kuhns?"

Wyman didn't recognize the female voice on the other end of the phone.

"Umm. . .Sadie's not available right now."

"I see. Well, I'm the owner of the new bookstore in Shipshewana. Sadie came by here the other day and left a copy of her new book for me to look over. I've decided to try to sell a few copies, and if people show an interest I may want to have Sadie come in to do a book signing."

"I see."

"Will you please ask her to give me a call at this number?"

"Okay, sure."

When Wyman hung up he stood shaking his head. "Oh brother! What am I now—Sadie's secretary?"

"What was that?" Michael asked, stepping into the room.

"I was griping out loud."

"What's the problem?"

"It's Sadie's book." Wyman told his brother about the phone call.

"Do you think she has changed from the girl you first started courting?"

"Yeah. She's become self-absorbed."

Michael picked up his lunch pail. "What are you gonna do about it?"

"I'm not sure. Guess I should give Sadie a call and pass on the information." He punched in Sadie's home number and was surprised when Jana Beth answered the phone. He hadn't expected anyone to be in the phone shed and figured he'd need to leave Sadie a message.

"Is Sadie at home?" Wyman asked. "Because I have a message for her from the bookstore in Shipshewana."

"Sadie went shopping to buy a few things she'll need for her trip to Ohio."

"Ohio?" *This is news to me.* Wyman pressed his ear against the phone.

Michael went to leave, but Wyman held up his hand to stop his brother from going.

"Okay, I'll wait." Michael stepped over and took a seat.

"My sister's going there to try to get her books into some of the stores in Holmes County and possibly some of the other areas where tourists visit," Jana Beth continued. Our mamm's going with her, and they may go to Pennsylvania too."

Wyman lowered himself into a chair. He had no idea Sadie planned to go on a trip to Ohio or Pennsylvania. It hurt to find out from Sadie's sister, and he couldn't figure out why Sadie hadn't said anything to him about her plans. "When are they going to leave?" he questioned.

"In a few days, I believe. I'm surprised she hasn't told you about it."

"Yeah, me too." Wyman struggled to keep his composure. He'd begun to think he didn't matter to Sadie at all. *If she really cares for me, she should have let me know about her plans right away. I've tried to be understanding and patient in order to stay in her good graces, but it's getting harder all the time.* He clenched the phone in the palm of his hand. *All I want is to marry Sadie and raise a family with her, but apparently her wants aren't the same as mine.*

"Are you still there, Wyman?"

"Jah. Please tell your sister I called, okay?"

"Of course, I'll let her know as soon as she gets home."

When Wyman ended the phone call, he leaned forward until his head was nearly resting on his knees.

"What's going on with Sadie?" Michael asked.

Wyman repeated everything Jana Beth had said. "I can't believe she didn't let me know about this." Wyman slapped the table. "This whole book thing isn't getting better, it's getting worse. I had hoped things would've changed for us by now, but they sure haven't."

"I can say from experience that relationships will become difficult at times. You definitely have a problem with Sadie."

"How well I know."

"Do you need me to hang around longer so you can talk more about this?"

"No, I'll be leaving here soon myself. See you tomorrow, Brother. Danki for listening."

Michael gave Wyman's shoulder a squeeze before heading out.

Wyman couldn't believe that Sadie had managed to hurt him again. Michael and Lovina had patched things up by going to a marriage counselor, but that wasn't an option for him and Sadie.

Wyman turned off the gas lantern overhead and walked out of the store, making sure to look the door. *It would be a lot easier if I were competing with another man for Sadie's attention, but first a quilt and now a book? I have no idea how to contend with that.*

Chapter 29

Sadie felt a sense of excitement that alternated with apprehension as she and her mother entered the quilt shop. She'd called first, to see if they might be interested in meeting with her to look over the book she'd written. The manager had agreed and said Sadie should come in half an hour before the store opened for the day.

Upon entering the building, Sadie was greeted by a middle-aged Mennonite woman. "You must be Sadie Kuhns."

Sadie smiled and nodded then gestured to her mom. "This is my mother, Grace."

The woman shook their hands. "It's nice to meet you."

Sadie handed her a copy of the book. Unsure if there would be any interest in taking her book on consignment, she'd only brought one copy. "This is the book I wrote, comparing Amish quilts to those found in Hawaii." Sadie felt quite timid and vulnerable at the moment. "Of course, there's a lot more than just information about various quilts in the book, but that is the main focus."

The woman turned the book over and studied the back cover, which gave an overview of what was inside. Next, she flipped through several pages. "This looks quite interesting. Would you mind if I hold on to it for now and get back to you with my answer in a few days?"

"Well, umm. . .we may not be in the area that long." Sadie glanced at her mother.

"I think we can stay a few days before moving on," Mom said. "Sadie, why don't you give her one of the cards you made up with your name and phone number on it?"

"Yes, yes, of course." Sadie fumbled in her purse for one of the cards. *I feel like a child right now, barely able to think for myself. I'm glad Mom came on this trip with me. Don't think I could have done it alone. By myself, I'd probably say all the wrong things or not think of anything sensible to say at all.*

"I see you've included some scripture verses, like here on this page." The store manager pointed. "Is there a reason you added those?"

"Yes, when my friends and I visited the Hawaiian Islands a few years ago, we were impressed with how at most of the luaus, a prayer was said before the meal. Also, many of the Hawaiian people we met talked about their belief in God." Sadie's confidence grew as she spoke more about the book and the reasons behind each of the things she'd included.

"Since there are a few Bible verses and apparently some reference to Christianity, you may want to see if the Christian bookstore in town would be interested in selling your book."

Sadie moistened her lips, feeling cautious hope. "Thank you for the suggestion."

The woman glanced at the clock on the far wall. "I hate to cut this short, but it's time for the quilt shop to open, so I need to put the sign in the window and prepare to greet customers this morning."

Sadie shook the manager's hand and said she'd look forward to hearing from her in a few days.

As she and Mom left the building, a question popped into her head. *Should I call the Christian bookstore first or just make a trip over there unannounced?*

✳

That evening, as Sadie and her mother relaxed in their hotel room, Sadie got a call on the prepaid cell phone she'd purchased before leaving Indiana. Since they'd be gone a week or two, it wouldn't have been fair to ask Wyman to loan her his phone again, so the prepaid option worked best.

When Sadie answered the phone, she was pleased to hear Wyman's voice.

"Hi, Sadie. I've been wondering about you and called to see how things are going on your trip." He spoke rapidly, and she sensed an air of apprehension in his tone.

"Mom and I are fine. We visited a few stores in Holmes County today. Some places seemed like they might be interested in selling my books. None of them gave a definite answer, but they all said they would call and let me know."

"That's good. Do you know when you'll be coming home?"

"Probably not for a few weeks. We're just getting started, and we still plan to go to Pennsylvania to speak to some of the bookstores, quilt shops, and gift store owners there."

"I see." There was a pause before Wyman spoke again. "I miss you, Sadie."

"I miss you too."

"Sure wish you could find a way to sell your books without traipsing all over the country to visit stores."

Sadie rolled her eyes. "We're not going all over the country, Wyman— just some high tourist areas in Ohio and Pennsylvania. I thought I'd explained that when I called you the day before I left home."

"Guess you did, but anyplace other than here seems like a long way, and I—"

"Sorry, Wyman, but I'm getting another call. It might be important, so I'd better see who it is. We can talk again in a few days, okay?"

"Okay, sure, whatever you say."

Sadie heard the disappointment in his voice, but in case the other call was from one of the owners or managers of the stores they'd visited today, she didn't want to miss the opportunity to speak to them.

"I'll talk to you later, Wyman. Bye." Sadie clicked off, but when she tried to access the other caller, she realized that she had apparently hung up on them, for there was no one on the line.

"Oh, great."

"What is, Sadie?" Mom looked up from the magazine she'd been reading. "Did Wyman say something to disappoint you?"

"No, but another call came in while we were talking and I must have hung up on them."

"I'm sure whoever it was will call again."

"I hope so. If it was someone from one of the stores we visited today, I'd like to talk to them."

The phone rang again, and Sadie answered in haste. "Hello."

"Hi Sadie, it's your daed. Is your mamm free to talk?"

"Jah, she is, but. . ." Sadie wanted to tell her father that she didn't want to tie up the phone in case one of the stores tried to call, but she couldn't do that to Mom. No doubt she'd be eager to hear from Dad, and he was most likely looking forward to talking to her. "Mom's right here. I'll give her the phone."

Sadie handed the cell phone to her mother and then went to the bedroom to give Mom some privacy. Since most of the store managers they'd spoken to today said they'd get back to her in a day or so, none of them would probably call tonight anyway. She needed more patience.

✳

Grace laid the magazine down while she spoke to her husband. "Good evening, Calvin. I'm glad you called. I was just thinking about you and the girls."

"Hi. How are things going there?"

"All right. Today Sadie and I went around to the bookstores, gift shops, and quilt shops here in town. The manager of the quilt shop we spoke to suggested that we speak to the owners of the Christian bookstore. Since there are some scriptures and mentions of the Lord, it could appeal to

Christian readers. This might expand the playing field for Sadie to get her books accepted in some of the businesses."

"Makes sense to me."

"It was a long day, and I sure got my quota of steps in."

Calvin cleared his throat. "How much longer till you and Sadie will be coming home?"

"As I mentioned before we left home, we'll probably be gone a few weeks."

"I was hoping you might come home sooner."

"Is something the matter?" Judging from the tone of her husband's voice, Grace wondered if there might be a problem at home.

"I don't like to complain, because it makes me seem ungrateful, but—"

"What's wrong, Calvin?"

"I'm already tired of the girls' cooking."

"You are? Why's that?"

"The suppers they've fixed so far haven't been nearly as tasty as yours."

Grace lifted her gaze to the ceiling. Since they'd been married, Calvin had never wanted anyone to take care of him but her. Maybe Grace catered to him a little too much, but she liked to keep her husband happy. It was hard not to feel a bit prideful over his disliking of the girls' attempt at cooking their evening meals. But she'd hoped her daughters would have learned more of the ins and outs of good home cooking from her. When she returned home, she'd have to give them a refresher course on adding the proper amounts of seasonings to certain recipes to enhance the flavors.

"I'm sorry you're not happy with the suppers they've made for you, but I'm sure they've done their best."

"I suppose. Just wish they'd try a little harder. Seems to me that they've both got their minds somewhere else."

Grace looked over her shoulder to check for Sadie. "Maybe you could see if Saul's wife would have you over for some suppers to give the girls a break."

"That would help things out. She is a good cook. Can I complain to you a little more, Grace?"

"All right, go ahead."

"It's about my lunches. I've been forcing myself to eat the sandwiches the girls have made, and I have to say—they are flat tasting and dry compared to yours."

"I have an answer for that. Ask the girls to make your sandwiches with softened butter or plenty of mayonnaise spread on each slice of bread. That should help."

"Okay."

"When you explain to Jana Beth and Kaylene what you expect them to fix, please try to say it in a pleasant way. We don't want to hurt their feelings."

"I'll do my best."

"Other than the girls' lack of cooking skills, how's everything else going there?" Grace asked.

"About the same—nothing new, except that I took Sadie's horse, Lady, out today instead of using my horse or yours. That animal was sure eager to go. I had to hold her back at times."

"Lady doesn't get much attention, and she has a good deal of spirit in her that will hopefully wear off. That's why I prefer using Annabelle, my docile mare."

"I understand. Say, I looked at some brochures the other day of Pinecraft. I've been thinking we should go there one of these days like many snowbirds do."

"That would be fun."

"Wouldn't it? Maybe we could plan a trip sometime in the future and take the family along."

"I agree."

Grace could tell her husband missed her, the way he continued to find things to talk about. It reminded her of their courting days, when they didn't want the time to end, knowing they'd have to go their separate ways for a while.

"I suppose I've kept you on the phone long enough, plus I'm sitting in this overly warm shed, and it's losing its luster."

She chuckled. "No doubt that old, hard seat is uncomfortable to sit on after a while. In any case I should let you go."

"Okay, have a good night, and I hope things go well for you and Sadie during the rest of your trip. I miss you both."

"We miss you and the girls too. Please give them our love."

"I will. Good night, Grace."

"Good night, Calvin." Grace clicked off the phone and set it aside. *I don't want to spoil things for my daughter. She's trying hard to do this, and I want to be supportive of her, but I sure miss home.*

She continued to sit in silence. There'd been times when she'd wished Sadie had not written a book. But Grace had come to realize that she needed to accept and support her daughter's endeavor, which was why she'd agreed to accompany Sadie on this trip.

Grace closed her eyes. *Lord, please help us find some stores that would be willing to sell her books, so we can return to Indiana, where hopefully things can get back to normal for all of us.*

Chapter 30

Bird-in-Hand, Pennsylvania

$\mathcal{J}$hings went fairly well today, don't you think?" Sadie's mother asked as they ate supper at the Bird-in-Hand Family Restaurant. They'd loaded their plates with a variety of tasty foods at the buffet table.

Sadie shrugged. "I guess so, but I had hoped for a little better response from the stores we went to."

Mom blotted her lips with a napkin. "Two of the quilt shops gave a favorable reply."

"But they only took ten copies of my books on consignment. That's not very favorable to me." Sadie's gaze flitted around the room. "I wish the manager of this restaurant had been here this evening so I could ask if she might be interested in selling some of my books on the racks we saw in the front entryway when we came in."

"We can check back with them tomorrow morning." Mom gave Sadie one of her hopeful smiles. "Or at the very least, you could give them a call."

"I suppose." Sadie fingered the knife lying beside her plate. "I thought writing the book was difficult, but going around and trying to promote it is even harder."

"Jah, but then, all good things take time."

"I'll admit, I'm not very patient. It's an area in my life I need to work on."

Mom nodded. "We all do, Daughter. Everyone gets discouraged and impatient at times."

It felt good to let down somewhat at the restaurant as Sadie and her mother filled their stomachs. They'd been speaking in Pennsylvania Dutch most of the time, to keep the conversation more intimate for themselves around the English people who sat nearby.

Sadie stifled a yawn. "I'm exhausted. When we get back to the room it will be nice to relax for the rest of the evening."

"I agree, and I'm debating about whether I should take advantage of that jetted tub in our room." Mom took a sip of her iced tea.

"You should do it. Why not pamper yourself once in a while?" Sadie glanced to her right when she heard the young woman who had waited on their table speaking to another waitress. She tried not to make herself obvious but couldn't help hearing their conversation. Apparently, the young woman needed five hundred dollars to repair her car. Tearfully, she told the other waitress that she didn't have that much money and wasn't sure how she would get to work each morning without a vehicle. She'd been fortunate today to have a friend drop her off, but that friend was moving out of town and wouldn't be available to help her in the future.

I should do something to help out. When the two women stopped talking and moved toward the kitchen, Sadie looked back at Mom.

"What are you thinking about, Daughter? Your boyfriend, perhaps?"

"Uh, no, not at the moment, but I do miss being able to spend time with Wyman." Sadie drummed her knuckles on the table. "Whenever we're together, he doesn't seem to understand the amount of stress I'm under or have any interest in what I'm trying to accomplish."

Mom finished her piece of ham before responding. "You could try speaking to Wyman in an understanding way and convey to him the amount of hard work it takes to do this."

"I don't think he cares. Wyman hasn't been acting like himself lately. Who knows what's rolling around inside his head."

"You did admit to me that you're under stress. Maybe that's coming through in the way you respond to him. Or he may just have other things on his mind. Try not to read too much into the matter." Mom gestured to

Sadie's plate. "And please try to enjoy the rest of your food."

Sadie's troubled thoughts continued to twist around in her head. It wasn't only her relationship with Wyman that had Sadie concerned. Her sisters, and even Mom and Dad, had distanced themselves from her at times. *Or maybe I'm the one who's distanced myself from them,* she pondered. *My life has been super busy since my books arrived, and it probably doesn't help that all those boxes I received are still piled up all over our house.*

Sadie forked a bite of mashed potatoes with gravy. *When Mom and I go home, I'll see about buying a storage shed to store the boxes in.*

Mom offered Sadie a dimpled grin. "How about when we're finished eating, we take a walk through the gift shop? Maybe we'll find something to bring back to our family."

"Okay."

Sadie's cell phone rang, and she pulled it from her purse. In so doing, a card that must have been at the bottom came to the surface. "Well, for goodness' sake."

"What is it?" Mom leaned slightly forward.

"It's the card I thought I lost—the one with Clara Williams's phone number on it. Remember—she's the woman who said she could help promote my book?"

"Jah, I remember, and I'm glad you found her card, but don't you think you should answer the phone? It could be important."

Sadie held the phone to her ear and responded to the call. "Hello."

"Hi, is this Susan?"

"No, I'm sorry, you must have the wrong number."

"Okay." *Click!*

"Who was it?" Mom asked when Sadie put the phone back in her purse.

"I have no idea. They asked for Susan."

Mom gave a small laugh. "Wrong numbers do occur, even on the recorded voice messages some people leave on our machine in the phone shed at home. By the way. . .when we've finished eating, I'd like to use your phone. I want to call home and leave a message. Maybe someone there will call us back and we can see how things are going. Besides, your father appreciates me checking in and letting him know how we're doing. Sure don't want him to worry about us."

"Uh-huh." Sadie studied the card she'd found in her purse. Tomorrow morning, Clara would be the first person she'd call. If there was a chance that she could help Sadie's book to sell, it would be worth it.

Better yet, Sadie thought, *I'll give Clara a call when we get back to the hotel this evening. In the meantime, though, I'm going to seek out our waitress and give her the money she needs.*

✳

Middlebury

Jana Beth opened the oven door to check on the meat loaf she'd made for supper this evening. "I hope this meal is to Dad's liking. It smells good, and it's browning up nicely." She glanced across the room to where Kaylene stood peeling potatoes. "He's sure been picky since Mom and Sadie have been gone. It feels like months instead of days have passed since they left home."

Kaylene shook her head and muttered, "Tell me about it. We've been stuck with everything, and Dad's been so grumpy—complaining about our cooking and comparing everything we make to the way Mom fixes it."

"We are not our mother." Jana Beth gave a huff. "I hope they come home soon. There has been too much hubbub in this house since our sister took on the project of writing her book. I'm not happy with the negative comments we get after our attempts at cooking suppers either."

"Same here. It's not much fun being in charge of the cooking and cleaning—especially when we get so little appreciation for our efforts."

Jana Beth breathed deeply of the fragrant aroma coming from the oven. "If the meat loaf tastes even half as good as it smells, then I don't see how Dad can have any complaints."

Kaylene blew an errant hair off her forehead. "I'll make sure the potatoes are extra creamy, with plenty of butter and milk when it's time to mash them."

"We'd better be prepared, though. As hard as we've both tried to make a pleasing supper, our daed may find something to complain about."

Kaylene groaned. "I hope not. It's hard to put up with all his grumbling. Makes me think I never want to get married."

Jana Beth shrugged. "Not all men are grumblers, you know. For the most part, our daed's kind and polite about things. I think it's mostly that he misses Mom so much."

"You're probably right, because I'm missing her too." Kaylene set the kettle of potatoes on the stove and turned on the gas burner. "These should be ready to mash about the time the meat loaf is done."

"Do we have much ketchup in the refrigerator?"

"Why are you wondering about that?"

"Well, I had a thought. Before the meat loaf is done maybe we could brush some ketchup on the top of it to give more flavor."

"I suppose we could try it. What do we have to lose?"

"At least we have our sister-in-law's dessert that she dropped by after we got home from work." Kaylene picked up the dishcloth and wiped off the counter.

"What did Saul's wife make for us?"

"A chocolate cream pie."

"Yum, I can almost taste it." Jana Beth licked her lips.

"Rebecca's a good cook, that's for sure. I think when our mom gets home from the trip I'm going to start paying closer attention to how she cooks our meals."

"I probably should too."

Jana Beth got out the dishes and silverware to set the kitchen table. "I wonder how Wyman is doing in Sadie's absence. He sure seemed upset when he found out she was going to Ohio and Pennsylvania and hadn't told him about it."

"But she did call him the night before she and Mom left."

"True, although I would have thought she'd have given him some advance notice." Jana Beth blinked rapidly. "If I had a boyfriend as good looking as Wyman, I wouldn't do anything to ruffle his feathers or make him think I didn't care. Our sister seems to have a one-track mind lately, and it's all about her book."

✳

"Are you feeling all right, Son?" Mom asked as Wyman sat at the supper table with his parents.

"I'm okay. Why do you ask?"

"You haven't had any seconds." She gestured to the platter of ham. "Normally you'd eat two or three pieces."

"My appetite's diminished this evening," he admitted.

"How come? Aren't you feeling well?"

"He's probably pining for his aldi, and it's taken his appetite away." Dad looked at Wyman.

"Now, Ernest, don't start teasing our son. He has every right to miss his girlfriend. You remember our courting days and how we always wanted to be together. One time when I was with my folks visiting my uncle and aunt in Ohio, you became upset because we were gone longer than anticipated."

"Oh yeah, I was lonesome as a pup taken from its mother while you were away." He grinned at Mom and winked.

"I do miss Sadie," Wyman conceded, "but I'm also struggling not to worry."

"Are you worried about her safety as she travels around trying to promote her book?" Dad questioned.

"That's part of it." Wyman shifted in his chair. He wished the topic of Sadie and her book had never been brought up.

"What's the other part?" Mom asked.

"I'm concerned that the longer she's gone, the more chance there will be of her losing interest in me." There, it was out. Wyman felt better for saying the words. Truth was, with each passing day he became more concerned about his relationship with Sadie and worried that if she became too wrapped up in promoting her book, she might never want to settle down and marry. *Of course, I need to ask her first.*

Mom reached over and patted Wyman's hand. "If it's meant for you and Sadie to be together, it'll work out."

Dad smiled. "There is also the saying, 'Absence makes the heart grow fonder.' Maybe you should try to be more patient."

"I've been trying to, but I'm not succeeding."

Mom patted him again. "You've got to do what feels best inside. You'll know if things are right when the time comes."

He managed a nod, but inwardly, Wyman had a horrible feeling that the relationship he and Sadie once had was nearing an end.

✳

Bird-in-Hand

Back at the hotel, Sadie gave Mom her phone and listened as she left a lengthy message for Dad.

Sadie stepped into the washroom to freshen up. When she returned to the other room, Mom rose from her chair. "Here's your phone back. Think I'm going to relax in that tub now."

Sadie smiled. "Go right ahead. I'm done in the bathroom."

"I hope your call to Mrs. Williams goes well."

"Thanks." Sadie watched her mom disappear into the other room and then got comfortable while placing her call. Sadie felt pleased when the kindly woman said she would do all she could through her blog and other online sites to promote Sadie's new book. She also suggested that Sadie try to schedule some book signings or speaking engagements to get the word out about her book.

Sadie realized all this might keep her busy and that there would be little time for courting or spending quality time with her family. Even so, she was determined to see this through.

Who knows, Sadie thought as she prepared for bed, *if things go well, I might be able to make a trip to Hawaii and promote my book there. Surely there would be some visitors to the islands who'd be interested in reading a book such as mine.*

Chapter 31

*I*n the month since Sadie and her mother had been home, she'd begun to feel like her world had been turned upside down. Thanks to her blogger friend's posts and social media mentions, Sadie had been getting a lot of direct-to-consumer orders for her book. Packaging them up and getting them mailed out kept her busy enough, but now more bookstores had requested copies of her book. Sadie had purchased a storage shed recently, so that helped with getting the boxes of books out of the house at least. She'd also gotten several requests to visit stores for book signings and to speak about the book and her travels to Hawaii. This evening she would be speaking at a library in Fort Wayne and signing copies of her book that she'd brought along.

As Sadie sat at the kitchen table, autographing a stack of books that needed to be mailed that day, she paused to flex her fingers. *I hope things go well this evening, and that I don't make a fool of myself during my speech. What if my nerves get the best of me, and I choke up? Or what happens if someone asks me a question about Hawaii and I don't know the answer?* Sadie's heart beat a little faster than usual. *I wish Mandy could be there with me. She'd know what to say and could probably answer most any question that might be asked.*

Thoughts of Mandy caused Sadie to remember the last phone call she'd received from her friend. Mandy had said she felt better these days, and that it was good to have Ken's mother home from California again. Sadie hoped everything would go well with her friend's pregnancy this time.

"Did you get all the books signed so I can help you package them up for the post office?" Mom asked when she entered the kitchen, breaking into Sadie's contemplations.

"Not yet. I still have a few left to do." Sadie gestured to the books she hadn't autographed. "I sidetracked myself when I started thinking about my event this evening, and how I should respond if someone asks a question I don't know the answer to."

"If you don't know how to answer, then just smile and say it's something you're not sure of. There's no crime in that, you know."

"You're right, but I still get *naerfich* thinking about it."

"There's no need to feel nervous. I'm sure you'll do fine." Mom took a seat at the table. "Speaking of tonight's event. . .I just came from the phone shed and found a message for you from Wyman."

Sadie sat up straight. "Did he say if he was planning to go to Fort Wayne with me this evening?"

Mom stared at Sadie's books. "Wyman said he won't be able to make it."

"How come?"

"He didn't offer an explanation."

Sadie's shoulders slumped. "Since we've only seen each other a couple of times in the last two weeks, I figured he'd be eager to go along. We'd have plenty of time to talk on the ride down there and again on the trip back home." She fingered the embossed title on one of her books. "It would be nice to have help hauling the boxes of books in and out of the library too."

"Your driver said he would do that. And since your daed and I have other plans for this evening, you could ask one of your sisters to go along to help out."

Sadie shook her head. "The event starts at five o'clock, and we'll have to leave before Jana Beth or Kaylene gets off work, so there was no point in inviting them to go."

Mom reached over and gave Sadie's shoulder a tender squeeze. "You'll be fine with your driver's help."

"Jah, but it won't be the same as having Wyman with me." Sadie lowered her gaze. "I thought he'd enjoy hearing me speak, but I guess I was wrong."

"Things aren't going well for you and Wyman these days, are they?" Mom spoke in a sympathetic tone.

"I'm afraid not. He still isn't supportive and doesn't understand my need to let people know about the book I wrote." Sadie heaved a heavy sigh. "In fact, I think he's jealous of the time I spend contacting bookstores and preparing for signings and speaking engagements."

Mom picked up one of the books and placed it inside a padded envelope. Sadie had to wonder if her mother might be on Wyman's side. Mom hadn't said so, but Sadie suspected that she might think too much emphasis had been placed on her book and not enough on nurturing the relationship between her and Wyman.

There will be plenty of time for that once things quiet down, Sadie thought. *Bookstores, quilt shops, and libraries won't always be asking me to do signings or speaking engagements. When I have more free time again, Wyman and I can pick up where we left off in our courtship.*

✳

Wyman figured Sadie would be bummed about his decision not to go to her signing, but it was the way he felt. The reasons for his unhappiness ranged from Sadie's climb to wealth with the inheritance and the fact that her book dominated most of her waking hours.

Wyman was barely guiding his horse down the road, because he was thinking too heavily on his and Sadie's relationship. Benny had slowed to a slow walk, and Wyman didn't even care.

I'm not happy with how our courting has slowed to a crawl. My horse has more get-up-and-go than I do right now. He jiggled the reins, and Benny came to life. *I'm sure anyone would be on my side regarding my choice to stay away from Sadie's book signing this evening. Anyway, she's probably found someone else to help her haul in the books. That's most likely the main reason she invited me to go with her—not because she wanted to spend time with me. It would be hard to sit and listen to Sadie talk about her book. I've already heard more than I care to know.*

Truthfully, Wyman hadn't wanted her to write the book. He could see from the day she'd decided to take on the project that it was going to affect their relationship.

He shook his head. *It's strange how a material item can dominate someone's life. I wonder why Sadie can't see it too.*

Wyman had hoped things would be back to normal by now, but maybe it wasn't meant to be.

His vision blurred, and he wiped the sweat pouring off his forehead. Or was the moisture partially his tears? *I don't want to end our courtship, but Sadie's changed so much, and I don't think we have much of a chance anymore.*

✳

Fort Wayne, Indiana

A wave of heat washed over Sadie as she stood in front of a wooden podium at the front of a sizable room in the library. Several rows of chairs had been set out and were filled with people looking at her expectantly. Was what she'd planned to say good enough for this event? Sadie needed to speak for a certain length of time. She had rehearsed at home and written down several items to talk about. But now, so many doubts raced around in her head as she stood holding three-by-five cards in her sweaty palms.

Lord, please give me the courage to do this and put the right words in my mouth. Her knees felt weak as she clutched a copy of her book in the other hand while leaning against the podium for needed support. The microphone stood poised and ready as she leaned into it to speak. "I appreciate you all coming out this evening." Sadie paused for a moment and took a deep breath. "I'd like to tell you a little about my book, and then I'll open it up for questions."

It was strange to hear the sound of her own voice booming through the speakers. Sadie had finally made it—she stood, unbelieving, promoting her first book in front of a good-sized audience, and now she needed to get through this ordeal without any hiccups or embarrassing moments.

Sadie looked at her first card to make sure she stayed on track. She began by telling a little about the trip she'd taken with Ellen, Mandy, and Barbara. Then she talked about her quilting and how she'd come up with the idea to make a blended quilt.

Pausing for a moment, Sadie set the book and notecards aside and reached into the tote bag she'd brought along. When she withdrew her quilted wall hanging, there were several oohs and aahs from the audience as she opened the quilt and held it in front of her. Sadie continued to hold it while she explained what the patterns were and talked about the similarities between Amish and Hawaiian quilt patterns.

A latecomer entered the room and took a seat near the back. Sadie felt relieved seeing it was her blogger friend. It was nice to see a familiar face and know she had the support of this helpful, pleasant woman.

Sadie draped the wall hanging over the back of a chair and talked for a few more minutes about some things she'd discovered among the Hawaiian people that reminded her of the Plain people's simple lifestyle.

Once Sadie mentioned everything she could think of, she opened the meeting up for questions. She felt relieved to be finished with the first half of the event. Sadie now hoped the questions and answers would pose no problems.

A young English man sitting in the first row of chairs raised his hand. Sadie nodded in his direction and smiled. "Do you have a question?"

"Yes. I would like to know if you are a member of the Amish church, or are you still on *rumspringa*?"

"I'm a church member. I joined soon after my friends and I returned home from our trip to Hawaii."

"So if you weren't a church member, how come you went there on a cruise ship rather than flying? Wouldn't you have been allowed to fly if you'd wanted to?" the same man asked.

"I suppose we could have, but we thought taking the cruise would be more of an adventure, and we'd be able to see some important things on each of the four major islands."

An elderly woman raised her hand, so Sadie called on her.

"Did you learn any Hawaiian words while you were in Hawaii?"

Sadie nodded. "A few, like *aloha*, which is commonly used as a greeting for 'hello' or 'goodbye.' We also learned how to say 'thank you,' which is *mahalo*."

Several other people asked questions, including a few more from the young English fellow. He was the only man in attendance. It seemed a bit odd to Sadie that he'd be taking an interest in her quilt and the book she'd written.

When it came time for Sadie to sign books, the librarian in charge of the event led the way to a table where her books had been set out. She was also given a pen for signing, as well as a bottle of water.

Sadie's throat felt parched, so she took a few sips from the bottle before speaking to the first person in line. It wasn't easy adapting to this new part of being an author. She didn't have someone by her side who could show her the ropes and give some needed reassurance. But at least Clara, who'd come here this evening and waited off to the side, had given her a thumbs-up.

Sadie still wished Wyman could've been with her this evening, or her mother, for that matter. Her driver sat in the back of the room scrolling on his phone, waiting to haul the leftover books back to his van once the event ended. This wasn't how she'd envisioned her first big engagement, but Sadie had no control over it. She would simply do her best to get through it.

"Thank you for coming tonight." She smiled at the middle-aged woman. "Would you like me to personalize my autograph or just sign my name?" Sadie would not have known exactly what to say if Clara hadn't given her a sense of direction when they'd talked on the phone the other day. On her own and being so new at something like this, she would have been even more nervous than she was.

As more people came through the line, and Sadie spoke a few words to each one, she felt herself begin to relax. This was actually kind of fun, and it had been a great experience for her. If she got more invitations to speak or sign books, she wouldn't feel so apprehensive. Slowly, the rest of the people came through the line, and before long she was nearly finished. Everyone was kind and polite, which made Sadie feel more comfortable.

The last person in line was the young English fellow. He stepped up to the table, grabbed a book from the pile, and placed it in front of Sadie.

"Would you like it personalized?" she asked.

"Nope. Just sign your name. That's good enough."

"Oh, okay."

While Sadie autographed the book, he leaned closer—so close that his head almost touched hers. "I have a few more questions I didn't get the chance to ask. Would you mind answering them for me?"

Before Sadie could form a response, he added, "Maybe we could go someplace for a cup of coffee. There's a restaurant not too far from here."

Sadie stiffened. *I'm not feeling comfortable with this person.*

"Sorry, but Sadie's answered enough questions this evening," Clara intervened. She stepped up to the table and handed him her business card. "If you want to know anything else about Sadie's book, you can email me, and I'll get a message to Sadie and get back to you with her answer."

Frowning, he took the card and clasped the signed book in his hands. "Okay. Whatever you say." He stepped away from the table but then turned back around, lifted his cell phone, and snapped a picture. Before Sadie had the presence of mind to say anything, he turned and sauntered out the door.

A cold chill ran up her spine. *Who is this man, and why was he so persistent? Was he really that interested in my book, or could he be a reporter? I hope there's not a picture of me in tomorrow's paper.*

Chapter 32

Middlebury

Sadie sat on the front porch, waiting for Wyman. He'd called yesterday and left a message, saying he'd be coming by this evening to see her.

Maybe he wants to apologize for not going to Fort Wayne with me two evenings ago. Sadie frowned. *He should have been there. I needed his support and encouragement.*

She'd been over this so many times, it was like a revolving door. While it was true that she and Wyman didn't see each other as much as they had previously, when they were together he seemed sort of detached and didn't even ask how things were going with the sale of her book. His disinterest fueled Sadie's concern. Their relationship was crumbling, and she felt powerless to stop it.

Sadie's attention was drawn to the road when she heard the unmistakable sound of a horse and buggy. She continued to watch as it approached the driveway. Sure enough, it was Wyman's spotless rig.

Rather than wait on the porch, she walked out to the hitching rail to greet him.

"*Guder owed,*" Sadie said when Wyman got out of his buggy. "It's nice to see you."

"Good evening." Wyman glanced at her then looked away as he secured his horse to the rail.

Something was wrong. Sadie sensed it by his cool tone of voice. *Maybe he's working up to saying he's sorry for skipping out on my signing a couple of days ago.*

"I felt bad that you couldn't go to my signing event at the library in Fort Wayne the other night." She took a step closer to him.

"Yeah, well, I figured there was no point in me going, since you'd be occupied most of the evening."

"We could have visited in the van, and it would have been nice to have you there. Maybe you can go to my next signing, which will be at the library in Goshen this Saturday."

Wyman looked down at the ground then back at Sadie. "How many more events are you planning to do to promote your book?"

Sadie's forehead wrinkled. "I'm not sure at this point. Clara Williams, my blogger friend, is working on my schedule for the summer months and possibly into the fall. She hasn't given me an updated list yet, so I can't answer your question."

"I see." Wyman folded his arms. "This isn't working for us, is it?"

"Wh—what do you mean?"

"Clear back when you first made that blended quilt, your feelings for me started to change."

Sadie shook her head. "No, they didn't."

"Well, maybe not your feelings, but the amount of time you were willing to spend with me got less and less."

She opened her mouth to respond, but he held up one hand. "Please, hear me out."

"Okay."

"While you were writing the book and later when you began to promote it, you were too busy for me." Wyman's words were rushed. "Even during the few times we were together, all you ever talked about was your book, the quilt, or Hawaii. You didn't seem interested in me or the things I enjoy doing—many of which we used to do together."

"I am still interested in you, Wyman. It's just that—"

"You're too busy for me now."

Sadie saw the tension in his neck and shoulders and wondered what she could say to smooth things over and make him understand.

"I'm sorry if I let you down. If you'd just try to understand that I—"

"It's over between us, Sadie. Your life has taken a new direction, and I don't fit in." His sharp tone cut deep.

"That's not true, Wyman."

"Jah, it is. You're a successful, not to mention wealthy, woman who's written a book and now has readers who want to meet you and get their books autographed." He touched his chest. "I'm just an ordinary fellow working at my daed's feed store, and I'll never be anything more than that."

"I've never thought of you as ordinary, and I just think—"

He shook his head. "Unless you change your mind about running all over the place to tell others about your book, it's time for us to go our separate ways."

You're asking me to give up something I feel is important. Tears gathered in the corners of Sadie's eyes and threatened to spill over. "You can't mean that. There has to be some way we can work things out."

"You can give up your silly notion of becoming famous."

Her heart ached, and she needed to protect herself from any more harm. Heat flushed throughout Sadie's body, and her fingers curled into the palms of her hands. "I am not trying to become famous, and I can't believe you would say such a thing!"

"Okay, well, maybe you're not focused on being famous, but it seems to me that you've become selfish—always thinking about yourself."

Sadie stiffened. *Was I selfish when I gave my sisters money to buy their horses? And what about the time I gave five hundred dollars to the waitress at the Bird-in-Hand Family Restaurant? That was not a selfish act.* Of course, Wyman knew nothing about any of that. It wasn't like Sadie to tell others or brag about her good deeds, and she saw no reason to tell him now.

"You're right, Wyman," she said in a near whisper. "It's probably for the best that we go our separate ways, since we don't seem to see eye to eye on anything these days." Holding back the sob rising in her throat, Sadie turned and dashed for the house.

✳

When he returned home, Wyman unhitched the horse and led the animal into the barn. While removing the harness and bridle, his thoughts took over. *Michael and Lovina are doing well these days. I've heard my brother go on and on about how wonderful their marriage is since they went for counseling.*

He tossed the horse's gear up on the hook. *Meanwhile, I'm miserable, alone, and left wanting a relationship that didn't work out for me. Is having someone to love too much to ask for?*

Wyman walked his horse into the stall and closed the door. Taking time to collect his thoughts, Wyman grabbed the hoof pick and got busy cleaning out Benny's hooves. "It looks like you've got a small stone in this first one. At least it didn't bother you while we were out today." He cleaned out the frog, released the leg, and was pleased to see that his horse stood fine.

Wyman finished taking care of the feet and moved on to brush his horse's coat. It was a chore to do some days, but right now the peaceful chewing sound Benny made seemed soothing.

He continued to brush until he'd had enough. "Okay, boy. You're taken care of for now." He stepped out from the stall and headed into the house.

Wyman came in through the kitchen and stopped at the sink to wash his hands. On the counter sat a glass container full of cookies his mother had made. After drying his hands, he grabbed two out of the jar and closed it. *This won't stop the hurt in my heart, but Mom's baking might satisfy my longing for something sweet.*

Wyman ate his treat and headed for the living room. He found his mother in her chair, mending a vest that belonged to Dad. "How'd it go? Did you see or talk to Sadie?" she asked.

Wyman plopped down in a soft chair. "I did, and we are no longer an item. We've broken up as of today."

"Sorry to hear this, but maybe it's for the best."

"What's for the best?" Dad scooted in and took a seat.

"Our son has broken up with the Kuhns girl."

"I see. Are you all right with that?" He looked at Wyman. "I mean, you two have been together for a while, and I figured by now things would be getting serious—maybe even a wedding in your future."

"I'd hoped for that too, but things have been unraveling for Sadie and me for some time. We've spent more time apart than together lately, and it's gotten worse with those book signings she's expected to do. Sadie's just too busy for me these days."

"Are you sure about this, Son?"

"Jah, Dad. I've tried to be patient, gain Sadie's approval, and prove to her that I can be dependable. But where did it get me?" Wyman shook his head. "It's all been for nothing, and that's the truth."

His parents remained silent while Wyman continued to rant. "Sadie needs to come down off her high horse and live a normal, Plain life again." Wyman stared down at his feet. "I didn't want to break up with her, but I couldn't keep taking this crummy treatment from her."

His parents nodded, and then Dad spoke again. "Whatever happens in the future, we will support your decision."

"I'm sorry, Wyman. Your heart is obviously breaking, and you deserve better than this." Mom spoke softly but with feeling.

"Danki for hearing me out. I'm going up to my room now to take it easy the rest of the evening." Wyman strode out of the room. He still loved Sadie, and his days without her would be empty.

*

Goshen, Indiana

Saturday evening when Sadie entered the library with Clara Williams, she was surprised to see another large crowd of people seated and waiting for her arrival. Although she didn't feel quite as nervous as she had at the

Fort Wayne event, Sadie's heart wasn't in it. All she could think about was Wyman, and the fact that they'd broken up. Could the things he'd accused her of possibly be true?

I need to put this out of my mind—at least for tonight, she told herself. *These folks came to hear about my book, so I'll put on a happy face and share with them, like I did the other night.*

Sadie stood with Clara near her signing table until the librarian in charge introduced her. Then, to help keep her mind on track, Sadie grabbed the cards out of her handbag from the time before. Stepping up to the podium, Sadie began her speech. When she'd said everything on her agenda, Sadie asked the audience if they had any questions. Several hands went up, and she patiently answered each one.

Several seconds passed before another hand shot up. Sadie was surprised to see that it was the same young man who'd been at her Fort Wayne signing. It seemed a bit odd that he'd be at this event too. The man seemed rather peculiar, and it caused Sadie to tense up. *Why is he back? I hope Clara will say something to him again if he gets out of line.*

"What is your question?" she asked.

"I'm curious about the Amish way of life and am wondering if you've ever considered giving up your quaint, old-fashioned way of living and becoming English, as you Plain folks like to call those of us who are not Amish."

Since the man's question had nothing to do with her book and was of a personal nature, Sadie didn't know how to answer, or even if she should. She wondered if it would be possible to bypass this question and say nothing at all. But that would be rude. Sadie felt that she ought to give him some kind of a response.

Sadie cleared her throat. "To answer your question, sir, I have never considered leaving the Amish faith and going English."

"Not even once?"

Sadie felt a tightness in her chest, and she drew a quick breath and released it before speaking. "No, not even once."

"Okay, then I have another question. Did you ever go wild during your running around years, before you joined the church?"

A flush of heat traveled from Sadie's neck up to her face. The questions this man asked had nothing to do with her book, and it frustrated her.

"I think we should stick to the topic at hand," the librarian intervened. "Sadie is here to talk about her quilt, the book, and offer information about Hawaii, not discuss her personal life."

"Okay, whatever." The man slumped in his chair.

Sadie answered questions from several other people until it was time to sit at the signing table. Most everyone in attendance had purchased a book. As the line went down, she spotted the young English man moving toward her table. *Oh no, not again. I hope he doesn't have more personal questions for me to answer. I'm feeling stressed out. I wish he hadn't come here this evening.* She looked toward Clara, who stood talking to the librarian. She hoped they would say something if this fellow got out of line.

His turn came a few minutes later; when he stepped up to the table, he leaned in close to her. "Sorry if I embarrassed you with my questions. I'm just curious about the Amish way of life and want to know more, that's all."

"There are some books you can buy or check out here in the library that include information about the Amish way of life," she responded.

"I'm well aware, but reading about it is not the same as getting firsthand information." His dark eyes appeared as if they could bore a hole through Sadie as he stared at her for several seconds. She wished she could just blink her eyes and disappear.

Before she could think of anything intelligent to say, he pulled out his cell phone and took a picture. "Thanks for your time, Sadie." He gave a quick wink and hurried off.

Clara moved away from the librarian and came up to Sadie. "Wasn't that the same man who attended your last signing?"

"Yes, it was."

"I was listening to your conversation, and he was rude. If that young man hadn't stopped bothering you with his unrelated questions I would have asked him to leave."

Sadie smiled. She appreciated the interest and the support this dear lady had offered.

Sadie's lips pressed tightly together. *Too bad Wyman doesn't care about me anymore. I'm sure he would have put that young man in his place if we were still courting and he'd been here tonight. I hope it's the last I ever see of that arrogant English man.*

Chapter 33

Middlebury

Sadie couldn't believe how quickly four months had gone by. Book signings, speaking engagements, and sending out book orders kept her busier than ever. It wasn't busy enough to keep her from thinking about Wyman, though. She went to bed each night and woke up in the morning with him on her mind. It hurt to know the way he felt about her—not caring to share in the thrill of her book's success and believing she'd become selfish.

Her books had gone through a second printing, and thanks to her blogger friend's internet promotions, there had been almost more orders than Sadie could handle.

As she sat at the desk in her room, signing another stack of books that needed to be sent out in the mail, Sadie thought about her parents' and siblings' reaction to all of this.

Mom and Dad seemed tolerant, although she'd heard a few grumbles when the last load of boxes arrived a few days ago. Sadie figured as long as she kept them in the storage shed, there shouldn't be a problem. After all, there weren't any boxes piled up in the hallway, like there had been when the first batch arrived.

Sadie's sisters still complained about her being gone so much, which meant most of the household chores and meal preparation fell on them.

Sadie had considered the idea of buying a house of her own and hiring someone to do the cleaning and help with packaging books to send. But she'd been too busy to look at any homes that were for sale.

Besides, she thought, tapping the end of the pen against her chin, *I'd be lonely living all alone.*

Once more, an image of Wyman came to mind. She stared at the gorgeous ducks she'd gotten on their lovely date together at Winona Lake. It was a nice of Wyman to arrange the surprise for Sadie, having the fancy meal and enjoying the view of the water from their table. She wished for that chance to be with Wyman again. It didn't need to be in a fancy restaurant or somewhere away from Middlebury. If only things could be better between them.

Sadie held one of the ducks and studied it awhile before she put it back. *If he had proposed to me back when things were going well in our relationship, we might be married or at least planning a wedding by now.*

Forcing her focus on something else, Sadie glanced at the clock on the table beside her bed. In two hours she was supposed to go with Clara to Das Dutchman Essenhaus restaurant, to eat supper and talk about something the older woman had said was important. Sadie was curious as to what it could be. Perhaps Clara had found a new way to promote Sadie's books. In any case, she needed to hurry and sign the rest of the books on her desk so she would have time to get ready before the nice lady arrived to pick her up.

✱

"Where'd Sadie run off to tonight?" Jana Beth asked as the family took their seats around the kitchen table. "Is she doing another book signing?"

"No events for your sister tonight," Grace responded. "Her friend, Mrs. Williams, came by to pick up Sadie shortly before you, Kaylene, and your daed got home. They went out for supper."

"It figures that she wouldn't be here to help cook or eat the meal. Sadie's hardly ever home anymore."

Kaylene's reddened face and Jana Beth's downturned lips told Grace that her daughters still struggled with envy toward their older sister. While

Grace had only attended a few of Sadie's events, Jana Beth and Kaylene hadn't gone to any. Their excuse was that most of the signings and speaking engagements had taken place either while they were at work or when they'd be leaving their jobs for the day. The girls could have asked their boss for some time off, but Grace was almost sure that neither of them had fully accepted their sister's success. For that matter, Kaylene and Jana Beth were still somewhat envious because Sadie had inherited so much money. She'd heard them discussing it again the other day.

They need to get past this, Grace thought as she scooted her chair closer to the table. *Jealousy does no one any good—it eats away at a person and causes dissension. We all need to be content.* The words of Hebrews 13:5 came to mind. *"Let your conversation be without covetousness; and be content with such things as ye have." Yes, that's what we all need to practice every day.*

"Let's bow for prayer." Calvin glanced at each family member, and all heads bowed.

When they'd finished praying, he scooped two pieces of meat loaf off the platter and slid them onto his plate. "I can't wait to take a bite of your good meat loaf, fraa." He grinned at Grace.

Grace smiled, until she noticed her daughters' somber expressions. Kaylene's previous smile had disappeared as she took the platter and dished hers before passing it to Jana Beth, who mumbled something under her breath. Grace was tempted to ask for clarification but decided to leave it unsaid.

No one spoke as the broccoli, cheesy potatoes, and pickled beets made the rounds. Then Calvin forked a piece of meat loaf into his mouth. "This is sure tasty. You make the best meat loaf, Gracie."

"Danki." Grace nibbled on her food as the tension in the room continued to grow. She wasn't sure what Kaylene had on her mind, but the avoidance of eye contact was evident. Jana Beth also appeared to be annoyed as she slumped in her chair.

While they ate, things were quiet until Kaylene asked Grace a question.

"What makes this meat loaf taste so good, Mom?"

Grace smiled. *Ah, so this is what's bothering them.* "It's not hard to make. I just follow the recipe handed down from my mamm."

Jana Beth sat straight in her chair. "When we tried making this from your recipe, it didn't taste the same."

"It probably wouldn't, because when I first made the meat loaf myself it wasn't very good until my mamm showed me how to play with the recipe and make it my own."

"Can you show us how to make it better?" The question came from Kaylene.

"Of course. After supper I'll show you exactly what to do."

Kaylene smiled and tilted her head. "I have another question. What have you and Dad done with the money you got from Aunt Sadie Ruth?"

Calvin took a good-sized bite of meat loaf, so that left Grace to answer her daughter's pointed inquiry. She rested her arms on the table and cleared her throat. "If you must know, I was able to take care of a large bill we needed to pay, so a nice chunk of the money remedied the problem. The rest of our inheritance is in the bank, hopefully drawing some interest."

I hope that satisfies her curiosity, and since the subject is now open, I'm curious too. "How about you, Daughter? What did you do with the money you received?"

"I put mine in the bank, because I'm saving up to get an open carriage. But of course, when I do get one, it'll use up a good amount of my money." Kaylene's mouth twisted.

"That's how it is—you save up money and then you have to spend it." Dad took a bite of cheesy potatoes.

Jana Beth spoke up. "I'm going to hang on to my money until I need it for something important."

Kaylene sipped her water and then set the glass down. "If I had Sadie's money I could get whatever I wanted."

Jana Beth laid her fork down and wiped at her frown with a napkin. "I still wish Kaylene and I had gotten more money."

Grace drew a deep breath. "We've been over this several times, girls, and the answer is always the same. My sister's will stated what she wanted each of us to have, and we have all received our share. Remember too that Sadie has been most generous with the money she got, and many of the things she included in her book could be helpful to others."

Jana Beth lowered her gaze. "You're right, Mom. I apologize for spouting off. The truth is, I did enjoy reading Sadie's book."

"Same here, and I'm sorry too." Kaylene's chin quivered a bit. "I'm trying to work through my feelings of envy, but they resurface sometimes. I should be more grateful."

"We can't let the desire for money stand in the way of our strong ties with loved ones." Calvin's voice was calm but firm.

Grace quoted to the girls the words from Hebrews 13:5 that she'd reflected on only moments ago.

The girls' heads bobbed as they finishing eating what was left on their plates.

Grace appreciated her husband's sound advice, and she hoped that through all of this, their younger daughters would learn to be more selfless and appreciative of what they had.

✳

Sadie and Clara had been eating for nearly half an hour, and so far, their conversation had been centered on the lovely weather they'd been having and how good the buffet was at Das Dutchman Essenhaus.

Sadie was on the verge of asking Clara what she had wanted to talk about, but the woman spoke first.

"I have an idea I'd like to run past you, Sadie." Clara leaned closer, and Sadie couldn't miss the look of expectation on her face.

"What is it? Have you found another way to promote my book?"

"No, but I've been thinking that since your book has been selling so well, it might be time for you to write a second one."

"A—another book?"

"Yes. It could include another original quilt pattern, with perhaps more information about the Amish way of life. If we promote it well, it could become a bestseller."

"You really think so?"

"Absolutely." Clara gave a throaty laugh. "Most self-published books don't do nearly as well as yours has, Sadie, so you obviously have something to offer that people want to read about."

"But what I wrote about in the first book was mostly the similarities between the Amish and Hawaiian way of life, as well as information about their quilt patterns. I doubt that anyone would be interested in reading a book that focuses mainly on the Amish way of life."

"Au contraire. . . Don't you remember all the questions that have been asked of you during your talks? Many people asked about things related to your Plain way of living."

Sadie nodded. She remembered those questions quite well—especially the ones the young English man had asked during her first two events, plus three other times he'd shown up at her signings. The way he'd looked at Sadie and the fact that he'd taken her picture on more than one occasion had made her feel like crawling under the signing table or covering her head with her arms.

"I appreciate your suggestion, Clara, but coming up with a new quilt pattern and knowing what else to put in a second book would be time consuming. Then there would be more signings and speaking engagements—all of which would take me away from my family a good deal of the time."

"Of course, but think of the joy you would bring your readers by offering them a second book." The older woman paused to drink some iced tea.

Sadie's thoughts became so fuzzy, she could barely focus on the rest of her meal. She was not ready to commit to anything yet. "I feel a bit overwhelmed by all of this. Could I take some time to think about it?"

"Certainly, but I would advise you not to wait too long. Your book is selling well right now, and you're establishing a fan base, so you need to act upon this soon." The older woman smiled. "If you decide to proceed, I'll begin blogging about it right away. Then by the time the book is printed, people will be eager to place orders."

Sadie's mind spun with all the possibilities. If she wrote a second book and it was successful, would she be expected to write a third, fourth, fifth, or even a sixth book? *Oh my! Will there be no end to what's expected of me?*

✳

With so many unanswered questions floating through her mind, it had been difficult for Sadie to sleep that night. The next morning when she climbed out of bed, her head felt like it had been stuffed with a roll of cotton batting. Sadie had wanted to discuss Clara's idea with her parents last night, but by the time she'd returned home, they'd both gone to bed.

She ambled over to the window and raised the shade. Looking down into the backyard, she watched as a cluster of sparrows ate from one of the feeders. *Clara said I need to make a decision about writing another book soon, but I want Mom's opinion on this, so I'll talk to her after Dad and my sisters leave for work. I'd rather not discuss this in front of Jana Beth or Kaylene, because I'm almost certain what they would think. Since neither of them offered me much encouragement on my first book, they'd probably say it's a silly idea and that I should be content to stay home and help out around the house.*

Sadie washed up and got dressed then hurried downstairs to the kitchen to help with breakfast. Mom was already there, and so were Sadie's sisters, so she made idle talk while the four of them got the morning meal put together.

Soon after they'd finished eating, Kaylene, Jana Beth, and Dad left, so Sadie figured it was a good opportunity to talk to her mother. "There's something I'd like to discuss with you, Mom."

"Can it wait awhile? I have an appointment to see the chiropractor this morning, and my driver should be here any minute." Mom gestured to the dishes still in the sink. "Would you mind doing those by yourself this morning?"

"Well, no, I don't mind, but I'd really hoped—"

Toot! Toot! Toot!

"Oh, that's my driver." Mom peered out the kitchen window. "I'd better go. I don't want to be late. We'll talk later, Sadie." She grabbed her dark outer bonnet and put it on her head, then slipped into her jacket and went out the back door.

With slumped shoulders, Sadie made her way to the kitchen sink and filled it with warm, soapy water. *Guess I have no choice but to wait till Mom gets home, because I can't make such a big decision on my own.*

✳

Sadie had finished washing and drying the dishes and was about to put them away when she heard a horse and buggy enter the yard. She hurried to the front door to see who it was. Watching as Ellen got out of her rig, Sadie stepped out onto the porch and waved.

A few minutes later, after Ellen secured her horse, she reached into the buggy and lifted Irene into her arms.

Sadie felt a tug on her heartstrings. She always felt a bit envious whenever she saw Ellen or Barbara with their children and remembered that she'd felt the same way when Mandy and Ken had come to visit last Christmas with their cute little boy.

I'd better accept the fact that I may never get married, Sadie told herself. *I may end up a wealthy old spinster with no husband or children. If I fill my time writing books, will it offer me a sense of fulfillment like being a mother would?*

Sadie's musings came to an end when Ellen stepped onto the porch with Irene. Sadie smiled. "It's good to see you. It has been awhile."

"Jah. I came by tell you that I had a phone call from Ken last night."

"Come in." Sadie led the way, and soon they were seated in the living room, with Irene on Ellen's lap. "What did Ken have to say? Is everything all right with Mandy?"

"Mandy's great. She had her boppli—it's a girl, and they named her Miriam Victoria, after Mandy's mamm and Ken's mom, Vickie, whose real name is Victoria."

Sadie clasped her hands and lifted them slightly. "That's wunderbaar. I'm happy for them." Another pang of envy shot through her, but she put on a brave smile. "Are Mandy and the baby both doing well?"

Ellen nodded and stroked her daughter's head. "Motherhood is so rewarding, and I have some news in that area too."

"Oh?"

"Rueben and I are expecting our second child." Her face fairly glowed.

"That is good news. Congratulations."

"Danki." Ellen leaned over and set Irene on the floor so she could run around and play. "Tell me now, how are things going with you?"

"Okay, I guess, but I'm feeling kind of torn."

"About what?"

Sadie told Ellen everything Clara had said to her the evening before. "It's nice to know she has such confidence in me, and I appreciate the fact that she's willing to keep promoting my book, but. . ."

"But you're not sure if you want to write another one?"

"Exactly." Sadie reached up and rubbed the back of her neck. "When I'm gone from home so much while doing signings and speaking engagements, I miss my friends and family. Writing another book would take up a lot of my time too." She leaned against the sofa cushions and sighed. "Writing my first book put a wedge between me and my family at times, and it ruined things with me and Wyman."

"Have you seen him lately?"

"No, other than at our biweekly church services."

"So he hasn't tried to win you back?"

"No, and even if I decide not to write another book and I quit going around to talk about the one I've already written, I've lost Wyman." Sadie swallowed hard. "I believe it's too late to get him back."

"What are you going to do?" Ellen spoke quietly, in a soothing tone.

Sadie slowly shook her head. "I honestly don't know."

"Would you like my advice?"

"Of course."

"Pray about the matter—ask God what He wants you to do with the rest of your life."

"That's good advice. I should have thought to do it sooner, instead of lying awake most of last night trying to reach a decision by myself." Almost the minute Sadie spoke the words, a sense of peace came over her, like a warm quilt covering her body on a cold night. *Prayer. Yes, making my request known to God and asking Him to guide and direct me is precisely what I need to do.*

Chapter 34

Sadie entered the phone shed the following morning and closed the door. Taking a seat on the folding chair, she rehearsed what she would say when she called Clara to give her decision. She'd spent another restless night, praying and going back and forth in her mind about the ramifications of writing a second book and how it would affect her and the family. The attention Sadie had gotten from *The Blended Quilt* had been flattering; and even though she'd received many positive comments from those who'd attended her signings, being in the limelight had affected certain areas of her life in a negative way.

She picked up the phone and dialed her friend's number. When Clara said, "Hello," Sadie greeted her and got right to the point.

"I've given your suggestion about writing a second book a lot of prayer and thought, and I've decided not to pursue it."

"I'm sorry to hear that, Sadie. Would you mind telling me why?"

Sadie explained her reasons and ended it by thanking Clara for everything she had done to promote *The Blended Quilt*.

"I understand, and as long as you want me to, I'll keep encouraging people to buy your first book."

"Thank you." Sadie sat very still, allowing the relief she felt to sink in. It seemed like a huge weight had been lifted, and Sadie felt a complete sense of peace.

"I hope we can get together from time to time," Clara said. "Or at least talk on the telephone. After spending time with you these last several months, I feel as if you're my friend."

Sadie fingered the writing tablet next to the phone. "I feel that way too."

"I'd better let you go, Sadie. I'm sure you have a busy day planned."

"Yes, I do. After I get some more books signed and ready to mail out, I plan to spend some time grooming my horse. Due to my busyness, the poor mare's been neglected."

"All right, Sadie. Have a good day, and I'll talk to you soon."

"Goodbye, Clara."

✳

"On your way home after work this afternoon, would you mind dropping off some bags of feed that a few of our regular customers ordered?" Wyman's dad handed him a slip of paper. "I'd do it myself, but I'm meeting your mamm at the dentist's office. We'll both be getting our teeth cleaned, and we're going out for supper afterward."

Wyman was on the verge of asking why his father hadn't asked Michael to make the deliveries, until he thought it through. Short of a miracle, his brother would never be able to lift heavy feed bags again.

"Yeah, sure, Dad, I'll deliver the feed. I will work off this list and load the sacks into the back of my market buggy now."

"Sorry I can't help," Michael apologized from where he sat behind the counter.

Wyman flapped his hand. "Don't worry about it."

With a nod, his brother offered him a wide smile. Michael had been more cheerful since his marriage had gotten back on track, while Wyman had been getting his priorities straight—doing more praying and asking the Lord to work in his life. He was happy for his brother but still felt a bit envious. He wished things could have worked out for him and Sadie. However, he'd reached the conclusion that it was not meant to be. His hope was for them to remain friends, though, with no hard feelings between them, but they hadn't had much verbal communication in several months.

I should've been more understanding toward Sadie. I'm just as much at fault as she is for ruining things between us.

Looking at the list of names of people who needed orders dropped off, Wyman saw that one of the places he would need to go was at Calvin Kuhns's house. If Sadie was at home maybe he'd get a chance to speak with her and at least apologize for anything he'd said or done to hurt her.

✳

Sadie stepped into the barn to groom her horse. She was eager to tell her family about the decision she'd made that morning, but she would wait until Dad and her sisters got home from work. It might be best to tell everyone about her conversation with Clara while they ate supper.

Sadie entered her horse's stall and had picked up the curry comb, but it dropped in the straw. She retrieved it, shaking off the debris, and turned to begin brushing Lady when someone stepped out of the shadows.

Her heart pounded erratically as she stared at the man who had attended several of her book signings, asking too many questions and taking pictures without her permission. Sadie's worry returned, like it had before, when the unnerving fellow blocked the doorway of the small cubical. "You frightened me. Wh–what are you doing here?"

His brown eyes appeared even darker in the dimness of the barn as he took a few steps toward her. "I came for you."

Sadie's elbows pressed into her sides as she stepped back, bumping into her mare. Her heart beat so hard, she feared it might explode. This man was obviously a stalker and up to no good. Sadie shuddered to think of what he might do to her. All she could think was to find a way of escape. But where could she go when he stood blocking the stall door?

Sadie screamed, although she didn't know what good it would do, since no one was at home right now. With Dad and her sisters still at the trailer factory, and Mom having gone over to their widow neighbor's house with a loaf of zucchini bread, Sadie was at the mercy of this frightening man.

"Say, now. . .calm down." He took a few steps toward her. "There's no reason for you to get so upset."

Sadie's trembling legs felt like two sticks of rubber. "Please, leave me alone."

He moved to the left and reached out, as if to touch her. With barely enough room to slip past him, Sadie pushed the stall gate open and dashed toward the barn entrance. She was almost to the door when Wyman rushed in, carrying a sack of feed, which he promptly dropped on the floor.

"What's going on, Sadie? I heard you scream. Did you encounter a *maus* or some other critter?"

Sadie shook her head and pointed with a trembling hand. "Th–there's a *mann* in my horse's stall, and. . ." Her voice faltered.

Wyman tipped his head. "A man? What man?"

"She's talking about me." The dark-haired fellow came up behind Sadie, and she quickly stepped closer to Wyman.

"Who are you?" Wyman asked, pointing to the man.

"My name's Chuck Sawyer, and—"

"He came to some of my book signings and asked all sorts of questions. Then he showed up here and threatened me."

Chuck looked at Sadie with raised eyebrows. "I did not threaten you in any way."

"Yes, you did. You trapped me in my horse's stall and said you came here for me."

Wyman placed his hand on Sadie's trembling arm. "I'm gonna call the sheriff."

Chuck's eyes widened as he held up one hand. "No, don't do that. I did say that I came for Sadie, but not in the way she must have thought."

"What, then?" Wyman asked.

"I'm a television producer, and I'm looking to do a reality show about Amish people who have unusual occupations." He gestured to Sadie.

"Since she's an author, I thought that would give the show an interesting slant. If she'd given me a chance, I would have explained."

Sadie shook her head vigorously. "I'm not interested, sorry."

"I could offer you a pretty good sum of money for being on the show, and the exposure could help sell more copies of your book."

"Sadie's a millionaire; she doesn't need your money." Wyman's words were clear and concise.

Chuck's eyes widened as he gave Sadie an incredulous stare. "So you're a wealthy author?"

Her head moved quickly from side to side. "No, I inherited some money from a deceased relative, and I don't consider myself an author, since I've only written one book."

The producer pulled his fingers through the back of his hair and emitted a loud whistle. "Wow, she's an author as well as a millionaire. Now that would sure add interest to my show. I bet we'd get top ratings."

"I just told you. . .I don't consider myself an author, and I have no desire to be on your TV show."

"But you don't understand. This could be big—for you and our ratings."

"She said she's not interested." Sadie felt relieved when Wyman spoke up. "We'd appreciate it if you'd leave here right now."

"Okay, okay." Chuck reached into his pocket and pulled out a card. "Here's my business card. If you change your mind, don't hesitate to give me a call." He walked away, glancing back at Sadie one last time before going out the door.

Sadie stood looking at Wyman, and her voice quavered when she spoke. "Danki for standing up for me. I'm glad you came by when you did."

Wyman gestured to the sack of feed. "Came to deliver this for your daed." He put his hand on her arm again. "You okay, Sadie?"

"Jah, but I feel pretty shook up. That man frightened me when he kept asking questions and taking pictures during my book signings. Then, when he showed up here in the barn, I was really scared."

"I'm sorry you had to deal with that. Hopefully you'll never hear from him again."

Wyman's tender expression was nearly Sadie's undoing. She wanted him to wrap his arms around her so bad. Instead, he just stood looking at her with an expression she couldn't decipher. Was it merely concern she saw on Wyman's face, or could it be a look of love? Was it possible that he still loved her? Sadie had never stopped loving him.

"I've made some decisions." She looked up at Wyman.

"Oh?"

"Although I will continue to design and make quilts, I'm through writing books."

"Really?"

"Jah, and I owe you an apology for putting my book and promotion ahead of our relationship. It was wrong, and I've been miserable without you. Will you forgive me?"

He gave a nod. "If you'll forgive me for the things I've said and done in the past that hurt our relationship. I should have been more supportive and encouraging of you." Wyman placed both hands on Sadie's shoulders. "If you're willing, I want to marry you."

Tears gathered in the corners of Sadie's eyes. "Oh yes, Wyman, I'm more than willing."

He pulled her into his arms and sealed their love with a sweet, tender kiss. While Sadie felt glad for the experience and opportunity she'd had to share her blended quilt pattern with others, she knew without reservation that nothing could make her as happy as becoming Mrs. Wyman Kaufman.

Epilogue

*W*yman stood behind Sadie with his arms around her waist, drinking in the beauty before them. Never in a million years had he dreamed of taking an ocean voyage, much less with his bride of a few weeks.

He bent his head forward and kissed the back of her neck. "I love you beyond measure."

She turned to face him, her face mere inches from his. "I love you too, dear husband."

Wyman felt thankful that he and Sadie had both gotten their priorities straight and could spend the rest of their married life enjoying whatever time God allowed them to be together. Learning to be content with the simple things in life was something else they had both learned, and Wyman felt good about that.

✳

A couple of loud blasts from the cruise ship's horn caused Sadie to turn around. Her breath caught in her throat as the island of Kauai came into view. It was every bit as beautiful as she remembered. It would be wonderful to see Mandy again and get caught up on each other's lives. However, the best part of this day was having someone special to share it with—a man who loved God as much as she did—a man who loved her as much as she loved him.

A vision of the lovely covering Sadie's mother and sisters had made as a wedding present for her and Wyman's bed came to mind. They'd used

Sadie's Blended Quilt pattern, and Sadie had brought her original Blended Quilt wall hanging along on this trip. She would present it to Mandy as a way of saying thank you for allowing her and Wyman to stay free of charge at the Palms Bed-and-Breakfast for the next week. After that, she and her new husband would board another cruise ship to take them to a different island, where they could see many other interesting and beautiful sights.

Sadie thought about her dear friend Ellen, and how excited she and Rueben had been when their second child was born—a precious little boy they'd named Daniel. Sadie looked forward to the day that she and Wyman became parents. It would bring her such joy to teach their children about God and bring them up to appreciate the simpler things in life.

A verse of scripture she'd committed to memory came to mind: *"I have learned, in whatsoever state I am, therewith to be content."* Philippians 4:11.

Sadie closed her eyes and said a silent prayer. *Thank You, Lord, for Your many blessings, and for helping me learn to set my priorities straight. Please give Wyman and me wisdom in the years ahead, and help us to be a blessing to everyone we meet.*

Sadie's Coconut Carrot Cake

Ingredients:

1 cup coconut oil

2 cups sugar

3 eggs

2 cups flour

2½ teaspoons baking soda

2 teaspoons cinnamon

1 teaspoon salt

1⅓ cups shredded coconut

2 cups grated raw carrots

1 (8 ounce) can crushed pineapple in juice

½ cup chopped nuts

Preheat oven to 350 degrees. Beat oil, sugar, and eggs together. Add flour and dry ingredients, and beat until smooth. Add coconut, carrots, pineapple, and nuts. Pour into a greased 9x13-inch pan and bake for 50 to 60 minutes. When cool, frost with coconut frosting.

Coconut Frosting
Ingredients:

1 cup shredded coconut

3 ounces cream cheese

¼ cup margarine or butter

3 cups powdered sugar

1 tablespoon milk

½ teaspoon vanilla

Toast coconut. Cool. Cream the cream cheese with margarine. Alternately add powdered sugar, milk, and vanilla, and beat until smooth. Add half of the toasted coconut. Frost the cake. Top with rest of the coconut.

Discussion Questions:

1. For a while, Wyman had a hard time sticking with any job. He became bored easily and was always looking for something better. This affected his relationship with Sadie. Have you ever known someone like that or become easily dissatisfied yourself? Is it best to keep changing jobs, hoping to find the right one, or should a person stick with a position they don't like?

2. Sadie got caught up in the excitement of making her blended quilt and didn't help around the house as much as she used to. This caused some dissension between Sadie and her sisters. Do you think Sadie was inconsiderate or selfish? Or was she simply so caught up in her new project that she wasn't aware that she was shirking her duties?

3. When an older woman's purse was snatched in a parking lot, Sadie came to her rescue and got the purse back. Have you ever been faced with something similar—either having something taken from you or been on the scene to rescue and return an item for someone else? How did you feel about the situation? Would you have accepted or given a reward for the good deed?

4. After Sadie inherited a large sum of money, she was able to quit her job and concentrate on writing a book. How did self-publishing a book affect Sadie's life? Do you think it changed her personality? How did it affect her relationship with her friends and family? Was there something she could have done to make things better?

5. How did Sadie's parents and siblings feel when they received a smaller inheritance from their aunt's estate while Sadie got such a large one? How would you react if you were in a similar situation—either on the less receiving end or acquiring more than the rest of your family because of an inheritance?

6. Wyman's brother and his wife, Lovina, were faced with some problems that affected their marriage. The answers came when they agreed to see a marriage counselor. If your marriage were in trouble, would you be willing to see a counselor and follow their advice to make some necessary changes?

7. After Sadie's friend Mandy suffered a miscarriage, she sank into depression. Have you or someone you know ever been so depressed you could barely function? What are some things a person can do when depression takes hold?

8. When Sadie was in the sewing room looking over patterns to create the blended quilt, she'd said that she wouldn't quit until she came up with the right combination. Have you ever started a project and struggled to get it done? If you didn't finish it, did you have any regrets? If you were able to finish your project, how did it make you feel?

9. Why do you think Sadie was so determined to write a book about her blended quilt and the trip to Hawaii she'd made with her friends? Have you ever wanted something so badly that you put the goal of achieving it ahead of your relationship with others?

10. Wyman liked to keep his buggy clean and looking good. Is there a point when a person can let an object become his or her main focus? What can someone do to avoid this temptation?

11. Do you think Sadie and Wyman's relationship went downhill because he wasn't supportive enough, or did it have more to do with Sadie putting her needs ahead of his?

12. When Sadie was trying to decide whether to write a second book, her friend Ellen gave her some sound advice. How do you handle your decision-making? Do you ever seek out a friend for clarification? Should prayer and seeking God's will be a part of it?

13. Were there any verses of scripture in this book that spoke to your heart or made you think about some area of your life that needs to be changed?

14. While reading this book, did you learn anything new about the way Amish people think or do things in their everyday life?

About the Authors

New York Times bestselling and award-winning author **Wanda E. Brunstetter** is one of the founders of the Amish fiction genre. She has written more than one hundred books translated in four languages. With over eleven million copies sold, Wanda's stories consistently earn spots on the nation's most prestigious bestseller lists and have received numerous awards.

Wanda's ancestors were part of the Anabaptist faith, and her novels are based on personal research intended to accurately portray the Amish way of life. Her books are well read and trusted by many Amish, who credit her for giving readers a deeper understanding of the people and their customs.

When Wanda visits her Amish friends, she finds herself drawn to their peaceful lifestyle, sincerity, and close family ties. Wanda enjoys photography, ventriloquism, gardening, bird-watching, beachcombing, and spending time with her family. She and her husband, Richard, have been blessed with two grown children, six grandchildren, and two great-grandchildren.

To learn more about Wanda, visit her website at www.wandabrunstetter.com.

Jean Brunstetter became fascinated with the Amish when she first went to Pennsylvania to visit her father-in-law's family. Since that time, Jean has become friends with several Amish families and enjoys writing about their way of life. She also likes to put some of the simple practices followed by the Amish into her daily routine. Jean lives in Washington State with her husband, Richard Jr., and their three children but takes every opportunity to visit Amish communities in several states. In addition to writing, Jean enjoys boating, gardening, and spending time on the beach.

New from Wanda and Friends!

Wanda E. Brunstetter's Amish Friends From Scratch Cookbook

A Collection of Over 270 Recipes for Simple Hearty Meals and More!

**A must-have cookbook that goes back to the
basics of cooking from scratch!**

Why does nothing compare to the memories of Great-Grandma's food?
Could it be because she made everything from scratch? Amish and
Mennonite cooks contribute recipes that celebrate the value of skipping
the factory-made shortcuts and cooking from scratch. Over 270 recipes
are organized into traditional categories from main dishes and sides to
desserts and snacks. Also included are kitchen tips and stories about
growing up around an Amish kitchen. Encased in a lay-flat binding
and presented in full color, home cooks of all ages will be
delighted to add this cookbook to their collections.

Comb Bound / 978-1-64352-708-6 / $16.99